Shadow

JUNE
FRANCIS
Shadows of the Past

CANELO

First published in the United Kingdom in 2019 by Canelo

This edition published in the United Kingdom in 2020 by

Canelo Digital Publishing Limited
Third Floor, 20 Mortimer Street
London W1T 3JW
United Kingdom

A CIP catalogue record for this book is available from the British Library.

Print ISBN 978 1 78863 795 4
Ebook ISBN 978 1 78863 710 7

Look for more great books at www.canelo.co

Printed and bound in Great Britain by Clays Ltd, Elcograf S.p.A.

Chapter One

Everton: March 1928

Fifteen-year-old Anne Anderson hummed the music to 'Hinky Dinky Parlez-vous' before bursting into song as she hurried through Liverpool's Stanley Park. She must find herself some full-time paid work soon, she thought, having been keen to do that ever since she had left school after her fourteenth birthday. However, her adoptive mother, Sylvia, was still insisting that she stay at home and help with the housework and with looking after her father and three brothers at their family home.

Anne thought how annoyed the old woman would be if she could hear her adopted daughter singing that cheerful wartime song, but it had such a catchy tune she simply couldn't help doing so. Anne loved singing, even the hymns they sang in Saint George's Church on Northumberland Terrace, which had a smashing view of the streets stretching down to the Mersey and across the water to the Wirral on the other side. Not for the first time, Anne wondered why everything she did seemed to get on Sylvia's nerves, or put her in her bad books. She supposed that it was still all the bad memories of what had happened to the family in 1912, and Sylvia's nervous collapse when her youngest daughter died in a tragic accident when she was only six or seven, but it was a shame Sylvia couldn't enjoy having a good sing at home.

Suddenly, a gust of wind whipped the red felt cloche hat from her head, which had been a birthday present from Emily, and sent it spinning through the air. Anne watched in dismay, then the wind seemed to slacken, and her hat plummeted to the ground. She hurried towards where it had landed, only to be beaten to it by a black, white and tan-coloured mongrel that pounced on her hat and began to savage it. Her birthday had only been a month ago and it was brand new, but Anne was filled with trepidation at the thought of having to do battle with the dog for possession of it, as she knew how upset thirty-year-old Emily would be if she went home without it. She watched in dismay as the dog shook the lovely object it its jaws while she built up the courage to tackle the animal, when a young man appeared out of nowhere. He seized the dog by the collar with one hand while with the other he gripped the hat and spoke to the dog in a tone of authority. The red hat fell on the grass and Anne lunged forward and picked it up gingerly, all the while keeping one eye on the dog.

She stood up, gazing with dismay at the saliva, bits of grass and soil that clung to the felt, which had been punctured by the dog's teeth. Tears started in her grey eyes before she raised them to meet the face of her hat-rescuer. It was a rather attractive face with a straight nose, a full-lipped mouth and a dimpled chin. His eyes were the rich brown of treacle toffee and a lock of dark-brown hair curled over his frowning brow.

'Is that dog yours?' she asked in a voice that trembled slightly.

The dog whimpered, straining against his hold, and when the man released his grip on its collar, they watched it bound away. 'No, and I presume he isn't yours either, but the hat is.' He teased her in a voice that held a hint of something more than a Scouse accent. Was it Irish or Scottish, she wondered, and was vaguely reminded of her adoptive father's Scots brogue which she loved so much.

'You presume right,' she said, 'and I have to add that I appreciate your coming to my hat's rescue. It's new and was a gift from my sister.'

'I'm sure it will be almost as good as new once you give it a clean and a brush,' he said.

She crinkled her pert nose. 'I see you're an optimist. It'll never be as good as new. I'll try to make it wearable again for when I get a job, but it's no good for church.' She began to walk towards the path that led to the gates close to the palm house and bandstand.

He fell into step beside her. 'What kind of job are you looking for?'

'Any I can get as long as it's not as a domestic. I have enough housework at home.'

'And where's home?' he asked, gazing down at her.

'Mere Lane. Do you know it?'

He nodded. 'Oh yes, my father and I moved into Leadenhall Street a short while ago.'

'So, you're quite close to where I live.'

He nodded. 'We've just moved from Gill Street not far from the TJ Hughes department store. My sister died of pneumonia and Dad couldn't stand the house after she had gone. We lived in this neighbourhood when my mam was alive but there was a fire and we had to find another house after that.'

'Oh, I'm sorry about your mother and your sister. How old was your sister?'

'Fifteen. No age at all. I would have had another sister too, but she died with my mam in childbirth, so it's just Father and me now.'

'How terrible for the pair of you.' Anne knew she shouldn't really be talking to strange young men in parks but there was something about this young man that seemed so open and honest. She liked that he was willing to talk about his family and so decided to tell him something of her own. 'I'm fifteen years old and I'm adopted. My adoptive mother had been on the verge of a nervous breakdown following the death of her little girl, Flora. It was a tragic accident and happened in 1913, the year I was born. Sylvia was past childbearing age by then, and Flora's death had almost broken her heart, so my adoptive father decided another baby girl might help her recover from her loss. I'm not sure I ever took her mind completely off the tragedy and it took her many years to recover, especially as, after war broke out, she began to fear for her first-born son Albert's life, who went away to fight in Flanders. I've been with them ever since.'

'Your brother and sister must be a lot older than you if he was in the war,' he said. 'The war started fourteen years ago, and though it ended ten years ago it's still very fresh in many people's minds.'

'Oh yes,' Anne answered. 'I'm quite the baby of the family.'

'It's very sad, but you must have been a great comfort to your mother after the loss of the little girl.' He looked at her sympathetically and Anne felt a strange fluttering in her tummy that she had never experienced before.

'I'm not sure about that. I find it hard to please her sometimes, but I love my adoptive parents and my brothers and sister. I was told my natural mother died giving birth to me and my father died before I was born.'

'Do you know who your natural parents were?' he asked.

Anne shook her head. 'No, and I don't let it bother me. Why should I when I have a good home and a family who care about me?'

'I don't blame you for feeling like that,' he said.

'I was told that my natural father was a pal of my adoptive father and had no family to care for me.'

They had reached the park gates. 'So, what's your name?' he asked.

'Anne Anderson,' she replied.

'I'm Andrew Fraser.'

Anne thought the name suited him.

They exited Stanley Park and headed in the direction of the Liverpool football ground on Anfield Road. He continued in the same direction as Anne, but now they were both silent, as if they had run out of things to say or both needed to digest the information they had learnt about each other before chancing getting to know one another better. As it was, they parted outside the football ground, Anne saying she needed to visit the bakery opposite. Andrew said that he had some painting to do at the house he and his father had only moved into recently.

He held out his hand. 'I'm glad I was able to help you. It was nice meeting you.'

She placed her much smaller hand in his and they solemnly shook. 'Thank you for rescuing my hat. It's been a pleasure meeting you, too. I'd best be off as I've the shopping to do.'

Despite her words, he still held her hand. 'What a delicate hand you have,' he said, holding her gaze.

'Perhaps it seems small because yours is so large.' She smiled at him but withdrew her hand.

'See you around,' he said, looking back at her with a wave of his hand as he headed up the road.

She waved back, thinking that living so close to each other they were bound to meet again. The thought excited her, but for now she thrust him to the back of her mind and consulted her shopping list. Anne could feel the familiar cold, damp touch to the air which meant a fog could be about to descend. She needed to get a move on if she was to finish her chores whilst Sylvia was still out visiting an old friend, who was also Anne's godmother, and before Emily came home.

Chapter Two

Anne groaned inwardly as she took a closer look at her red hat. 'Dratted dog,' she muttered, only to tell herself that she might never have got to speak to Andrew if it weren't for that gust of wind and the playful dog. Then she set to gently brushing the soil, grass and dried saliva from the fabric with a soft-bristled brush before placing her hat on top of a jug of steaming water and leaving it while she drank a cup of tea and listened for the sound of a key opening the front door. She could hear a ship's foghorn and, lifting a curtain, she saw that the fog was thick, even up here in Everton. After a quarter of an hour she removed her hat from the top of the jug and inspected it for any remaining marks.

Fortunately, her actions appeared to have done their job, so she carefully smoothed the felt back into shape with the side of her hand before putting the hat on and viewing herself in the mirror on the wall opposite the black-leaded range in the kitchen. She decided no one would be able to tell of the mishap and went upstairs to put her hat away on the high shelf in the cupboard in the bedroom. As she did so, there came the sound of the front door opening. She froze, expecting at any minute for Sylvia to call her and ask why dinner wasn't in the oven. To her surprise the voice that called out, 'Who's home?' belonged to Hugh, her adoptive father. She decided it must be much later than she had thought and wasted no time hurrying downstairs. Hugh was in the hallway as she reached the second stair from the bottom; he held out his arms to her and she jumped into them.

'Da, are you home early or has the clock on the mantelpiece stopped?' Her father worked as a foreman in the sugar factory, Tate & Lyle, not far from the docks.

'Due to the fog we were let off a bit earlier, which I'm glad of because it's scouts' evening and I want to get to the church hall early in case the lads start arriving early,' he said. 'Where's your mother and Emily?'

'They haven't arrived home yet,' she said, kissing his bristly chin. 'Which is all to the good because I haven't put the casserole in the oven. I'd better do that now.'

He lowered her to the floor and followed her into the kitchen, still wearing his tweed overcoat and a checked cap on his greying sandy-coloured hair, which was still thick despite his fifty-eight years. He was a fine figure of a man with broad shoulders and a nicely shaped head, set firmly on a strong neck. Few wrinkles marred his attractive features and those that existed could be written off as laughter lines. His eyes were grey, not that of steel but more like the colour of an early Scottish mist hovering over the surface of a loch.

Despite the troubles in the family's past, Hugh always said that taking in Anne had proved a blessing at a difficult time and she had brought him joy. 'Has your mother gone to Betty's?' he asked, and the words seemed to rumble up from his chest.

Anne nodded, thinking of the lifelong friend of Sylvia's whom Anne called Auntie Betty; she had been widowed at a young age in the 1890s and left childless. She was housekeeper to a doctor. According to Emily, Betty wasn't short of a bob or two and what with Anne being her goddaughter, Betty might leave her some money when she popped her clogs.

'I had thought Mother would be back by now,' she said.

'She hates the fog,' he said. 'Maybe I'd best walk and meet her if she's on her way home.'

'Don't get lost,' she called after him as he left the kitchen.

Anne opened the stove door and placed her hand in the oven, withdrawing it swiftly as the interior had reached a good temperature. *The casserole shouldn't take too long to cook in that*, she thought. In the meantime, she would set the table. Placing the casserole in the hot oven, she closed the door firmly before removing dishes from the sideboard cupboard and placing them on the yellow damask table-cloth. She sang 'Hinky Dinky Parlez-vous' as she did so and was reminded of Andrew, wondering if she would see him again and whether they could get to know each other better. He intrigued her, and she also felt sorry for him, having lost his mother and two sisters, albeit one had only been a newborn baby that he most likely had never seen.

She almost jumped out of her skin as a voice behind her said, 'Mother will skin you alive if she hears you singing that. She thinks it's common.'

Anne spun round and stared at the youngest of the Anderson boys. Gordon, who was twenty-five, was the shortest of the brothers and sadly did not possess Albert or Teddy's good looks. A kind and thoughtful boy, he was somewhat shy and lacking in self-confidence and had never had a girlfriend, but he remained a dutiful son, handing over his unopened wage packet to his mother each week. Teddy, on the other hand, had inherited his father's looks, and was now seriously courting a girl called Joan and wedding bells were expected sooner rather than later. As for Albert, he had shocked his parents by marrying a girl he had met down south during the war before the family had even met her. Indeed, the shock had been made worse for his mother because Albert and his wife, Gladys, lived in Bury St Edmonds and Sylvia had seldom seen him since he marched off to war. Gladys had inherited her father's house after nursing him during his final years. Anne didn't like Gladys; she'd always seemed quite snooty when they'd met and criticised the length of her skirts.

'I'd best sing a hymn then,' she said, and launched into 'Onward, Christian Soldiers'.

'Do you have to, our Annie?' She heard a groaning voice drift in from the doorway.

She stared at her other brother, Teddy, who had entered the kitchen unnoticed. 'And what exactly would you like me to sing?' she asked.

'Preferably nothing.' He glanced around the kitchen. 'Where's Mam?'

She told him Sylvia wouldn't be pleased if she heard him refer to her as 'Mam'; she thought it was uncouth and liked to be called 'Mother'.

'Anyway, she's at Auntie Betty's and Da's gone to fetch her. He arrived home early because of the fog.'

'What's to eat?' he asked.

'Beef casserole, but it won't be ready for a while. I forgot the time.'

'Then I'll have a jam butty while I'm waiting.' Teddy took a loaf from the bread bin and jam from the cupboard. 'What about you, Gordon? Do you want a butty?'

Gordon nodded.

Both brothers were carters, although they worked for different companies. It could be strenuous work, lugging sacks and boxes of various goods around. In the old days, the carters would drive a horse and cart to transport goods around the city, but in the last few years, the sight of horse-drawn carts had dwindled and now smart vans sporting the company name on the side did many of the city's deliveries. Teddy still drove a horse and cart – he loved his horse – but although he appeared physically strong, he was prone to suffer from a bad chest, a complaint he'd had since childhood, made worse by being out in all weathers. Anne liked Teddy's girlfriend Joan, who was sensible and kind.

When Hugh and Sylvia arrived home, the casserole was almost ready to come out of the oven. 'Good timing, Da,' Anne said, hanging up his overcoat for him. 'Has the fog cleared at all? I'm surprised it came down so thickly as there was a bit of wind out today.'

'It's living near the Irish Sea that does it,' said Sylvia.

'Rather from the Atlantic, I'd say, Mother,' said Teddy. 'We can't blame everything on the Irish. By the way, Da, it's club night tonight. Are you still thinking of going after the scout meeting? I'm not if the fog doesn't clear.'

Hugh and his sons were members of a social club connected to their local parish C of E church. Hugh had carried his connections with the church down from Scotland and had encouraged his sons to join too. None of them liked to miss their meetings and Hugh looked thoughtful. 'I'd rather you didn't go, Hugh,' said Sylvia. 'You don't want to catch your death of cold.'

'I'm going to the scouts early just in case some of the lads turn up despite the fog, but I'll give the club a miss, although I haven't missed a club night since I don't know when,' he said. 'I like to socialise with the other men; there's not many Scots here and I miss the Scottish episcopal service.'

Anne had been about to undo her father's boot laces, but now she went over to the oven instead and removed the casserole. Sylvia took it from her and placed it on the teapot stand in the middle of the table. Anne handed her a ladle and then sat down. 'Our Emily's late,' she said fretfully. 'I hope she hasn't had trouble in the fog.'

A moment later there was the sound of a key in the front door and Anne breathed a sigh of relief. 'Are you all right, Emily?' she said, as the woman who had been more of a mother to her than Sylvia entered the kitchen.

Emily had once worked at the British American Tobacco factory on Commercial Road but had to give up her job when Flora died and Sylvia was on the verge of a breakdown, and Anne was adopted. For years she had stayed at home looking after Anne and her brothers, while Sylvia refused to let her get a job outside the home. It had been a bone of contention for many years and it was only when Anne was ten, and able to take on more of those household chores herself, that Emily could leave the house to earn her own wage, but at a different job as she had developed bad knees.

Emily removed her headscarf, fluffed up her hair and sighed. 'I was almost wishing I was still the family drudge,' she said. 'What with the fog and my rheumatics it's taken me ages to get home today.'

'Well, you come and sit by the fire, luv,' said Hugh, taking her by the shoulders and manoeuvring her into a chair by the fire. 'And you were never a drudge. I'm surprised to hear that you looked at yourself in such a way.'

'Sorry, Da, but I reckon if I hadn't been expected to scrub the back-kitchen tiles on my knees every day, I wouldn't have such pain in them, so Anne, be warned and don't get down on your knees except in church.' Emily shot her mother a look that was loaded with years of resentment.

Sylvia clucked her tongue against her teeth. 'I give the orders to Anne in this house, not you, girl. You're too full of yourself now you've a job outside the home. I blame it on those Suffragettes.'

Emily shot back at her mother quickly, 'Women who are householders have had the vote for years now, Mother. But perhaps if I hadn't wasted my best years keeping house because you couldn't, I might have my own household now to give orders in and I'd have been able to vote for equal rights for all women earlier.'

'Don't be insolent. I needed help after what happened with poor Flora. Perhaps you don't have a husband because of your high and mighty ideas!' Sylvia's mouth was twisted in the beginnings of a sneer.

'Enough, Sylvia,' said Hugh in a warning voice. 'I still wear the trousers in this house and I'll not have Anne suffering the way Emily has and still does. We all know that Flora's death gave you a breakdown, which it took you a long time to recover from. Thankfully Emily was able to help keep us fed and our house clean until you were well again. Besides, you've no cause for complaint. You've been better off since she got a job.'

Sylvia opened her mouth as if to answer him back but then must have changed her mind because she clamped it firmly shut and began to help Anne dish out the casserole.

–

Later, when Anne and Emily were lying side by side in the bed they shared in one of the upstairs bedrooms, Emily explained that she did not hand over an unopened wage packet to her mother but gave her half of it for her board and lodging; the rest she kept for fares, lunches, clothes, money for the flickers twice a week and the little over she saved in a post office account.

'That woman has had enough off me, over the years. So, take my advice, Anne. When you do find yourself a job, don't go giving your wage packet unopened to Mother.'

'But I owe her and Da so much,' Anne said.

'It was Da's choice to take you in and he has no regrets, and even adopted you legally when a law was passed later allowing him to do so. You saved Mother's sanity, although I doubt that she'll ever get over Flora's death.'

'But it was you who looked after me like a mother,' Anne said, with feeling.

'Yes, I did most of the caring for you. Mother was too old to cope on her own while Da was out at the factory working all hours. You mightn't have realised but she's eight years older than Da, which means she's now in her sixties,' Emily said.

'How come? That's quite a gap.'

'Her mother owned this house and rented out rooms. When Da came down from Scotland looking for work, he lodged here. Mother never went out to work but stayed at home helping with the lodgers. Eventually she and Da married.'

'So, they were thrown together,' Anne said, diving beneath the bedcovers.

Emily nodded. 'And it wouldn't surprise me if she suggested it to him.' With those words, Emily kissed her cheek and wished her sister happy dreams.

Anne wondered why, even though her older sister didn't have a gentleman friend, she didn't leave home now she had a paid job. She remembered once being told that Emily had had a young fellow she was seeing, but that suddenly, he and his mother had vanished from the neighbourhood and never been seen again. Anne wondered if Emily had ever heard from him after that but was reluctant to ask in case she got upset.

Anne snuggled beneath the bedcovers, mulling over what Emily had told her, and concluded that lots of couples must make marriages of convenience. But she thought it was sad all the same that Emily had never married or had her own family. She thought of Andrew and his father living in a house that lacked a woman's touch and wondered if he had ever considered making a marriage of convenience.

Chapter Three

A few days later Anne entered Everton Library, which was situated on the corner of Beacon Lane and St. Domingo Road, opposite Saint George's Church, and went over to the counter to return her library book before perusing the shelves for another to borrow. She enjoyed reading local history, as well as some of the new writers, such as F. Scott Fitzgerald, an American. She also liked John Buchan's Richard Hannay adventure stories, but the problem with that was so did a lot of other readers. She had read *The Thirty-Nine Steps* only last year and it had come out four years ago. She had seen a notice in the library recently saying that the novel released last year called *The Witch Wood* by Buchan was now freely available and next year *The Courts of the Morning* would be published. Of course, not all his books featured Richard Hannay, and this evening she was in search of *Greenmantle*, which had been published a while ago. She had been intending to borrow it for ages but had been distracted by other books that had been recommended by the librarian such as *The Age of Innocence* by Edith Wharton, which was set in America. Sometimes she preferred a lighter read and had discovered Georgette Heyer who had written two historical novels, *The Black Moth* and *These Old Shades*. The latter was more romantic than the former but not as spicy as the famous

Elinor Glyn book *It*, which her mother would have been shocked to know she had borrowed from a friend who'd sneaked it out of her elder sister's bedroom.

Anne had a pleasant surprise when she came to the B's in her search for *Greenmantle* because to her delight, her hat-rescuer, Andrew, was there, standing with a book open in his hands, searching the pages. She cleared her throat and said, 'Hello, what's that you're reading?'

He raised his head and glanced in her direction and his eyes widened in surprise. 'It's you! I wondered when we'd run into each other again. I was starting to think I might have to place a piece in the *Liverpool Echo* asking if the girl who had her red hat savaged by a dog in Stanley Park could write to me at a PO box number, which I would give, of course.'

Anne's eyes shone with amusement. 'You're joking!'

He shook his head. 'I work for the *Echo*. I'm a cub reporter,' he said proudly. 'I was just giving it another week and if I didn't see you, I'd definitely have done so.'

Anne felt her heart swell at this news and wondered if she was blushing because her cheeks suddenly felt very warm. 'What's that like? A reporter's job sounds exciting.'

'It's not that exciting yet,' he answered. 'I have to attend local events and court cases. Eventually though, I hope to be given more exciting stories and go all over the place researching stories, and it's a grand job for a young man like me who wants to get on in life and loves to write.'

'We'll probably meet again if you come here weekly, because I do.' Anne was surprised by her own boldness, but she knew already that she wanted to see the young man again.

'Same time, same place,' Andrew said with a smile. 'Is there a specific book you're looking for, Anne?'

'You remembered my name,' she said, beaming up at him.

'How could I forget? And you're wearing the red hat,' he said. 'I'm glad it survived its ordeal.'

'Me too. But the book I'm looking for is *Greenmantle* by John Buchan.'

Andrew closed the book he had been reading and held it out to her and she was surprised to see it was the very book she was looking for. 'I didn't know girls read John Buchan,' he said.

'We're more liberated women now, Andrew,' she said teasingly. 'During the war lots of women proved they could do a man's job, so why shouldn't we read men's adventure stories too? But you had it first, so you should borrow it.'

'I should be a gentleman and say ladies first, but to be honest I've already read it and was just re-reading one of my favourite bits.'

'In that case I'll take it,' she said. Their fingers brushed as she took it from him, and she felt a thrill run up her arm. 'Thank you.'

They stood there smiling at each other.

'I suppose I'd better go, and have it stamped and be on my way,' she said. 'The family worry about me if I'm out too long at this time of day.'

'But it's not late,' he said, glancing at the clock on the wall, which said it was four o'clock. 'I'll walk back with you.'

Her eyes followed his. 'Perhaps I'll stay a little longer. Besides which, you haven't chosen a book to take out yet.'

'So I haven't.' He led the way over to the section of books on the British Isles and reached for one on Scotland. She gazed at his profile, taking in his pleasant features as he flicked through pages before replacing the book and taking out another.

'Are you searching for any part of Scotland in particular?' she asked.

'Greenock. It's where my father came from,' he said. 'One day I want to go up there. I was having a root around the other week and came across my parents' marriage certificate and it said he was a widower when he married my mother. That means he was married before he met her, so I want to try and find out more about his past. I also overheard he and my stepmother talking once and I think my grandfather is still alive somewhere, maybe in Scotland.'

'Couldn't you ask him about it?' Anne said.

'If you knew him you wouldn't ask that. He's a hard, secretive man and Mam's and the baby's deaths made him worse. I thought it might have drawn us together, but it didn't. When my sister Ruth died, it was the last straw. He almost ended up in a mental asylum.'

Anne said, 'It must be difficult for you both, having no woman in the house to care for you both.'

He shrugged. 'Father remarried again a few months after Mam died. He said he needed someone to look after Ruth and me while he was at work or his social club.'

'My da belongs to a social club too. And he's also from Scotland, perhaps he and your father have met.'

'My father's a member of the People's Church and goes to their men's club that meet regularly,' said Andrew.

'Da goes to St George's,' she said. 'Where does your father work?'

'Tate & Lyle.'

'So does my da. I'll ask him if he knows your father.'

'No, don't,' Andrew said firmly. 'Your dad might speak to Father and he'll get annoyed if he discovers I've been talking about family matters. When he's had a few drinks, he gets maudlin and says we've to stick together as we've only got each other.'

'What about your stepmother?'

'Her name was Sadie and she died in childbirth too, but there was a baby boy called Robbie who survived. My father didn't feel able to look after both of us, not with his job at Tate & Lyle, so our aunt, Marjorie, my stepmother's sister, came to live with us, only she left a year or so ago, taking Robbie with her. She hated leaving Ruth and me, but Father started pestering her after our stepmother died and she didn't want to marry him. I don't think he's the type of man who can manage without a woman around the house. I still keep in touch with Marjorie and she visits us occasionally, bringing Robbie with her so Father doesn't go to her house and prove to be a nuisance. Robbie's twelve now and will be leaving school and looking for a job soon.' He paused. 'I wonder if she could help you.'

'In what way?' she asked.

'Robbie's old enough to be alone in the house so she has a job in Nelson's jam factory. I'm sure she mentioned they'd be taking more people on soon.'

'That could be just the thing for me. Would you give me her address and I'll go and see her and ask her about the work and the hours?'

'All right. She's a good sort is Marjorie, I'm sure she'll be pleased to help you.' From his jacket pocket he took a notepad and pencil, scribbled a name and address on it and handed the paper to Anne.

She thanked him. 'I'd best be going now.'

He glanced at the clock. 'I'm ready to go, too. I'll take this book out,' he said, indicating a book with cowboys on the dustjacket.

Outside the sky was darkening and the lamplighters were at work. It wasn't quite spring yet and the cold fingers of winter still held a loose grip on the city. 'It must have been frightening in the olden days when gas and electricity were unknown,' Anne said.

'No bobbies patrolling the streets, either.'

'There were watchmen, though, weren't there?'

He nodded. 'But they were few and far between, generally hired by the moneyed classes to guard their property. One would find them down by the docks in the days before the warehouses started getting built. There was a time when cargoes were just unloaded onto the dockside.'

'But weren't there dock-gate men to stop people going into the dockyards and pilfering?'

'Yes, but one man against a gang wouldn't stand much of a chance preventing thievery,' Andrew said. 'The building of the Albert Docks changed a lot about the way of life around here in Victorian times and I'm sure you'll know that it was opened by the queen's consort Prince Albert, so was named after him.'

'Spoken like a true cub reporter,' she teased him. 'Seriously, I've never thought about it much, but I am quite interested in local history.'

They began to walk along St. Domingo Road and turned the corner into Mere Lane.

He asked what number she lived at. She told him, adding that it was up the other end, not far from the recreation ground, so a bit of a walk from Leadenhall Street where he lived. He accompanied her halfway along Mere Lane before saying he would have to leave her.

'My father just might walk as far as the corner of Leadenhall Street, looking for me, and see me with you. I don't want him getting agitated. It doesn't take much,' said Andrew.

'I understand. Goodnight,' she said. 'See you again.'

'I hope so,' he said. 'I'm interested in what you think of *Greenmantle*.'

'And I'll be interested in what you find out about Greenock,' she said, thinking how nice it was to have met someone who shared her taste in books.

–

The next day, she wrote to Marjorie, introducing herself and asking if she might visit her to ask her about the factory job. She received a reply two days later suggesting Anne visit her on Wednesday at four o'clock. The only person she told about it was Emily, who wished her luck and gave her some pennies for her tram fare and to buy a couple of buns to have with a cup of tea.

When Wednesday arrived, Anne told Sylvia she was going shopping. She did not like lying but decided it was a half-truth.

Marjorie lived near Barker and Dobson's, the sweet factory, and it was only a short walk from the tram stop on Oakfield Road. Anne arrived exactly on the dot and the door was opened to her by a woman she thought to be in her late twenties. Her features were pleasant, with eyes that were a lovely shade of hazel, like her nephew's, and her smile was welcoming. 'I see you're like Andrew who's always on time. Do come in, we've time for a natter before young Robbie comes in from school. I've the kettle on for a cuppa.'

'That's the gear,' said Anne, stepping over the threshold. 'I bought a couple of buns for us, as well as a gingerbread man for Robbie.'

'He'll love that as it must be ages since he's had one.'

'How old is he?' she asked.

'He's twelve, so will be leaving school in a year or so, although there's talk of the leaving age going up.'

Anne bit her bottom lip and looked down at the gingerbread man. 'I don't know why, but I thought he was younger.'

'Time goes by so fast. Sometimes, I find it difficult to believe our Sadie's been gone that long. Robbie loves football and plays for a local team over at Newsham Park, but anyway, all boys love a sweet treat no matter what their age.'

'She was your sister, Robbie's mother?'

Marjorie nodded. 'We were so close.'

'She must have only been young when she married Andrew's father.'

Marjorie sighed. 'It was convenient. He needed a mother for Andrew and Ruth and, to tell the truth, she needed a father for the baby she was carrying. The father had gone and got himself killed in the war before he could make an honest woman of her.'

'I suppose that must have happened to a lot of girls,' said Anne, thinking of her natural parents and wondering if Andrew and Robbie knew the truth about the boy's father. She decided it was none of her business and asked Marjorie about the jam factory wages, what the hours were and how she should go about applying for a job there.

Marjorie's answers were satisfactory, but Anne was taken by surprise on being told she needed to produce her birth certificate. 'I've never seen my birth certificate,' she said. 'I'm adopted.'

'So, you've no idea who your real parents were?' said Marjorie.

'I regard the couple who adopted me as my real parents as they've reared me and provided for me, although adoption wasn't legal until I was older.'

'You're not curious about the mother who gave you birth?'

'I was told she died giving birth to me and that my father was already dead before I was born,' Anne said.

'Oh, well, maybe your adoption papers would be sufficient if your parents don't have your birth certificate.'

'I'll see what Da and Mother say.' Anne gulped her tea before taking a bite out of her bun. She mulled over Marjorie's words and, if she was honest, they had roused in her a curious desire to see her birth certificate and perhaps find out more about her natural parents.

For the rest of her visit, they talked about Andrew and his job as a reporter. Anne bid Marjorie farewell, and as she headed to the shops on her errands, she couldn't get the thought of what her birth certificate might tell her about her natural parents out of her mind.

When she arrived home, it was to find Sylvia asleep on the sofa. Her mother always seemed to be tired and had little inclination to help with the household chores. It had always been the same and Sylvia only ever showed willing when Hugh was around to watch. It was the main reason why Emily was so aggrieved by matters at home and felt like she had been treated as a drudge. Anne knew she hadn't had it half so bad as Emily had but could understand why her older sister felt so resentful.

By the time Anne had put the shopping away and peeled potatoes and carrots and put them on to boil, Sylvia had woken and was demanding a cup of tea. She asked no questions of Anne, so it wasn't until after Hugh came in that Anne brought up the subject of having to produce her birth certificate if she applied for a job at Nelson's jam factory.

Hugh and Sylvia exchanged glances and there was something in their expressions that immediately caused Anne to feel suspicious. 'What is it?' she asked. 'I do have a birth certificate, don't I?'

'Of course you do, Anne,' said Hugh, but his eyes didn't meet hers. 'It's just a matter of finding it. You've never needed it before.'

'What about my adoption papers?' Anne asked, feeling frightened suddenly.

'They're with the certificate, I imagine,' Sylvia said. 'They could be anywhere in a house this large and they may have been lost altogether.'

Anne put a hand to her head. 'I can't understand how you could have misplaced two such important documents.'

'Don't take on so,' said Hugh firmly. 'You're our daughter every bit as much as our other children but you need to understand, dear, that sometimes things go missing and we just need a bit of time to search for them.'

'But there's an opening at Nelson's now and I need them found in the next few days, Da. I'm fed up being at home and want to be out working, earning my own money,' cried Anne.

'Don't upset yourself. Perhaps if I write a letter to the company explaining the situation?' he suggested, his Scottish accent more obvious as he became emotional.

She thought about that suggestion and nodded. 'It could be a temporary solution,' she said.

He sighed with relief and, going over to Anne, hugged her. 'Never forget we love you,' he said, the words muffled against her hair.

Anne felt comforted momentarily but couldn't help noticing Sylvia's stern gaze on her father as they finished preparing the table for dinner.

Chapter Four

That evening Anne almost forgot the scene from earlier on by losing herself in the pages of *Greenmantle* as she sat in the parlour where it was quieter. She managed to finish it in a couple of days, and lent the novel to Gordon, saying, 'I need it back by the weekend. I have to return it on time as someone else is wanting it.'

'I don't have as much time to read as you do,' he complained.

'Make time,' she said. 'Don't go to the park on Sunday to watch the football.'

He pulled a face. 'I like watching the football,' he said mournfully.

'Read it in bed then,' she advised.

'Mother will tell me off for having the light on late.'

'Then tell Da before you go to bed that you need to finish it as it's my library book and I have to take it back.'

His blue eyes brightened. 'I'll do that.'

Anne found it upsetting that Gordon should be so under their mother's thumb at his age. Sylvia was one of those women who considered she knew what was best for her children and husband, although she tried to keep that domineering side of her nature hidden from Da. As it was, Hugh showed an interest in the book and asked Gordon and Anne whether they had read *The Thirty-Nine Steps*.

He was delighted when they answered in the affirmative and suggested they read Sir Walter Scott's books if they enjoyed history and a good adventure story.

–

The day before she was due to meet Andrew again at the library, Anne wrote a job application letter to the Personnel Department at Nelson's jam factory and spoke to her father about it. As promised, he produced a letter for her to go in the envelope with it, telling them about the situation.

'Did you not find my birth certificate then, Da?' she asked, still troubled by its loss. If there was no paperwork to prove who she was, how could she be sure herself?

'I'm sure this will be enough for now,' he said quickly.

Anne thanked him, sensing he didn't want to discuss the matter further.

She posted the application on her way to the library the next day. When she met Andrew in the library, she told him that she had enjoyed *Greenmantle*, but not as much as *The Thirty-Nine Steps* because although it featured Richard Hannay, it was more of a war story than the other and she missed reading the descriptions of the scenes set in Scotland. She also told him of what her father had said about Sir Walter Scott and asked whether Andrew had read any of his books.

'Yes, when I was younger and enjoyed reading about knights in armour and damsels in distress. *Ivanhoe* is probably his most famous book. I should imagine you'll find it on the shelves here as it's a classic.'

Together they went in search of it and Anne read the description on the back and decided to borrow it. She looked up at him. 'Have you found anything to take out yet?'

'I was hoping to find something on Liverpool's connection to the slave trade and the cotton industry. It's for a story I'm researching, but I can't find anything. I think I'll have to go to Liverpool's Central Library on William Brown Street and search the archives,' he said. 'In the meantime, I'll read something lighter, maybe a detective story.'

'Is what you're looking for research for an article for the *Echo*?' Anne said.

He nodded. 'It's my first big project and I suggested it to the editor; so far I've only written small stuff.'

'I know,' she said. 'I've been reading it when I can and thought you made a church spring fete sound fascinating but that you were capable of better stories to work on.'

He thanked her and hesitated for a moment, then took a deep breath before asking her, 'Would you be interested in going to the flicks with me one evening?'

'I'd love to,' she said, blushing.

'Great!' Andrew grinned. 'Let's go in a week's time to the first house.'

They agreed that the following Monday, when they would have met at the library, they would instead go to the Paramount where a Western featuring Gary Cooper was showing. There were rumours that he'd be starring in a talkie in a year or two.

–

That evening Anne could hardly sleep for thinking about the outing. She had more cause for excitement when she received a letter from Nelson's inviting her for an interview that coming Friday and so immediately wrote a letter accepting and posted it.

The following days seemed to drag by but eventually Friday came and she dressed in her best clothes and set off for her interview, clamping down on her nerves. She need not have worried. She had a testimonial written by the headmistress of her last school which had been given to her when she left, as well as a letter of recommendation from the vicar at Saint George's to show them, and so these went some way to make up for the lack of the missing birth certificate and adoption papers. She was told that she could start work the following Thursday and work the first shift from eight o'clock until two o'clock, though the shifts would change. She was told to bring in her birth certificate and adoption papers as soon as they were found.

Anne agreed and left with a spring in her step, looking forward to telling her da and Mother that she had the job. When she got home and shared the exciting news, they congratulated her, but she couldn't help but notice the looks that passed between them when she mentioned that Nelson's were still expecting her to produce her birth certificate sometime in the future.

That weekend could not go fast enough for Anne, but something slightly unsettling happened when she was scrubbing the front step. She was singing 'Dashing Away with the Smoothing Iron', her actions in rhythm to the music, when she suddenly sensed she was being watched. She glanced across the road and saw a man leaning against a garden wall staring at her. He was dark-haired beneath his cloth cap and was dark-complexioned. His grey flannel trousers and tweed jacket looked clean but well-worn. Maybe that could be because they were his working clothes. She could only guess, but when he raised an arm and beckoned to her that was enough to send her scurrying indoors to tell her da about him.

Hugh told her to stay in the kitchen and hurried outside. Anne dashed into the parlour and peered around one of the curtains. She watched as Hugh crossed the road and spoke to the man who replied with a threatening gesture. She wished she could hear what was being said as she saw Hugh seize the man by the back of his collar and the seat of his pants and march him along the pavement until both were out of sight.

Anne thought it was safe to return to her cleaning, and when a hot and bothered Hugh returned she was finishing scrubbing the step. 'Up off your knees, lass,' he said.

'It's all right, Da,' she replied. 'I'm kneeling on a cushion.'

'Never you mind, lass. This is the last time you get down on your knees out here. Now let's go inside and have a cup of tea.'

She did not argue with him; after all, she didn't want to be scrubbing steps if she could possibly avoid it. She emptied the dirty water from the bucket down the grid in the street and then removed her pinny as she followed him inside. Her mind was full of questions as he had stood waiting for her. She wanted to ask him about the man as she placed cups and saucers on the table, but his grim expression was enough to put her off. She placed two scones she had baked earlier on plates and buttered them before making a pot of tea. Hugh poured the tea and told her to sit down and have a rest. Her father's breathing settled down and he appeared thoughtful. She imagined he was going to tell her about the man outside, but instead he began to talk about his home in Scotland; he told her it was not that far from Glasgow and the village was called something that sounded like Cardross. He had grown up on a farm with his two brothers and his mother.

'What about your own da?' she asked.

'He had itchy feet and went travelling, leaving us to tend to the farm business.'

'Why didn't you stay on the farm and take it over?'

He hesitated before saying, 'I wasn't cut out for it and leaving seemed a good idea at the time.' He took a bite out of his scone. 'You should visit Scotland someday and meet the Scottish side of the family.'

'Perhaps we could go together, Da?'

'Perhaps,' he said. 'We'll see. I have a little money put aside for you so maybe we could go...'

There came the sound of a key in the front door and the next minute Emily entered the kitchen and the conversation was turned to who she had met at Great Homer Street Market on her way home from work, and she showed them what she had bought. But Anne couldn't easily forget the strange incident from earlier and wondered who the man had been.

Chapter Five

Anne was wearing what she now called her lucky red hat and her best costume consisting of a straight navy-blue skirt that came just above her knees and a bolero jacket with a crêpe de Chine pink blouse beneath it. In a shopping bag, she carried her library book and two oranges as well as her purse, although naturally she presumed that Andrew would be buying her ticket for the picture palace.

She hummed the music to 'Sonny Boy', made popular by Al Jolson in his second talkie 'The Singing Fool', which had been released that year, as she waited, having arrived at the library far too early. But she didn't have to wait long as the next moment she heard her name being spoken and there was Andrew smiling down at her. He looked smart in a brown suit with a pinstripe, a cream shirt with a maroon tie and a beige trilby hat. She could have sworn that he had shaved because his chin and upper lip were completely lacking what Da had rudely called bumfluff when Gordon was of the age to start shaving. Of course, Da had been completely unaware she was within earshot. She did not like asking Andrew how old he was but reckoned he was two or three years older than herself.

'You look lovely,' he said, his expression appreciative.

'So do you,' she said, then altered that. 'I mean you look smart.'

'Shall we go?' He offered her his arm, so she slipped her red kid-gloved hand inside it as they headed to catch a tram that would take them into town and to the Paramount Cinema.

As soon as they had seated themselves on the first tram that was going the right way, she asked him whether he had managed to do his research at Central Library.

He turned his head and gazed at her profile. 'You remembered.'

'Of course, I remember everything you told me.' Even as she spoke, she felt herself blushing. 'I was reminded of you telling me that you wanted to go to Greenock in Scotland when my da spoke to me about his own home in Scotland. He grew up on a farm. I thought how interesting it would be to go up there with him one day.'

'Where did he live?' Andrew asked.

'A place called Cardross, I think. When he gets excited or emotional his accent can be really strong.' She paused. 'Anyway, your research – did you find what you needed?'

'On the whole, yes. I have to confess that I find it disturbing that a lot of Liverpool merchants made their fortunes out of the African natives' misery and that some of our finest buildings and institutes were funded by that money,' he said.

'The slave trade ended years ago, don't forget,' she said. 'Brought about by men and women who felt just as strongly about it as you do now, stronger even.' She also added that the Suffragettes had considered that women were often regarded as possessions, just as slaves had been, and fought for improvements in the way they were treated.

'I bet you'd have been a Suffragette.'

'Mother would have been against it. She believes a woman's place is in the home.' She paused. 'Which reminds me, I start work on Thursday. I applied for the job at Nelson's and was hired anyway despite not having the right papers. Da and Mother said they might have them but that there's so much paperwork upstairs that it's taking them some time to find them.'

'I'd have thought they'd have them in a safe place.'

'Me too, but apparently safe places can change.' She heaved a sigh in frustration. 'Anyway, once it turns up, I have to take it into the Personnel Department at the factory.'

'What hours are you working?'

'Normally they're from eight o'clock until two o'clock.'

'And on Monday?'

'I don't know yet. I'll let you know as soon as I find out.'

'How? Should I drop by at your house and ask?'

She thought about that and shook her head. 'The family will want to know all about you. If they knew I was going to the flickers with you now, Mother would probably have a fit. I'm still only young.'

He grinned, causing his eyes to crinkle attractively at the corners. 'So, this is a secret liaison.'

She smiled. 'You make it sound exciting and dangerous.'

'I can't see the danger in it, but I find being with you exciting and interesting. I do hope you like Westerns. I should have asked.'

'How can you doubt me enjoying a Western, even a silent one?' She paused. 'I hope you like oranges. I bought a couple for us to eat while watching the film.'

'I love oranges, they're my favourite fruit. Even if they weren't before, they would be now,' he said, his eyes twinkling down at her.

There was a pause as the tram stopped and they gazed out of the window to see where they were. 'Only a couple more stops,' he said, and in no time at all they were stepping down from the tram. He went first and held out a hand to help her down and he kept hold of it as they made their way to the pavement, careful to avoid an automobile, van, a horse and cart and other pedestrians.

'I didn't think it would be so busy,' she said.

'By the time we come out it will have quietened down,' he said.

They entered the Paramount and soon they were seated in the upper circle gazing down at the stage and screen. A pianist was playing popular tunes of the day but stopped and began to softly play an altogether different tune when the lights were dimmed.

Anne knew she would never forget the evening. She enjoyed the romance between the hero and the leading lady, and the feel of her hand in Andrew's and the way their legs sometimes touched during the film.

Her eyes were shining as they left the picture palace and came out onto the darkened road lit by gas lamps. 'I hope a tram comes quickly. It's getting late,' she said, hurrying them both to the tram stop.

'Surely you can come up with some excuse about why you're late getting in from the library?'

'You mean tell a lie?' she said quietly.

'Not a complete lie. You can say you went to the flickers with a different friend instead of me.'

She was unsure what to say to that. 'I don't like telling lies, but they'll say I'm too young to be stepping out with a boy,' she said.

'No one likes fibs but it'll only lead to trouble if you tell the truth and you'll face a barrage of questions from your family.' Andrew looked at her honestly and she could sense he only had her best interests at heart.

They had reached the tram stop where they stood, gazing at each other. 'Well, what is it, Anne? Truth or white lie?'

She decided that she wasn't ready yet to end their secret liaison as her parents would probably prevent her from seeing Andrew again and she enjoyed his company.

'White lie,' she answered. 'I'll tell them I went to see the film with Marjorie who works at Nelson's.'

'When you get to work you can let Marjorie know whether you'll be able to meet me at the library next week too. I'll be seeing her at the weekend when she comes over with Robbie.'

That reminded her and she gasped, feeling the library book in her bag. 'Oh no, I forgot! Now *Greenmantle* will be late and I'll have to pay a fine on my book.'

'I didn't take one out last time. If you want, I could take it back tomorrow and get *Ivanhoe* and give it to Marjorie to pass it on to you.'

'That sounds like a good plan,' she said.

They said goodnight on Mere Lane and she dug into her bag and handed over her library book. He glanced about him. 'This is one of the most attractive streets around here. What with its fancy brickwork and with the houses having attics and the front rooms having bay windows and there being tiny front gardens with brick walls instead of fences.' He glanced down at her. 'I wonder whether they were built in Victorian or Edwardian times and what class they were intended for.'

'Must have been Victorian times because Da came down from Scotland and lodged here at the beginning of the 1890s and married the daughter of the owner.'

'I presume she must have had a domestic at the time who slept in the attic,' said Andrew.

'You're probably right,' she said. 'I think I heard that when Liverpool began to grow in Victorian times, the hard-working working class and master mariners moved up to this kind of street and some of the mansions owned by merchants and shipowners were demolished as they moved further away from the city, and streets of two-up, two-down terraces were built for those who flooded in to work on the docks.' She paused. 'Anyway, I'd best go in. Goodnight, God bless,' she added, reluctantly parting from him.

She looked back once and saw that he was still watching her. Could it be that he was seeing her safely home from a distance? The thought warmed her heart.

–

'What time is this to be coming in?' demanded Sylvia.

'I've been to the flickers,' Anne replied.

'On your own?' asked Emily, who was darning a stocking.

Hugh, who was reading the *Echo*, stared at Anne as if waiting for her answer.

'No, with Marjorie who works at Nelson's.'

Gordon glanced at her thoughtfully. 'Is she the Marjorie who has a nephew, Robbie, who plays footie for his local team?'

Before she could think up a lie, Anne found herself saying, 'I think so. Do you know him?'

'We've met. He has a good left foot. I've spoken to her, too, when she's come to watch him play in Newsham Park near where they live. She's a good woman.'

This was a turn-up for the books, thought Anne. Gordon played football all over Liverpool with a local amateur team, though she decided it was unlikely that Gordon would mention anything to Marjorie about them supposedly going to the flickers together.

'She mustn't know I'm your sister,' Anne said.

'I've seen no reason to mention it until I heard you talking about applying for a job in the jam factory.'

'She's a very nice person,' Anne said.

'That's what I thought. There's not many single young women who'd take on their late sister's baby and rear it as their own,' said Gordon.

'I agree,' Anne said.

'She also lived with ol' man Fraser for a while, keeping house and caring for his two kids from his second wife. Then she got fed up with him and left.'

'When you say ol' man Fraser, I presume you mean Liam Fraser who works at Tate & Lyle and goes to the People's Church?' Hugh said, looking over his paper at them. 'I heard on the grapevine that he's not too good and that he mightn't last the month out.'

Gordon nodded. 'How well do you know him, Da?'

'Well enough to know not to have anything to do with him.' Hugh's face clouded over.

'He's not a nice man and he has Irish blood,' Sylvia said.

'There's a lot of good Irish people, Sylvie, just like there's good Germans,' said Hugh. 'His race has nothing to do with matters. You're intolerant.'

'And you're too tolerant,' she said, pushing herself up from the easy chair. 'Anyway, Anne, to change the subject, what was the film like?'

'It was a Western with a dash of romance.' Anne was careful not to say too much. The talk of Liam Fraser and her father's dislike of him had unsettled her, as had Sylvia's reaction. Something about the subject of Liam Fraser was causing contention between her parents. She was glad now that she had chosen to tell the white lie.

'Worth the money?' Sylvia asked.

'I'd say so. I must admit, though, that I'm looking forward to when Gary Cooper is going to star in a talkie Western.'

'What do you think, Hugh, maybe we should have an evening out at the flickers?' asked Sylvia, appearing to try and smooth over the tension.

'If you like. Maybe Emily would like to go with us – my treat,' he said, glancing at his daughter.

'Thanks, Da, I'd like that,' she said.

Anne sighed with relief and decided to make herself a cup of cocoa and take it up to bed with her. She felt tired with all the excitement of the evening. Picking up Emily's magazine *People's Friend* on her way out, she wondered when next she would see Andrew and whether he would mention his father not being well.

Chapter Six

Anne was feeling a mixture of nerves and excitement as she stood outside Nelson's factory on Long Lane, Aintree, watching workers entering through its gates. She was hoping she might see Marjorie but there was no sign of her, so she made her way into the factory's arrivals office and was escorted to the area where she would be working on a regular basis. She found the girls and women easy to get along with and the job of sticking labels on glass jars easy to pick up with practice. The factory was also filled with the pleasant smell of boiling jam. The time passed swiftly, and it was soon time to go home. As she headed out through the factory gates, a young man fell into step beside her.

'Hello. I saw you earlier. You're the new girl.' The young man had a head of blond hair and bright blue eyes. Anne thought he seemed very confident.

'Yes, I'm Anne. Who are you?' she responded.

'My name is Pete. I'm on the packing line. Sometimes us fellas like to play tricks on the girls on the line.' He had a cheeky expression.

'I hope you won't play tricks on me as I'm still learning.' Anne didn't want to get into trouble.

'I can't promise that!' The man grinned as he ran off down the road in front of her and Anne thought his face was not altogether unattractive, but she was too fond of Andrew to entertain that thought for more than a moment.

–

Having seen no sign of Marjorie during the previous week, she decided to visit the library on Monday evening regardless of not getting a message to Andrew, but to her disappointment, he wasn't there. She had really liked Marjorie and had an inkling that Gordon had a soft spot for her too, although she guessed she might be a little older than him. She wondered if Andrew had mentioned the matter to Marjorie when he had seen her at the weekend and hoped she could trust Marjorie to keep quiet about her white lie regarding the visit to the flicks. But even if Marjorie were to tell Gordon, she reckoned he could be trusted to keep her secret too. As it was, it was her brother who handed the novel *Ivanhoe* to her late afternoon on Sunday after seeing Marjorie in the park. Anne was surprised.

'How did you come by this?' Anne asked, despite guessing that it must have come from Marjorie.

Gordon looked a bit sheepish himself. 'To be honest, Marjorie and I know each other a little better than I let on. We've been walking out together from time to time.'

'I like her,' Anne said. 'I like her a lot.'

'So do I.' Gordon smiled. 'Andrew passed it to Marjorie over the weekend and asked if she could give it to you in work, so you'd have a chance to read it before next going to the library. When I saw her today, she told me, and she knows you're my sister... so here it is.'

'Did she say anything about me and Andrew?'

'No, but I worked it out.' He smiled. 'You're going to have to be careful if you're going to carry on seeing Andrew. Da and Mother won't like it. You heard what they said about his father.'

'I know but I like him, and he likes me,' cried Anne.

'Da and Mother won't care about that,' said Gordon. 'Their excuse will be that you're too young to be going out with boys.'

'I'm not a kid. I've left school and I've got a job.' She scowled. 'I wish I knew what Da's got against Andrew's father.'

'I doubt he'll tell you. It's been going on for years.'

'Maybe it's something to do with work or something that happened in Scotland,' she suggested.

'Anyway, whatever it is, Da's not going to approve, so perhaps you should stop seeing him now.'

Anne shrugged. 'If Da met Andrew he'd soon see that he isn't the least bit like his father.'

'From what Marjorie says about father and son, I'd agree with you,' Gordon said, picking up her crossword and scanning it.

'I'll think about what you've said.' She opened *Ivanhoe* and turned to the first chapter. 'You can finish the crossword if you like. I'm going to read.'

He sat in the other easy chair and fell silent, so that when Emily came in to tell them tea was on the table, she found them completely engrossed.

Anne had discovered a folded sheet of paper between the pages of the book and soon realised it was a short note from Andrew.

Dear Anne,

*I'm sorry I wasn't at the library as usual on
Monday. I hope you enjoy the book and that you
can manage to be at the library next week at the
usual time. Father is not well, so I won't be able
to stay long but hopefully we'll have time to talk.*

Warmest thoughts flying your way,

Andrew

She sighed happily and tucked the note in the pocket of
her blouse.

-

Come Monday, she went to the library, taking her library
book to return it. She saw Andrew almost immediately as
he had been watching out for her. She followed him over
to where the daily newspapers were available to read for
those who could not afford to buy one. They sat down
at a table and, as he opened a copy of the London *Times*,
she asked after his father, deciding to remain silent about
what Hugh and Sylvia had said about Liam Fraser. She
told him that Hugh and Sylvia had accepted what she had
told them about going to the flickers with Marjorie. She
also told him that Gordon knew that Marjorie had once
cared for Andrew's father and that her sister, Sadie, had
been married to him before she died.

'It appears that Da knows your father,' she said, 'but
I didn't get the impression that they liked each other.
Gordon knows I've been seeing you, too.'

Andrew looked thoughtful and did not say anything
for several minutes and then he said, 'My father can be
a difficult man and other folk think so too, not just me,

it seems. We did the right thing keeping quiet about us meeting. Do you think Gordon will remain silent?'

She nodded. 'For a while anyway.'

'Do you want to continue meeting?' he asked, not looking at her and nervously flicking through pages of the newspaper he was holding in his hands.

'Of course. I get an enormous amount of pleasure from doing so,' Anne said.

He grinned in relief. 'I'm flattered.'

'You should be, as I can honestly say there's never been anyone else in my life like you.'

'Then perhaps we should see more of each other. How do you fancy meeting outside Nelson's on Wednesday at two o'clock and we can go for a trip across the Mersey to New Brighton followed by a walk along the prom?'

'I love the idea, and my mother is out all afternoon so won't miss me,' she said, smiling.

Andrew stared at her and Anne felt that strange fluttering in her tummy.

–

On Wednesday, Anne left the factory to find Andrew waiting for her across the road. He drew her hand through his arm and they set off to catch a tram that would take them to the Pier Head. Easter was now behind them and with no April showers to spoil their outing, they happily joined the crowds taking the ferry to New Brighton, a seaside resort on the other side of the River Mersey.

'How have you managed to take time off from work?' she asked as they stood at the side of the ship watching a couple of seamen casting off. 'They must be strong,' she said, diverted. 'Those ropes are really thick.'

'I'm writing an article about the ferry boats of the Mersey,' he said. 'Did you know there used to be a priory in Birkenhead a long time ago, and one of the first ferries was a rowing boat that would carry the monks backwards and forwards to Liverpool to a chapel over here near the waterfront and then sometimes they would walk up to the church of St Mary in Walton. It was well before the Reformation.'

'No, I didn't know that. You always share such interesting facts. I presume that information will go in your article?'

Andrew nodded. 'I'm also going to include something on the history of New Brighton and how it grew to be the place it is now. It's a shame that the tower isn't there any more. It was like the one in Blackpool, but it closed years ago because it fell into ruin.'

'I'd heard about it from my big brother, Albert. Never mind, we can walk to the end of the pier – it's very long. Anyway, I'm sure the *Echo* readers will enjoy your piece,' Anne said, holding her face up to the sun and the slight breeze that blew up from the estuary.

Andrew gazed at her peaches-and-cream profile and felt a swelling sensation in his chest. He really liked her but knew he was going to have to wait a while before he could take matters further. She was too young to be thinking of marriage. He would need to earn more money, so he could provide them with a home and support them both in a few years' time. There was also the problem of her da not liking his father. He wished he knew what all that was about, but it was almost impossible trying to get any sense out of his father, whose deteriorating mental state and occasional bouts of violence worried Andrew, especially as they were directed towards himself.

It was Anne nudging his elbow on the rail that brought him back to a realisation that he was wasting these moments they had together. 'Are you thinking about where to find the information you need?' she asked.

He smiled down at her and could not resist placing a kiss on the tip of her pert little nose. 'I can do that in Liverpool's Central Library. I just want to get the feel of New Brighton again as I haven't been there for years.'

'I have heard that there are caves in New Brighton where smugglers used to stow their contraband,' Anne said.

'You're right, but I don't think the public are allowed inside as they're considered unsafe.'

'Pity,' said Anne. 'It would be exciting going into a smuggler's cave.'

'You're clearly a girl with a taste for adventure,' he replied, looking at the excited gleam in her eyes. 'But onto more mundane matters. I know it's some way off, but have you any plans for Whit Bank Holiday Monday?'

'Probably what I always do and go and watch the Lodges march to Newsham Park with Emily. I like a parade and love the music. Mother will only stay for a short time and then return home. She always expects there to be trouble.'

The Protestant associations, or Orange Orders, had marches throughout the year and the next big one was on Whit Monday and they were going to Newsham Park. The marches caused tension between the mainly Irish Catholic community and the Protestants and sometimes squabbles broke out.

'As will my father,' Andrew said. 'I think it is an old-fashioned tradition that just causes trouble, but I'll walk alongside so I can keep my eye on him. Robbie and Marjorie will go with me.'

'Da will go to keep his eye on his womenfolk. It's a shame the two communities are still at loggerheads. I might see you afterwards, though,' said Anne. 'It can be fun in the park as there are games for the children and picnics.'

'We'll try and meet up in the park. How about on the bridge over the boating lake?'

She agreed. 'Won't I see you before then?'

'Of course. The library next week, same time,' he said. 'Whitsun is still a few weeks away but I can't see you as often with Father not being well. I have a little help from a local woman who's looking after him today, but she doesn't always have time.'

Anne sighed. 'So, what do we do?'

'I'll come up with something,' he said, sounding more hopeful than he felt.

Anne enjoyed their afternoon together just as much as she thought she would and could hardly bear the thought that this outing would probably be their last for a while. They held hands as they walked along the prom and gazed down at the crowded beach before leaving the crowds behind and strolling in the direction of Perch Rock Lighthouse. A short distance beyond, there was a clear view across the Mersey to the Bootle docks to the north and the Liver Building at Pier Head; they could also see the as yet unfinished Anglican cathedral at St James Mount.

'I love Liverpool,' she said. 'I'm not saying it's perfect but it's exciting, interesting. Most of all it's my home.'

'What if you had to leave it one day?' he asked.

'I'd have to have a good reason,' she replied.

Andrew wanted to ask if she would follow her husband to another place when she was older, but instead dropped the subject and said it was time they were catching the ferry back.

She did not argue, knowing she needed to get back herself, but was sorry that their day was over so soon. When they said goodbye at the top of Mere Lane, they were both walking on air.

—

The following Monday, Anne was looking forward to seeing Andrew, but she could tell that something was wrong as soon as she saw him in their usual spot by the daily newspapers. 'Are you all right?' she asked.

Andrew unclenched his fists and forced a smile, not wanting to tell her that his father had lost his temper that morning and punched him in the solar plexus. 'It's nothing that an hour in your company won't fix.' His voice shook, and he changed the subject by asking her what she thought of Sir Walter Scott's writing.

'He's terribly wordy.'

Andrew agreed that Scott was wordy, adding, 'But in those days his readers had more time to read and wanted a longer book to fill up the hours.'

They talked about books for the rest of their visit to the library, but Anne wished that Andrew would confide in her about what was wrong. She remembered what he had said about his father being a difficult person and, now that he was quite ill, Anne wondered if that had something to do with it.

After recommending she read *Winnie the Pooh*, which he said lots of adults enjoyed, she had the book stamped and they left the library. Andrew suggested going to the milk bar on Breck Road. 'I know it's a bit of a walk, but we can have a milkshake or a Vimto and spend some more time together before having to go back home.'

She liked the idea, especially as she sensed he wanted to stay away from home longer. She wished he felt able to talk to her about it. On their way towards the milk bar, she spotted Joan, Teddy's girlfriend, and guessed she was going to Mere Lane to see Teddy. She hoped Joan had not noticed her with Andrew.

Anne found it difficult to get the thought out of her mind of Joan telling Teddy about having seen her with a boy and her Da finding out. Gordon already knew about her and Andrew and she didn't know how much longer their secret would hold. She and Andrew bid each other a farewell when they got to Mere Lane.

'Are you sure you are going to be alright?' she asked.

'I'm grand. Seeing you has cheered me up no end. Have a nice afternoon and don't worry about me or about your brother's girlfriend seeing us.'

—

She need not have allowed herself to worry too much as when she got home, Hugh and Sylvia were more concerned with the news that Joan was expecting Teddy's baby. Teddy and Joan had broken the news to his parents that afternoon.

The news stunned Anne because she had believed a couple had to be married before they had children. Teddy had told his parents that there was no need to threaten him into making an honest woman of Joan because they were in love and wanted to marry each other anyway.

Anne could see that her parents were shocked, her mother more so, as Teddy was now standing up for himself.

'We've already had the banns read in church, Mother,' he told her. 'I'm a grown man and can make my own decisions.'

'You know your own mind and we won't stand in your way, son. We'll be happy to welcome Joan to the family,' Hugh said, and Sylvia kept her mouth in a tight line as her husband spoke. Anne thought Sylvia might not agree. It was decided the wedding would be in a fortnight's time and that the couple could live with the family on Mere Lane. Anne wondered how Sylvia would take to a strong-minded woman like Joan living under her roof.

-

It was on Teddy and Joan's wedding day that the issue of Anne having been seen walking out with a boy finally raised its head. The family had all come back after the service at St George's for tea and sandwiches and it was there that both Gordon and Teddy brought the subject up. Anne had felt for some weeks that it would be hard to keep it a secret now that Joan and Teddy and Gordon and Marjorie all knew. Gordon told her that the four of them had all agreed it should be Anne breaking the news that it was Liam Fraser's son she was walking out with.

'So, who is this boy that you've been seen out with, Anne?' Hugh asked. 'You're still a young lass and we want to meet him before we can approve of him.'

Anne couldn't bring herself to tell them all the truth just yet. Sylvia suggested that Anne bring the boy home to meet them and Anne reluctantly agreed that she would suggest it next time she saw him, knowing that would not be until Whit Monday. She had no idea how she was going to tell them the truth. Perhaps once they met Andrew, they would understand that he really wasn't like Liam at all.

Chapter Seven

The Anderson household was up early on the Bank Holiday Monday, after Hugh had attended a service the day before at the People's Church situated on Shaw Street in Everton, one that was popular with Orange Lodge members. Hugh was a member of the Royal Black Institution and had been so since his twenty-first birthday up in Scotland. His father had been a member and he had been keen for his eldest son to follow in his footsteps. Hugh seldom bothered with the lodge since leaving Scotland, but lately he had been thinking about his father and so had decided to attend the People's Church in uniform the evening before the march, although he had no intention of marching. He had dressed in smart black trousers, a black beret and a blazer with the insignia of the Black Instituion's Sir Knights on the front pocket. He also wore a sash diagonally across his chest. This was despite his father having deserted his family to go travelling years ago.

When Anne asked him about the uniform, Hugh said that the purpose of the uniform and the marches was to honour their traditions, not to upset people. Anne had to admit that she always felt a stir of excitement when the Lodge musicians began to play as they led the men and the women who marched with them. As the marchers proceeded past them, Anne and Emily joined the other spectators in singing 'Sons of the Sea Bobbing Up and Down Like This', at which point everyone bobbed up and down, which made her laugh. As the song finished, there was a sudden commotion at the front of the spectators.

A group of men had charged out of one of the pubs as the procession passed by and a confrontation had ensued. It didn't take long for tempers to flare and a violent clash followed quickly, with many bottles and bricks being thrown. Anne and Emily were terrified when they heard a voice shout, 'There's a man injured!'

They could see that there was blood pouring down the side of the face of the man on the ground. Anne thanked God that it was not Hugh before realising that Andrew was on his knees beside the stricken man, along with Robbie and Marjorie. They were then hidden from sight as more innocent bystanders gathered around the man on the ground. She wondered if the wounded man was Andrew's father because he bore a likeness to the man she had seen watching her when she washed the front step. A couple of policemen arrived and attempted to clear the scene. Again, she could see Andrew and the man on the ground who was obviously attempting to say something to Andrew. Seeing the terrible look of torment on his face, she did not hesitate in dashing forward and forced her way through the throng. Anne reached out to Andrew and placed a hand on his shoulder. He looked up, almost not recognising her for a moment.

When he spoke, his voice was shaking. 'My father has been attacked. It's serious.'

They both stared down at the now unconscious man, and despite the blood pouring from his head, she was positive he was the man who had watched her while she scrubbed the doorstep. Before Anne could speak, Emily was beside her and a man carrying a doctor's bag appeared, pushing through the crowd to reach the gravely wounded man. He brusquely ordered Andrew to get out of the way and one of the policemen told her to step back to give the doctor more room, which she did. Now separated from Andrew once more, Anne was desperate to offer him comfort, but Emily held her back and there were now too many people crowding around Liam Fraser for her to see what was happening. Suddenly Hugh appeared next to Anne, and between him and Emily, they managed to remove her from the scene.

Anne protested tearfully as Hugh ordered Emily to take her straight home, but Emily firmly insisted and, feeling wracked with worry for Andrew, Anne gave up the struggle and went with her.

On the way back home, Emily gently quizzed Anne about Andrew and how they knew each other. Anne could find no reason to hide the truth now. All she could think of was Andrew's tortured face as he looked down on his prone father, who had appeared almost lifeless.

The girls returned to Mere Lane to find Sylvia sitting by the fire reading a copy of *Woman's Weekly*. She glanced up and stared at them in surprise. 'Why are you two back so soon?' she asked.

'There's been a terrible incident at the march,' Emily said, lowering Anne into a chair.

Anne snuffled and attempted to wipe her tears away with her sleeve.

'What on earth has happened?' asked Sylvia. 'It's not your father, is it?'

'No, Mother,' Emily answered. 'It's Mr Fraser. A missile was thrown and hit him on the head. It's his son Andrew that Anne has been stepping out with.'

All the colour drained from Sylvia's face. 'You have to be kidding me!'

'Not at all!' Anne flushed and attempted to stand up but when she tried, her legs would not hold her up. She gripped the arms of the chair. 'I must go back there. Andrew needs me.'

Sylvia said icily, 'How come the two of you know each other? Does Hugh know about it?'

'We're… we're friends,' Anne managed, stumbling over the words.

'Where's your father, Emily?' Sylvia asked, looking highly agitated.

'He's at the scene,' said Emily. 'It's pandemonium, Mother. I don't know what he's going to do.'

'This won't do. He needs to speak to that young man – best he brings him here and we talk to them both together. I'm going to go and find him right away.'

Anne stared at Sylvia as she hurried out of the room, thinking that what she and Andrew had feared was now happening, but it was to be far worse than either of them had thought.

–

A couple of hours later Hugh and Sylvia arrived home, but they were not alone, having brought Andrew with them. The first thing Hugh said was, 'Make me and the lad some tea, please, Emily.'

Emily wasted no time in doing so. As for Anne, she asked Andrew how his father was and flinched when he told her that he had a serious head wound and had been taken to Newsham Hospital. He had been hit with a half-brick and a nurse was at his bedside.

'So, say what you want to say, Mr Anderson, then I must go back to the hospital,' Andrew said, glancing briefly at Anne. 'Although I suppose I can guess what you're going to say and that I'm to keep away from Anne because you don't like my father and because we are too young to be courting.'

'It's more than that, lad,' said Hugh, sighing heavily.

'Oh, get on with it, Hugh, or do I have to do it for you?' said Sylvia in exasperation. 'Andrew, Anne, there is no way of sugar-coating this news so brace yourselves for a shock.'

Suddenly Anne could feel her legs shaking, realising that something horrible was about to happen but not knowing what.

'It's time you both know the truth… you are brother and sister.'

Andrew reached out and gripped the table. 'I don't see how that can be,' he said, his voice faint.

'Me neither,' Anne said, her head swimming, and feeling as if her world had come crashing down. 'How can it be?' Her voice was trembling.

'Yes, explain. We deserve that, at least,' said Andrew harshly.

Sylvia looked to Hugh, but he appeared to be struck dumb, so she sighed and continued, 'When our small daughter, Flora, died in a terrible accident…' She paused but was interrupted by her husband.

'Due to your negligence!' Hugh thundered. 'You should never have left her alone in a room with an unguarded fire.'

Sylvia shivered and seemed to shrink as she wrapped her arms around herself and let out a moan. 'Hugh, please don't blame this situation all on me!'

Hugh's face was clouded in anger and something else Anne couldn't quite understand, before he turned his back on Sylvia and hurried from the room, which was now filled with a deathly silence.

Emily went over to Anne and sat on the arm of the chair and placed an arm around the shaking girl. 'You must know how much we all love you,' she said. 'We've tried to protect you all these years.' She squeezed Anne's hand before continuing. 'My little sister, Flora, died of burns when she fell into an unguarded fireplace. Mother was on the verge of a nervous collapse. It just so happened that Liam Fraser's second wife, Sarah, had died in childbirth, leaving a baby daughter without a mother to care for her. Struggling to survive, she was put with a wet nurse and luckily, she made it through.

'Hugh and Liam were both Lodge members at the time, and when Liam heard about Flora's death after the accident, he suggested that his baby daughter become part of our family as he couldn't care for her alone. Da went and visited the midwife and fell in love with you and brought you here.'

Andrew cried out in an anguished voice, 'He lied to me and told me that the baby and my mother had both died!'

'That little baby was our Anne, but a while later Da adopted Anne legally as soon as he could because your father started making a nuisance of himself, wanting her back,' continued Emily.

Sylvia burst in, saying, 'Hugh told him he no longer had a legal right to her, and Liam asked for money to stop bothering us. He only did it once before he moved out of the neighbourhood, only to return not so long ago. That's why there is so much bad blood between them.'

Andrew and Anne looked at each other in anguish. Andrew said despairingly, 'Can you prove any of this?'

'Of course,' Sylvia said. 'You only have to ask a couple of the Lodge members who were around at the time because they knew of it and we have the birth certificate.'

Anne felt just as filled with despair as Andrew did, convinced that she was now hearing the truth, instead of the lie she had been told about her natural father having died before she was born.

'I don't want to believe it,' she moaned. 'You told me my father was dead and never mentioned I had a living brother or a sister. You are supposed to love me. I thought I could trust this family.'

'We loved you from the moment we set eyes on you,' said Emily. 'Please, don't hate us.'

'How could I hate you, Emily? You cared for me like a mother and I still love you for that. But I'm lost about where my life goes from here.'

'Me too,' Andrew said. 'I had the next couple of years planned out, but now...' He paused. 'As soon as Father is conscious, I'm going to ask him if this is true!' He squared his shoulders. 'Right now, I'm going back to the hospital.'

He looked at Anne, and they both experienced the horrible sensation that they might never see each other again.

'Oh, Andrew,' Anne sobbed, 'this is awful.'

'I can't believe all my dreams for us are in tatters.' Anne thought she could see tears in his eyes as he spoke the words with feeling.

'But it might not be true!' Anne knew in her heart there was nothing they could do.

'See you around, kid.' Andrew tried to smile, but the effort was too much for him and he dashed out into the street.

Anne burst into tears and would have followed him if Hugh had not held her back. She felt as if her heart were breaking and couldn't believe that they might never see each other in the same way ever again.

Chapter Eight

Anne heard the news that Liam Fraser had passed away without speaking to Andrew again. She was to catch sight of Andrew at his father's funeral the following week, and it was a full-blown funeral paid for out of the local Lodge funds. Hugh had insisted that they all go despite the situation, as Liam was a fellow Lodge member like himself. It broke her heart all over again to see Andrew so brave and stoic at the graveside. They shared a look with each other that spoke volumes and she would have gone to him if the Anderson family had not watched her like hawks; either Gordon met her in his delivery van or Teddy with his horse and cart to take her home each day.

She had tried to speak to Hugh about the situation, but he was silent on the matter and so were the rest of the family. When she decided to visit Marjorie, Gordon accompanied her, and Marjorie told her that Andrew thought it best if they kept their distance.

When Anne burst into tears, Marjorie hugged her and added, 'He said that he'd never feel like a brother to you, so it was best this way.'

'I can't bear it,' sobbed Anne. 'I love him.'

'You have to be brave,' said Marjorie. 'He's doing what he thinks is best.'

'Is he at home?' Anne asked.

Marjorie shook her head. 'He's gone to London. He won an award for young journalists and has applied for a job at one of the big national newspapers.'

'He never mentioned entering a competition to me,' said Anne.

'Me neither,' Marjorie said. 'Probably didn't want to say anything in case he failed.'

'I bet he gets the job and I'll never see him again,' said Anne dejectedly.

Marjorie also told Anne that Andrew had visited Somerset House on London's big thoroughfare, the Strand, where all the public records were kept, and had discovered that a baby girl had been born to his mother and the baby had survived. He remembered his mother mentioned naming the baby Jane if it had been a girl, so it puzzled him that she had been named Anne.

Anne could scarcely believe Andrew would leave without saying goodbye to her, but it was obvious that he did not want to see her ever again. She felt weak with longing for him, while at the same time being worried sick about Da, who was a changed man. In the weeks after the revelation and the death of Liam Fraser, he had lost weight and looked as if he carried the woes of the whole world on his shoulders. Then he caught a cold which descended to his chest and he developed a hacking cough. It seemed as if he had no strength in him to fight the illness.

Sylvia was so concerned she wrote to Albert, their eldest son. Within the week he arrived at the house with his wife Gladys. Anne and her siblings had never taken to Gladys. She was high-handed and interrupted all the time with opinions that were none of her business and it seemed to Anne that the feeling appeared mutual.

Hugh seemed to get worse, and the doctor said it was a nasty bout of bronchitis which had soon developed into pneumonia. The family couldn't believe that their beloved Da had taken such a nasty turn for the worse and they all shared in watching over him throughout the day and night.

Anne volunteered to take a night shift sitting with him and, watching his grey features, Anne wished that he was well enough for her to ask all the questions that were racing around her mind. One night, Anne felt Hugh grip her hand tightly and she sensed that he was trying to say something to her, but her brother Albert had insisted on keeping her company and she never found out what it was Hugh might have wanted to say.

After several long, painful and exhausting days, Hugh passed away. The unexpectedness and speed of his death was a shock to all of them, for they all loved Da dearly and it was a great sorrow for the whole family.

—

Albert had never been close to his father, rather he had been Sylvia's favourite, and now he suggested that his mother leave Liverpool to live with him and Gladys in Bury St Edmunds. She refused, saying she wanted to be there when her first grandchild was born. To his siblings' surprise, he decided that he and Gladys would remain in Liverpool as he was helping Sylvia deal with the necessary paperwork to do with Hugh's death. The couple continued living with the rest of the family, much to everyone's dismay except for Sylvia. Gladys got on everyone's nerves with her opinions and laziness, doing little housework, leaving it to Emily, Anne and Joan. Albert, meanwhile, lorded it over everyone, and all the while Hugh's children could hardly credit the way things had changed in their household so quickly.

In September, to everyone's relief, Albert broke the news to them that he and Gladys were moving to Rhyl, a seaside resort on the North Wales coast. They had bought a small hotel, saying it had been a dream of his for ages to do so. Anne guessed that he had been able to fulfil his dream with his share of the money Hugh had left and Gladys's inheritance from her father. She was just glad to see the back of them, still engulfed in sorrow over Andrew's departure to London and Hugh's death.

In the weeks after their departure, Sylvia seemed to struggle without her favourite son, who had been a crutch for her to lean on, and a month after they left, she seemed to suffer a funny turn. While Emily was all for sending for the doctor, her mother insisted on simply taking to her bed and being waited on hand and foot, saying she could not afford the doctor's fee. Eventually, exasperated by her demands, they all clubbed in together with their wages to get the doctor in.

The outcome of the doctor's visit was that Sylvia was prescribed some little blue pills and told to get out and about more, and also that a holiday by the seaside would do her a world of good. Emily wrote to Albert explaining the situation and a plan was hatched for Sylvia to go and stay with Albert and Gladys for a while. Apparently, the hotel was receiving some financial input from Sylvia, who had saved the money Hugh had left her in a bank. Emily, Teddy and Gordon had also inherited a sum of money.

Anne received only a little of what the others received individually. She would not have been surprised by this if she had not remembered Hugh mentioning having a decent sum for her set aside several months ago when he had talked with her about Scotland, but she could not be bothered making a fuss about it to Albert.

–

Anne's job at Nelson's factory was a helpful distraction. One day during the lunchtime break, as she sat in the canteen, the young man who had spoken to her before, called Pete, came over to her again.

'Can I join you?' He sat down next to her before she could answer.

'It's a free country.'

'I heard about your da passing away. I'm sorry for you.'

'Thank you.' Anne thought this was a different side to him that she was seeing and the concern in his eyes looked genuine.

'You need to have a bit of fun, to take you out of yourself,' he said.

'I don't know about that. It's hard to laugh when you are missing someone.' She meant Andrew as well as her father when she said this, but couldn't tell Pete that.

Wasps were a nuisance at the factory and Pete was charged with putting jam and water into containers to attract the wasps so they would drown. That afternoon, as her shift ended and she left her place on the line, Anne was shocked to see Pete running towards her. He held out his arms in front of him and she saw, to her horror, that they were covered in jam and almost a whole swarm of wasps were buzzing around him, some of them which were stuck to the jam on his fingers. She yelled out in surprise and soon all the other girls on the line were screaming too. Pete was laughing out loud at them and Anne could see now that this was a practical joke designed to cause pandemonium. However, Pete cried out himself as one of the wasps stung his face and Anne burst out laughing at his trick backfiring. It wasn't long before the foreman came over and gave Pete a good talking to, making him go to the bathroom to wash the jam off. The foreman was quite a good-natured man and Pete wasn't in any real trouble.

Pete fell into step with her again as she left the factory after getting her coat with the other girls.

'Did you like my little joke?' His same cheeky grin was plastered all over his face, and Anne thought he looked very pleased with himself even though he had a big red swelling on his forehead where the wasp had stung him.

'You're a daft idiot, what were you thinking? Does the sting hurt? It looks painful.'

'Nah, I'm fine. I was trying to get your attention.' His eyes twinkled mischievously.

'Mine? Why?' Anne couldn't think what he meant.

'How about coming to the flickers with me? We'll have a laugh and you need cheering up. We can see a Buster Keaton movie. He's funny.'

Anne told him that she'd have to think about it and hurried off home, but he had made her laugh, it was true, and it felt like a real tonic after all the sadness at home.

–

Albert came soon after and took Sylvia with him to his hotel in Rhyl to recuperate, and it was blissful to have the house to themselves without all of Sylvia's testy demands. One evening, over a Madeira cake that Anne had made, she spoke to Emily about the conversation with her da about Scotland and of her conviction that he had intended for them to visit Scotland one day together because he had set money aside for it. 'I'd still like to go there one day,' she added.

'Surely you could do so next year, maybe in spring? You don't want to go in summer because of the midges,' said Emily. 'You have some money Da left you still, surely?'

'I'm not sure it will be enough. I do have some money I've saved from my wages as well, but I could do with more, what with Christmas approaching,' Anne said.

Emily agreed, adding that one never knew what might happen before then.

'I also decided that perhaps I should search for my adoption papers while Mother is away, and Albert isn't around to spy on us. I remembered that Da had kept his important papers in an old leather suitcase, but couldn't find it even with Gordon's help.'

'Albert could have taken it with him,' Emily suggested.

Anne could have wept. 'It's difficult not doing anything to improve my situation but wait. I just wish Andrew would get in touch, instead of my having to wait to hear news of him from Marjorie. I keep thinking there must be some way that it's not true that Andrew and I are brother and sister. I would be able to sense it inside of myself. I don't think I could feel this way about him if he was really my brother.'

'At least you know where he is. I'd love to know what happened to my sweetheart, Larry. As it is, I don't know if he's dead or alive,' said Emily sadly.

'I wish I could help you find out.' This sparked a thought. 'Maybe I could, while I'm trying to find out about my own family?' The idea excited her. It would be wonderful to see Emily happy.

'He could be anywhere now… but it does nag away at me. Perhaps it was his mother who was to blame. She didn't want him to marry me! Or maybe he could have died?'

'That would be sad to find out,' agreed Anne, 'but at least you would know one way or the other and not always be wondering.' Anne promised herself that she would try her best to find out what had happened to Larry. She owed it to her sister, who had given up her life to care for the family.

'Is there any cream?' asked Anne.

'No, but there's jam. Nelson's – I love strawberry jam, thank goodness for your job!' Emily said, licking her lips.

Anne said, 'Did I tell you about this bloke at work, Pete? He's a bit of a prankster, but he's funny. He asked me out to the pictures.'

Emily suggested that if he asked her out then she should accept as there was little point in her moping about after Andrew.

Anne thought that was easier said than done and wished there was a way of finding out more about her birth and the circumstances around it. She didn't even know where exactly she had been born, thinking just somewhere in Liverpool was not enough information. She needed to find her birth certificate. Strangely, it was only then that she thought of the old biscuit tin Sylvia kept on top of the wardrobe. Anne had resisted climbing on the bed and getting it down to search inside of it, believing that Sylvia had looked there when Anne had told her she needed it. So, later that day, she asked Gordon to get the tin down for her, telling him it had to be done now before Mother returned from Rhyl.

Anne was delighted to discover the certificate and the adoption form squashed in between old birthday cards, a marriage certificate, an insurance policy and a sealed envelope. She took the tin and its contents to her bedroom. Gordon followed her and sat on the bed beside her as she unfolded the birth certificate, and both read it carefully.

Gordon said, 'I see Mr Fraser didn't register the birth. It says here that it was the midwife and gives the place of birth as the Sandon Hotel, Oakfield Road, and the baby was named Jane.' He glanced at Anne. 'Don't you think that's odd?'

She said, 'Andrew told me that his mother had mentioned calling the baby Jane if it was a girl, but I find it strange that I was born in a hotel and the parents are Mr and Mrs Fraser.' She heaved a sigh. 'And it gives the midwife's name and she's a Cissie Jamieson.'

'It also gives the mother's home address but that caught fire when the house next door was on fire. I wonder why she wasn't taken to the nearest hospital?' Gordon said.

'Let's have a closer look at the adoption papers,' said Anne.

They did so and saw that the child Jane Fraser was going to be known as Anne Jane Anderson.

Gordon and Anne stared at each other and he said, 'Interesting, but where do you think this will lead you? The parents named are still Andrew's parents.'

'I feel in my bones that I need to follow this trail as there's something odd about the whole thing, and while I'm feeling hopeful, I'd like to help Emily find out what happened to her sweetheart, Larry, too. Do you know anything that could help me trace him?'

Gordon said, 'I do remember going with her to a greengrocer's on Netherfield Road, and she and the assistant seemed to have a lot to say to each other.'

'Perhaps that was Larry,' said Anne. 'I'll see what I can find out without saying anything yet.'

'I don't know how Mother and Da missed looking in this tin when you asked for your birth certificate. It's probably been here all the time,' Gordon said, leaving her bedroom to put the tin back on the wardrobe. 'Let's go and have a cuppa now.'

Anne kept the birth certificate and adoption papers and then led the way downstairs and made tea. She was thinking that it was likely that Gordon would tell Marjorie about what they had discovered, and she would pass it on to Andrew who just might write to her. And even though it was wrong, she hoped that he would. She resolved to visit the Sandon Hotel as soon as possible. She did so the following evening and was stunned to see that it was nothing other than a commonplace pub near the Anfield football ground. Disappointed and puzzled, she turned away, aware that she just could not go inside alone, and so went home.

Chapter Nine

When Anne returned from work, it was to find Joan preparing a hot dinner. They'd had word through the post that Sylvia was coming home after feeling much improved and Albert would be bringing her back. Joan also planned on making scones. 'I thought we'd better have something to offer them with a cup of tea in case Albert doesn't want to stick around for dinner,' said Joan, now heavy with child and moving about cumbersomely. 'I can't see Gladys and Albert having children after all this time. She's no spring chicken and she's a few years older than Albert.'

'Just like Mother was older than Da,' said Anne. 'The girls at school used to think she was my grandmother.'

'She was past forty when she had me and then Flora, so Emily told me,' Gordon said, who had popped in during a delivery to see if his mother and brother had arrived yet. 'Da was only in his mid-thirties.'

'Getting on in age to be adopting,' Anne said thoughtfully.

'She probably wouldn't have if Da hadn't brought you home.' Gordon said grimly. 'When Flora died it was as if a black cloud descended on the house. Then Da said something had to be done. When he turned up with you shortly after, everything began to get better.'

'Didn't Mr Fraser have any women in his family who could have helped?'

'No, he wasn't a Liverpudlian, so had no family here. They were all up in Scotland,' Gordon said. 'I don't know why I'm telling you all this when you know the bloke was Andrew's father. Da thought it would snap Mother out of her depression and it did up to a point. She never got over the loss of Flora. Sometimes Da blamed her and sometimes she blamed herself; really it was an accident, but you certainly helped her concentrate her thoughts elsewhere, other than on her grief. As for Da, he loved the bones of you. Me, Emily and Teddy all took to you as well. Albert wrote from the Front saying they were making a mistake and told Da that he should never have adopted you because it wasn't fair on Mother.'

Anne said, 'As it was, Emily did most of the hard work caring for me – she should have married and had children of her own. Instead, she was so overworked that it almost crippled her.'

Gordon said simply, 'Well, she did have that boyfriend, Larry, but I don't think she's had much opportunity to meet anyone else since then.'

Anne was feeling odd. For what felt like forever she had believed her natural mother had not wanted her and had willingly given her up; now she was starting to understand that it had not been like that at all. Her mother had sacrificed her life giving birth to her. She was so caught up in her thoughts that she did not catch what Joan said and asked her to repeat it.

She said, 'Emily's chap was called Larry Williams and he lived with his widowed mother. She was very posses-sive, just like Mother is of Albert. Teddy says he was

72

always Mother's favourite and no girl would ever be good enough for him. Gladys wouldn't have stood a chance of getting him if she'd met him on home turf. Mind you, if she had a baby that might change things. Mother would probably think she was perfect then!' Joan took a packet of Woodbines out of her pinny pocket and offered Gordon one before lighting up.

'Mother will have a fit if she sees you smoking, especially with the baby being due so soon,' Anne said absently, while mulling over the name Larry Williams.

'That's why I'm having one before she arrives,' Joan said. 'She's still living in the old days when women weren't considered equal to men.'

At that moment, there was the sound of a key in the front door and both Joan and Gordon shot out the back to stub out their cigarettes, so it was Anne who welcomed Sylvia and Albert. 'You're looking much better, Mother,' she said, kissing Sylvia's cheek. 'Have you had a good time?'

'Lovely,' said Sylvia, removing her hat. 'The hotel is grand. Albert and Gladys have worked hard getting it up to scratch. I saw photographs of what it was like when they bought it.'

'Well, I'm glad you've enjoyed yourself,' Anne said. 'I'll put the kettle on.'

Sylvia sniffed. 'Can I smell cigarette smoke?' She glared at Anne. 'Was it you?'

'You can smell my breath if you like, Mother,' Anne said, breathing into her face.

Sylvia brushed her away. 'All right, so it wasn't you. Anyway, where's Joan? Is she still keeping well?'

'She's as healthy as a horse, and almost the size of one now,' Anne said. 'She's just popped out into the back to get some herbs out of the window box for the stew. Now doesn't that smell good?'

'It certainly does,' said Albert, watching Anne pour boiling water into the teapot. 'And how are you, Anne? Not still missing Andrew Fraser, I hope.'

'I don't know why that should bother you, Albert,' she replied, thinking his comment spiteful. 'You've never cared a ha'penny about my happiness.'

'Don't speak to Albert in that tone,' said Sylvia. 'Now hurry up with that tea.'

Anne poured tea into cups and offered the sugar basin and milk jug before opening the back door and calling out, 'Joan, hurry up with those herbs! Mother and Albert are here.'

Anne had been thinking of something since her father's death and, facing Sylvia, said, 'Mother, were Da's brothers informed when he died? I was surprised that they didn't turn up for the funeral.'

'Of course they were told,' Sylvia snapped. 'At least his brother Donald was, because he was the only one left alive. His youngest brother, Jamie, died in an accident on the farm, leaving a daughter. Donald couldn't leave the farm, but he sent his condolences. They never kept in touch much over the years and I don't think they know about Flora's accident or us adopting you. Why do you ask?'

'Da mentioned taking me to Scotland a few months ago, that's all.' Anne sighed deeply.

Albert said, 'Well, that's not going to happen now, is it?'

Anne did not answer, only poured milk into her tea and then sugared it, thinking, by hook or by crook, that she would get to Scotland one day.

Joan entered the kitchen, clutching some thyme and sage. 'How well you look, Mother. You should visit Rhyl more often.'

'Mother knows she's always welcome,' Albert said virtuously. 'But I mustn't linger. See you again sometime, Joan, Anne.' He kissed his mother's cheek and left.

—

The whole atmosphere in the house had altered now Sylvia had returned. It was not so relaxed and the five of them were soon fed up of hearing about how marvellous the hotel was and that it was situated so close to the seafront. Anne had taken Emily's advice and had been glad to accept an invitation from Pete to go to the flickers to escape.

They had a nice time and saw *The Cameraman* with Buster Keaton. Pete talked non-stop, even while the film was showing, and she laughed a lot, even though the other filmgoers kept shushing them. But she didn't feel that spark like she had with Andrew.

Sylvia was not pleased about it when Anne came home late, not having told Sylvia first that she was going out with a young man from work. 'I would have thought you'd have learnt your lesson after the Fraser lad. Anyway, where is Emily?'

'Maybe she's gone the flickers, too,' Anne said. 'It's not as if you're on your own here. You have Joan and Teddy to keep you company.'

'I wish I was back in Rhyl,' Sylvia said. 'I'm going to write to Albert.'

–

A few days later there was a letter from Albert telling them that he was going to come back to see Mother again shortly, to help her as they weren't looking after her properly.

Anne and Emily agreed that Albert had cheek and was an interfering busybody, but there was nothing they could do to stop him.

–

Anne decided she would take a walk along Netherfield Road the following Saturday afternoon, which was where Gordon had said the greengrocer's shop was where Emily had spoken with the man they thought was Larry Williams. Suddenly she had felt guilty acting behind Emily's back, so she approached her sister over breakfast on Saturday morning and told her about the searches she planned to do.

Emily stared at her in astonishment and flushed. 'Why are you doing this? It's too late to make a difference to either of our lives. He could be married to someone else if he could have done the deed without his mother finding out.'

'But what if he still loves you and yearns for you?' said Anne.

'He knows where to find me,' responded Emily.

'There could be reasons we know nothing about as to why he didn't get in touch,' said Anne.

Emily was silent for what seemed a long time and then she said, 'He was very ill with consumption and our mothers decided to stop our relationship going any further.'

'So, what should I do?' asked Anne. 'Do you want to know what happened to him or forget him?'

'I could never forget him,' said Emily softly.

'What if I find out his whereabouts and then you can decide whether to make contact?' Anne suggested.

Emily nodded. 'Yes, that sounds like a sensible plan.'

'What's the name of the shop where he worked?'

Emily pondered on that, telling her the name Brookes, and adding, 'Netherfield Road is a long road and on a Saturday it'll be really busy. I wish you luck.'

But Anne's luck seemed to have deserted her because the previous owner of the greengrocer's shop had retired, and the new owner knew nothing about Larry or his family's whereabouts. Fortunately, one of the customers was listening to their conversation and could tell her where the previous owner now lived. Apparently, he had moved out to Crosby on the outskirts of Liverpool and the customer was even able to give her the address. Anne wondered if this person would remember Larry. She decided to go home as she was tired after having been in work that morning and would write or call on him another day.

Besides which, Pete had asked her to go to the flickers with him again, and while she knew she could never feel towards him as she did to Andrew, she had enjoyed his company. He was amusing but also had a serious side to him that she had not expected. Marjorie had also told her that he did not have a happy home life. His father was dead, and his mother was a gin-guzzler who neglected his younger brother. He was a decent bloke, but he wasn't Andrew and she wondered what Andrew would make of her going out with Pete, convinced that Marjorie would not keep that news from him.

Chapter Ten

Anne could not conceal her irritation when Albert drew up in his second-hand automobile a fortnight later. He entered the house and went into the kitchen where she and Teddy and Joan were talking. Teddy was making a pot of tea while Joan was ironing, and their mother was sitting listlessly in a chair by the fire.

'Where's Gordon?' Albert asked.

'He's gone to Marjorie's. They're having a day out in Southport with young Robbie,' said Teddy.

Albert said in a sneering voice, 'He was always a fool. She'll have him tied to her in no time, sharing the responsibility for ol' man Fraser's brat.'

'There's no need for that,' Teddy said stiffly. 'You've made a new life for yourself in Rhyl, so what we do here in Liverpool has nothing to do with you.'

Albert's face turned puce. 'You watch your mouth, brother. I'm the head of the family and Mother has asked me to take control of things for her and that includes keeping an eye on you all as well.'

'What things?' asked Teddy.

Sylvia said, 'My financial affairs. I'm too old to deal with insurance, wills and bills and other family matters. Hugh left things in a mess and Albert is sorting it out.'

Teddy stared at his elder brother in silence; Anne was aware of the tension in the room and wished she had followed on Gordon's heels. He was worth a dozen Alberts.

'Maybe you should have taken Mother with you when you and Gladys moved to Rhyl and she could have stayed with you permanently. We can manage our own affairs,' said Teddy, coldly.

Albert sniggered. 'Really? Well, I hope you and Joan manage when the baby arrives. How will you get by on your meagre wage with Joan having to give up work?'

'You can relax, Albert. We wouldn't be coming to you for it. I've set the money aside that Da left me and we saved while Joan was still earning.'

Sylvia pushed herself up in her chair. 'It will be nice having my grandchild in the house. It's something to look forward to without your father here, so I'd rather stay here and just visit Rhyl, say three times a year.'

'Thank you, Mother,' Teddy said, giving her a hug.

Shortly after, a sour-faced Albert left alone, and Anne noticed he had taken a tin with him, saying he hoped everything went off well with the birth. Anne realised the tin was the one that had contained all her mother's papers and was glad she had removed her birth certificate and adoption papers from it beforehand.

Sylvia was subdued after Albert had gone. But after a cup of tea and a brawn butty, she roused herself and, putting on her hat and coat, said that she was going to visit her friend Betty.

-

Anne decided to visit Central Library that evening and see how she could go about tracing the midwife, Cissie Jamieson, who had registered her birth. She was told that if she was a registered midwife then she could be found on their register, but some midwives were not registered.

Anne realised that would make tracing Cissie more difficult.

'If she was on call in a certain neighbourhood, the doctors in the area might be able to help you.'

Anne thought about that and decided to leave matters as they were for the moment and consider why she was going to all this trouble a bit more. Was it because she could not accept that Liam Fraser had fathered her and needed to prove it, so she could be close to Andrew again as his sweetheart? Or was it because if he wasn't her father, then who was? Likewise, the woman who was her real mother and who had given her own life to bring her into the world – who was she? Whatever the truth of the matter, it only made sense that Andrew should be aware of what she was doing. Because if she wasn't his sister, then they'd need to know what had happened to the baby girl his mother had given birth to. Surely he would want to know too.

In the meantime, she would have something to eat before going out with Pete that evening. She had accepted his invitation to a variety show at the Empire Theatre, which had opened two years ago; it was the second theatre to have been built on that site and was very popular. Many stars of the day played there such as Arthur Askey and Wilson, Keppel and Betty.

She had not expected Pete to turn up with his brother, but she enjoyed the occasion because the show was truly good entertainment with lots of variety singers and comedians. It was obvious that Pete and his much younger brother enjoyed it, too.

A fortnight later, Anne was woken in the middle of the night by footsteps passing her bedroom door, followed by whispers and a scream that caused her to sit up in bed. It was Emily who crept into her bedroom and told her that Joan and Teddy's baby was about to be born. They heard the baby's cries shortly afterwards and were relieved that all was well. The baby was a girl and that delighted Sylvia, who wanted her to be called Flora after the child who had died, but the parents refused, Teddy saying he did not want to be reminded of a tragedy in the family every time he looked at his daughter. They wanted to call her Amy and it was Sylvia who phoned Albert from the post office to inform him of her birth.

A congratulations card arrived a day later, which also informed them that they would not be seeing Albert or Gladys until well into 1929, as the Christmas and New Year period were going to be busy occasions at the hotel with parties and dinners and dances arranged.

Sylvia did not seem that bothered about not seeing her favourite son for several months. Anne guessed that was because she was so delighted with her first grandchild, and there would also be plenty going on in the neighbourhood during the approach to Christmas. If only Da had still been alive, Anne would have been a lot happier, despite not seeing Andrew. The preparations for the holiday only made her feel their loss more keenly. As it was, she was enjoying her work at the factory and had now been moved to the bottling section where the smell of the bubbling plums was mouth-watering.

There were also outings to the pantomime and carol services with Peter and with family and friends as Christmas approached. The festive two-day holiday came and went without a card popping through the letter box from Andrew. Disappointed, Anne tried not to dwell on it as she headed towards Marjorie's house to see how their Christmas had gone. Knocking on the door, she was astounded to find it opened by the very person who had been occupying her thoughts on her way there.

'Why didn't you let me know you were coming?' Anne blurted out, gazing up at Andrew with an entranced expression, thinking he was even more handsome than she remembered.

'I wanted to respond to your letter in person and apologise for leaving London without saying a proper farewell,' he said, taking both her hands. His eyes were shining, and she could tell he was as happy as she was to be reunited.

'How is life in London? Is the job all you hoped it would be?'

He squeezed her hands gently and she was aware of the warmth of his fingers through her new Christmas gloves.

'I like London,' he said. 'There's much I miss about Liverpool, but I had to leave because I cared for you in a way that wasn't at all brotherly, and if you can discover anything that would prove we aren't brother and sister I'd be made up. In the meantime, if there is any way I can help, by searching records in London for instance, let me know.'

Anne could not have been more pleased and was about to fling her arms around his neck, only for Andrew to hold her at a distance. She understood straight away what he could not bring himself to say. They must restrain themselves until they knew the truth, whatever that was. 'All right,' she said in a low voice. 'I get the message.' She stepped back. 'How have you got on trying to trace your grandfather?'

'I've been searching Father's past and with the help of the Lodge records and those of Tate & Lyle. I've discovered enough to take me to Scotland and Northern Ireland come spring,' he said.

Anne thought about her own search and promised herself if she could meet Andrew in Scotland then she would, no matter if they were brother and sister or not.

Chapter Eleven

Sylvia had never fully recovered from her previous illness and all the activity at Christmas seemed to add to her condition. Exhausted, she took to her bed the day after Boxing Day and stayed there, waited on hand and foot by Anne and Emily during the evening and some nights, whilst Aunt Betty volunteered to help Joan with the baby during the daytime. Joan tried to cheer up Sylvia by bringing baby Amy to her bedside, but instead of helping, Sylvia went on and on about her darling Flora, weeping copiously while recalling her loss.

At the beginning of January 1929, Joan was churched and Amy was christened. She was a beautiful child with blonde curls, deep blue eyes and dimpled cheeks. Anne was one of the godmothers and, a few weeks later, she decided to have a word with Emily, given that Sylvia was not in the best of health and had been asking for Albert. She found Emily in the kitchen sitting in the rocking chair, knitting a pink matinee jacket for the baby.

'I need to speak to you, Emily,' said Anne, pulling up a footstool and sitting a step away from the rocking chair. 'Should we tell Albert about Mother not being well? I can't see Teddy doing so after the way they spoke to each other last time Albert was here.'

Emily set aside her knitting and sighed heavily. 'I think we must, as it's what Mother wants, and he'd never forgive us if she died and he hadn't been sent for.'

'Do you think that she could die?' It was the first time Anne had thought that things could be so serious.

'She's just getting worse. I think something happened to her mind when she had that turn and now her body is following suit,' Emily said.

Anne couldn't help thinking that she was right. Emily limped off to the post office, her joints in terrible pain now that winter had arrived, and phoned Albert, explaining the situation to him. He was shocked and apparently annoyed with himself for letting Teddy get to him, so he did not scold her for not telling him sooner. 'I'll be there by this evening,' he said, ending the conversation abruptly.

Anne had told Joan of Emily's intention to get in touch with Albert and Joan had forcefully told Teddy to keep a civil tongue in his head when Albert arrived, and be thankful that they could leave him to deal with any decisions concerning his mother's welfare.

It was almost as if Albert's arrival foreshadowed the end for their Mother. Sylvia insisted that Albert stay by her side; even so she still deteriorated rapidly. The doctor was called and he told them it was heart failure made worse by too much excitement and worry. Not long after his visit, Sylvia slipped into unconsciousness and passed away with her children by her bedside. Anne noticed him later lifting down Da's small suitcase from the top of the wardrobe.

–

Anne did not feel her mother's loss as much as she had Da's, but it caused her grief all the same. Her sadness was worsened when Albert informed her that she was left out of Sylvia's will. This made her feel that she had failed to be a daughter to Sylvia as Hugh had intended. To add to her woes, Pete broke off their relationship, telling her that he was moving to St Helens where his paternal grandparents lived, as they had found a job for him in a chemical works there, and his mother had agreed to it and that his brother could go and live with his grandparents as well. Anne knew that even though there had been no romance between them, she would miss Pete. He had been a good friend to her at a sad time, but now she could concentrate on her search for Larry Williams, Emily's lost sweetheart, and then visit the Sandon Hotel and go inside this time.

That weekend, to distract herself from all the thoughts about Andrew and her real parents, she took the tram to Crosby. She was pleased that when she went to the address that she had been given, the door was opened by a kindly gentleman who was more than happy to help her. He invited her in out of the cold.

'Oh yes, I remember Larry well; he had a weak chest and a strong mother!' The man laughed and Anne couldn't help smiling over the cup of tea that he had made her in front of his cheery fire.

He told her that Larry now lived in Eastham on the Wirral, where his mother had bought a greengrocer's shop and the adjoining cottage.

'I was always of the opinion that his mother exaggerated a chronic bad chest to keep him under her control,' he said.

Anne wondered how Emily could care about this man, who sounded a weakling and was tied to his mother's apron strings. Still, there must be something about him that was attractive for Emily to have cared about him.

Anne told Emily what she had discovered when she returned home. Emily seemed cheered by the news and Anne promised her sister she would visit Eastham when the weather improved.

—

Anne was glad the worst of winter was now behind them and the evenings were lighter for longer. It would be her sixteenth birthday that month. Before then, she decided to visit Eastham that coming Sunday and suggested that Emily go with her, but Emily was too nervous and worried about having to face Larry's mother. She also worried about occasionally having to use the wheelchair she had purchased with some of the money her mother had left her, because her knees were so painful when she walked. It had meant that she could not return to working at the tobacco factory but had managed to get a desk job as a bookkeeper. It was only when Anne stood across the road from the greengrocer's shop in Eastham that she was filled with trepidation and kept going over the sentences she had been rehearsing for the past few hours in her head. She took several deep breaths before finally crossing the road and banging purposefully on the cottage door next to the closed shop.

It was some time before the door of the cottage opened and a man with a thatch of sandy greying hair came out. He glanced at Anne curiously. 'Don't you know it's Sunday and I'm closed?' he said in a Liverpudlian accent.

Anne gazed into his blue eyes and thought she liked the look of him. There was something kind and decent about him; she could see it straight away. 'I'm trying to trace a Larry Williams who used to live in Liverpool.'

'And who would you be, miss?'

'My name is Anne Anderson and I've come on behalf of my sister, Emily, who lost touch with Mr Williams a good few years ago. She would like to know what happened to him.'

He looked astonished and took a step back. 'Emily Anderson! You must be her little adopted sister all grown up. You were only a tot the last time I saw you.'

'Then you are Larry Williams?' She could not keep the excitement out of her voice.

'I am Larry Williams – and this shop is mine. My mother died last year and left it to me.' He hesitated before asking, 'How is Emily?'

'She has a few health problems, but she keeps going.'

'Is she married?'

'No, she has a job. Emily has been more like a mother to me than ours. Mother died recently… and Da died last year.'

Anne had managed to prevent herself from giving a cheer at the news Larry's mother was dead, knowing it wasn't seemly, but she couldn't help thinking it was another obstacle out of the way in bringing Emily and Larry together. Now she took a deep breath and decided to risk asking, 'How would you feel about meeting up with Emily in Liverpool?'

He looked thoughtful and did not reply immediately. She had hoped he would agree straightaway, but it appeared he was a cautious man and perhaps that showed he was a man of good sense. Even so, she prayed that he would agree, unless… Was he married? She gazed at his left hand but there was no telltale ring on the third finger.

'Are you sure that she wants to meet me?' he asked her guardedly, and she reassured him that she did and suggested that Larry meet Emily for tea at the Kardomah on Saturday afternoon at five thirty. He said that would be alright as the shop shut at four o'clock, and he agreed to be there.

As she made her way home, her spirits soared, thinking how pleased her sister would be at the news. Emily's response didn't disappoint; she was overjoyed that Anne had found Larry and was full of questions about him. 'Did he look well?' she asked.

'Very well. The clean air over there must be doing him good.'

Emily proceeded to bombard Anne with questions about her meeting with her long-lost sweetheart until Anne longed to scream *Stop!* She could not help thinking of Andrew, wishing that they might be sweethearts rather than siblings.

On Monday and Tuesday, Emily was in a right tizzy, up one minute and down the next. As for deciding what to wear, she kept changing her mind. Yet when Saturday finally dawned, her nerves had disappeared and she seemed perfectly calm, even having settled on what frock to wear before having a bath.

Anne indicated the wheelchair that had been brought in from the outhouse and was only used when Emily felt the pain was too much to cope with. 'You don't need the wheelchair? You'll be doing a fair amount of walking.'

'No! After all these years, I don't want Larry to see me for the first time in a wheelchair, and besides, I can't take the wheelchair on the tram.'

Anne remembered saying to Emily once that 'if you don't use your legs, you'll lose the use of them' and being told by Emily that she wouldn't be saying that if she knew how painful her knees were. After that Anne had kept quiet on the subject.

Emily said, 'I don't plan on deceiving him about my condition. I'll tell him.'

'I didn't think you wouldn't,' Anne said, going over to the dressing table and applying the remains of a lipstick that Marjorie had given her. She caught Emily's eyes reflected in the mirror. 'Would you like me to make up your face?'

Emily hesitated and then shook her head. 'I've never painted my face and I'm not starting now.'

'Even Mother used to powder her nose and apply a touch of lippy.'

'I'm not Mother.'

'No, but you could try a red lipstick. The shade is 'strawberry' and it's from the TJ Hughes make-up counter.'

Emily's cheeks paled. 'Surely you're not suggesting I should be encouraging Larry to kiss me when we haven't seen each other for years? What if his feelings have changed when he sees me?'

'Somehow, I don't think they have, and if you both still care for each other, I would have thought you'd want him to kiss you after being parted from him for so long. You can't have forgotten enjoying being kissed by him?'

'We seldom had the chance to kiss under the circumstances.'

'Of course, I wasn't thinking.' Anne realised afresh just how awful it must have been to have the person you loved suffering from consumption. It was what they called tuberculosis these days and it had been a death sentence for many years before, but treatment and managing the spread of the disease had greatly improved and to Anne, it looked like Larry had completely recovered. But it must have been terrible for a mother to have it and not be able to kiss her children or husband. 'Even more reason why you'd want to kiss to make up for those times when you couldn't,' she added.

'All right, if it will shut you up, you can apply some of the 'strawberry' lipstick and powder my nose.'

Anne let out a cheer and wasted no time responding to Emily's invitation. She also applied a touch of eye make-up and rouge, just enough to accentuate her features, knowing she must not overdo it, otherwise Emily might wipe her face clean of powder and lipstick altogether.

Fortunately, Emily made no complaint when she gazed at her reflection in the mirror and Anne prayed that all would go well for Emily and Larry. She should have thought more about the place she had chosen; it was a long way for Emily and Anne hoped she would get there and back alright.

-

Emily was feeling more tired and in pain than she had wished, and she could only hope that Larry would wait as she was likely to be late because her pace was slow. She was also concerned that they might not recognise each other after so long, but she need not have worried; he was standing outside the Kardomah, looking slightly anxious as he gazed about him. Then she saw his expression change as she approached, and he walked along the pavement to meet her. Despite the passing years, she thought he had changed little, still recognisable as the young man she had loved.

'Emily?' he said, pausing a couple of feet in front of her.

'Larry.' Despite Emily's voice being low, a thrill threaded through it. 'I prayed we'd meet again, but I never thought the wait would be so long.'

'Better late than never,' he said, taking her free hand and pressing it against his chest. 'I wrote to you, but you never answered my letters.'

A shadow crossed Emily's face. 'I never received any letters. Mother must have intercepted and destroyed them. She'd do anything to get her own way; she could be cruel like that.'

'Cruel indeed,' said Larry. 'But let's not spoil this time with regrets. We must make the most of it. Let's go and have lunch and talk.'

Emily thankfully accepted the arm he offered. 'Anne's told me about the shop and the cottage. It has a garden, doesn't it?'

He nodded. 'I grow some vegetables and have a couple of fruit trees.'

'What about flowers? If I had a garden, I'd grow roses, pinks, sweet peas and chrysanthemums.'

'I like flowers, too, but Mother considered them a waste of space. I'll come in the van and take you to see it next Sunday, if you'd like that?' He smiled into her eyes and a rosy flush bloomed on her cheeks. 'Even though it is winter, it's still very pretty.'

'I'd love it,' she said.

Chapter Twelve

A few weeks later, Emily had a birthday and invited Larry over to share some of the birthday cake she had made and to see Teddy, Joan and George and baby Amy. It was probably his fifth visit to the house to pick up Emily in his van to take her out.

Anne thought how happy the couple looked together and wished she'd had been with Andrew for her sixteenth birthday. Their eyes were shining, and their cheeks glowed with a healthy colour. 'You two look as fit as fleas,' she said.

'Good.' His expression altered. 'Though I can't help noticing Emily's limp has worsened.'

Emily had told him about her bad knees from scrubbing floors over the years.

'It's always bad when the weather is very cold or very wet, but all those years of being the household drudge have taken their toll.'

Larry's expression was a mixture of anger and tenderness. 'If only we had stayed together, and our parents hadn't tried to keep us apart. Things wouldn't be this bad for you.'

'No, but we can't go back and must make the best of things.'

'Exactly my thinking.' He smiled at Emily with love in his eyes. 'If you marry me there won't ever be any more scrubbing like a washerwoman.'

Emily's cheeks flushed. 'Marry! Are you sure? We've hardly been back together more than a few weeks! I'm a different person now to the girl you once knew.'

He shook his head. 'I can see that girl in your eyes – and I'll be eternally grateful to Anne for caring enough to make the effort to unite us. You are going to say yes, aren't you?'

'I'd be a fool not to. We have a lot of lost time to make up,' she said seriously. 'So, yes, please marry me. I feel better than I've felt in years,' said Emily.

'Me too,' Larry said.

'Which proves you're good for each other,' pointed out Anne, who was delighted at the turn of events. She could not conceal her pleasure at seeing them together and threw her arms about Emily's neck and kissed her. 'Can I be bridesmaid?' she asked.

'Of course!' cried Emily and, shooting a glance at Larry, added, 'I don't know how I'll manage without you afterwards.'

He nodded. 'Yes, I've been thinking about that too, and if Anne is willing, I have a plan.'

'What plan would this be?' Anne gazed at the pair of them, eager to hear what Larry had to say.

'I wondered if you'd come and live with us,' Larry said. 'It doesn't have to be a permanent arrangement. After all, you could meet someone and get married yourself.'

'That's a wonderful idea, and just until we get into the way of things,' Emily said.

'There is a spare room you can have,' Larry said. 'You'd have to give up the job at the factory. You'll pick it up in no time.'

'And for helping me in the house you won't have to pay rent or for meals,' Emily put in excitedly.

'Thank you! I don't mind giving that job up,' said Anne. 'I was always good at addition and subtraction and pounds, shillings and pence, so I could work the till once I'm shown what to do.'

'And we can share the housework and go shopping together,' Emily said. 'Just as we do now.'

'I'll work out your shifts and how much money per hour I can pay you,' Larry said firmly. 'As well as time off. If we spend too much time together, we could get fed up of living in each other's pockets. I remember Ma wanted me with her all the time and I found myself walking out when I couldn't stand it any more and needed to escape. I felt I couldn't call my life my own.'

Anne said, 'Mothers can be possessive. In fact, families can be possessive as well. I'll have to ask Teddy and Gordon first, of course.'

'They're not the possessive type and I'm sure they'll think it is a good idea. I can see life's going to be very different. Happier and definitely more interesting,' Emily said.

'You deserve some happiness.' Larry put his arm around his fiancée.

'And so do you,' Emily said, her voice a caress. 'I hope I won't prove too much of a burden to you.'

'I wouldn't have asked you to marry me if I wasn't expecting to be burdened by you,' he said.

Emily shot him a confused look, which made Anne laugh. 'He wants to be burdened by you, Em!'

'Exactly,' Larry said teasingly to Emily, before facing Anne and saying, 'Are you with us then?'

'Sure, if the wages suit me.' There was a mischievous twinkle in her eye as she said this.

'Anne!' exclaimed Emily, laughing too. 'I'm family. You should do it for love.'

'A labourer is worthy of her hire,' Larry said. 'I'm taking it for granted you don't mind giving up your job as a bookkeeper for love, Emily?'

'Of course not. It's expected of most wives, and their husbands are expected to work to support their wives and any children the couple might have. I like children and know I'll miss Amy.'

'Are you going to invite all the family to the wedding?' Anne asked.

'Too right I am. I want them to see that I can have a life of my own without them feeling sorry for me at being left on the shelf.'

—

The couple arranged the wedding for the Easter Saturday at the end of March and Emily and Larry were fortunate that the vicar had a gap between two other weddings, as it was a popular day to be married. Though Emily had written to Albert and told him of the wedding, he had made Easter the excuse for not attending, saying the hotel was fully booked and Gladys couldn't manage without him.

The sunrise of the wedding day was all that any bride could have wished for. Many a compliment came the bride and her attendant's way when they arrived at the church. Anne wished that their da could have been there to see them both. Anne wore a peach crêpe de Chine dress with a single artificial gardenia pinned to a peach-coloured felt cloche hat. Emily was dressed in a cream shot-silk suit with a coffee-coloured blouse and had chosen not to carry a bouquet, just a spray of roses and gypsy grass pinned to her Bible, and on a headband in her hair was a short lace veil. On her feet, she wore a neat pair of mock crocodile strapped shoes with low heels.

'You look stunning,' said Gordon as Emily entered the church. 'I wish Mother and Da were here to see you.'

Emily smiled and thought if she'd had had her way years ago, they *would* have been at her wedding, but she wasn't going to allow regrets to cast a shadow over her special day.

A signal was given to the organist, who launched into Mendelssohn's 'Wedding March'. Anne felt tears well in her eyes as Emily's fingers tightened on her arm and she took her first step down the aisle towards her future husband, who had turned his gaze to meet hers as she approached the front of the church. As she took her place beside him, he took her hand and gripped it firmly. Anne took her sister's Bible and stood back.

Larry said, 'You look wonderful.'

'And so do you,' Emily whispered through the lump in her throat. 'This is the happiest day of my life.'

'Dearly beloved…' The vicar's voice resonated through the church, causing all there to pay attention.

–

When the wedding photographer had finished taking some photographs outside the church, the wedding party headed back to Larry's cottage. Emily's face appeared a little strained due to the effort of staying on her feet so long, but she managed a smile for their family and friends as they came to offer their congratulations.

The bridal couple were booked in to a hotel on the Isle of Man for their honeymoon, and they were going to leave Anne in charge of the shop along with a Mrs Evans, the woman who occasionally worked part-time for Larry. Anne had already given up her job at Nelson's before the wedding and wasn't sad to leave.

After the happy couple had been waved off on their honeymoon, most of the guests had taken their leave and Anne was glad to have the house to herself with Larry's cat, Tigger.

She set to making herself a much-needed cup of tea and thought about the last few weeks and all that had happened. She had approached Gordon and Teddy before the wedding with the idea of moving in with Emily and Larry and had been a bit nervous about what they might say. But instead of being annoyed, Gordon shared the happy news that he and Marjorie were engaged to be married.

Anne was so pleased with the news and having Marjorie as part of the family because somehow it brought Andrew closer. She returned to the idea of tracing the family history. Gordon had told her that he had been interested in this too and had been doing his own research in his spare time, though he hadn't had much spare time since he and Marjorie had started courting.

Anne was also toying with the idea of tracing the Fraser ancestry as well – after all, that would mean she might meet up with Andrew in Scotland. She had written to the sugar factory where Liam had worked for so many years and asked them if they had any information that could help her.

She had visited Marjorie a couple of days earlier and discovered that Andrew had had a similar idea and was planning a trip to Scotland around the Whit weekend. She still missed his company dreadfully – the discussions they'd had, the books they'd shared, the laughter. If she managed to visit Scotland at the same time as Andrew intended on going up there, she wasn't to surprise him. She desperately wanted them to have a chance to be together and prayed that everything would work out alright in the end, even though it seemed unlikely that it would. She just hoped that Larry would allow her the time away if she worked hard in the meantime.

Gordon had said he would have liked to visit the family farm too, but he could not afford to take the time off work now he and Marjorie were getting married later that year.

Anne was disturbed from her thoughts by the ringing of the telephone as she poured herself a cup of tea to have with a second slice of wedding cake. She fumbled with the receiver and said hesitantly, 'The Williams' residence. This is Anne Anderson speaking.'

'Anne, is that you? Is Emily there? Can I have a word with her?'

Anne was surprised by the sound of Albert's voice, but she wasn't cowed by it so replied coolly, 'I'm sorry, but she and Larry have left on their honeymoon.'

'Already!' He sounded miffed.

'They had a boat to catch. Is there anything else I can help you with?'

'Did everything go off all right?'

'Of course. Emily is a wonderful organiser. She looked lovely and it was a very happy and touching ceremony.'

'It sounds like we weren't missed.' He sounded grumpy.

'Of course you were missed. Several of our old neighbours and friends asked why you weren't there. We told them the truth that you were too busy to attend with it being the Easter weekend and how busy you were in Rhyl.'

There was a brief silence, then he said, 'I'm sure they understood.'

'Of course. They have a living to make, too.'

'I would have liked to be there,' he said huskily. 'Emily and I were close once.'

'Well, if she was that important to you, you should have made more of an effort to be there. Anyway, you'll be able to see the photographs.'

'Who gave her away?'

'I thought you knew,' Anne said, surprised. 'No one gave her away. At her age, she didn't consider it necessary.' She paused. 'Look, Albert. My cup of tea's getting cold and I also need to get ready for working in the shop tomorrow, so I'll say ta-ra. I need to be in Larry's good books so he'll give me time off to go to Scotland.'

'Scotland? What are you going there for?'

'To see what I can find out about the Frasers. I'll also look in on the Andersons in Cardross as Gordon has asked me to find out what I can about them while I'm up there.'

'What is the point of looking up the Frasers? You were brought up by us.'

'But it's Fraser blood that supposedly runs in my veins,' she said in a tight voice.

Before he had a chance to make any more disapproving comments, she added, 'Ta-ra again, Albert. See you sometime.' Anne replaced the receiver and took a deep, steadying breath before sitting down with her cup of tea.

Chapter Thirteen

On the day that the newlyweds were due to return, Anne gave their bedroom a thorough clean, put fresh linen on the bed and a vase of freshly picked spring flowers on the dressing table. She was surprised by how much she was looking forward to seeing them; she had been a bit lonely, never having spent a night alone in a house before. When she opened the door to greet them, she thought that she had never seen Emily looking so well.

'Did you have a marvellous time?' Anne asked, though she thought she was stating the obvious judging by her sister's blooming cheeks.

'Terrible,' Emily replied, hugging her before smiling up at her husband.

'She's kidding,' Larry said. 'It couldn't have been better. For the time of the year, the weather was amazing. Very spring-like.'

'The hotel was wonderful too,' said Emily, drawing off her gloves. 'There were flowers and champagne and chocolates in our room, which had a sea view.'

'Well, I've no champagne but there's sparkling wine and some Guinness that Gordon bought from the off-licence,' Anne said.

'Not in the same glass I hope,' teased Emily.

'You are in high spirits,' Anne said, smiling.

'And why shouldn't I be?' Emily said. 'I've the husband I always wanted, I've had a lovely honeymoon and I've come home to a warm welcome, though I'm ready to put my feet up.'

'Did you do much walking?' Anne asked, concerned.

'She was amazing,' said Larry, placing his arm about his wife's waist. 'Inclined to show off by doing too much.'

'Foolish of me, I know,' Emily said, pulling a face. 'But I want to be a help to you now I'm home, not a hindrance. So I had to get plenty of practice in.'

'But I'm here to help you both,' said Anne.

'I know, love,' Emily said. 'But I'm determined not to live the life of an invalid.'

'That's understandable,' said Anne. 'But you will have to make sure you take time to rest every day or you'll exhaust yourself.'

'I'm not stupid.' Emily frowned, never liking being told what to do.

'Anne's right, no rushing about,' said Larry. 'Now let's go and unpack.'

The house had a whole different feel to it now Larry and Emily had returned, Anne felt, as if possession of it had been snatched away from her. Even Tigger switched his attention away from her to his master, except when Anne was cooking and creating delicious savoury aromas, then the cat would come and wrap itself around her ankles, threatening to trip her up, until she placed a tasty offering in his dish.

Naturally she also had to submit to Larry's orders in the shop. Her relationship with Emily was also different because now Larry came first with Emily. Although Anne and Emily gossiped together, Emily would now draw

Larry into the conversation as well. Some evenings Anne did make the effort to leave them alone, though when she wanted to listen to the wireless, the newlyweds would snuggle up on the sofa together and then she'd feel like a gooseberry.

During the next couple of months, Anne often thought about that phone call from Albert, and she had told Emily and Larry about both sides of the conversation.

'Good for you,' Larry said. 'He's a fool. One day he'll realise that family are more important than money. Losing their respect and affection is a big mistake.'

Emily and Anne agreed with him; he could be high-handed and domineering, much like their late mother, but they both still cared about Albert as a brother. Anne knew that she could never feel sisterly towards Andrew Fraser in the way she did with him or Gordon and Teddy. Even so, she was desperately hoping to bump into Andrew in Scotland, and that he would be pleased to see her. Just talking with him – that would be enough. She sighed, praying that was not wishful thinking. As she settled down in the Wirral, it felt strange for a while, having left the city she had called home all her life. The surroundings were so different from what she had been accustomed to, being more countryfied and village-like.

She had told also Emily and Larry about her wish to travel to Scotland and what she planned to do there, as well as her having written to the sugar factory, hoping they could help her with Liam Fraser's former address in Scotland.

'They'll have it,' said Larry. 'They'll have wanted references from the last place he worked at in Scotland when he applied for a job here in Liverpool. They'll probably still have it on file somewhere and the company in Scotland will have his last address.'

'Somebody else will have moved into the address by now I should imagine,' Anne said.

'Most likely, but there'll be neighbours who'll be able to give you some information,' Larry said.

'I hope so,' said Anne, thinking she needed a bit of luck.

—

Tate & Lyle's famous sugar factory was situated on Love Lane and Anne decided to visit their Personnel office to see what she could find out, bringing with her the necessary paperwork to prove her identity.

The secretary was very helpful. 'Oh yes, we had your letter. I've been looking into it.' The young woman told her to sit in a waiting area and after a little while she returned with an address on a piece of paper, which said that Liam had lived in Ann Street, Greenock and that prior to working at Tate & Lyle, he had worked at a sugar factory in his home town.

'He was still young when he came to work here, just like Hugh Anderson, your adoptive father.'

Anne was delighted with this small victory and thanked the woman, returning to Eastham without delay.

Upstairs in her bedroom, after she had arrived back at the cottage, Anne sat on her bed and gazed at the piece of paper, wondering if this could be the key to unlocking the secrets behind her birth. She felt sure that there was something she needed to find out and hoped that this was the start of finding the answers. Sitting on her bed under the eaves she gazed around, liking the way she had stamped her personality on the pretty little room. She had treated herself to the blue and white Wedgewood powder bowl and candle holders on her last birthday with money Emily and Gordon had given her. She kept trinkets in the bowl and white candles in the holders which looked attractive despite never having been lit. She also had several Beatrix Potter porcelain animals, which she had seen in Lewis's, and she had begun collecting them. Her favourite was Squirrel Nutkin. On one of the walls, she had pinned up a couple of photographs of Douglas Fairbanks, the film actor, and Ivor Novello, who not only wrote music but had a wonderful singing voice.

Looking out of the window of her bedroom, she could see the pretty garden was succumbing to weeds now that spring had sprung. Anne thought it would be a nice gesture to get out and pull some of them up, so Emily didn't feel she had to, and changed into an old skirt and blouse before heading out into the garden to do some weeding. After an hour or so, she'd had enough and was just about to return to the house when a voice hailed her, calling out, 'Good afternoon!' which caused her to whirl around and stare at the man gazing over the fence in her direction. The sight of him gave her quite a shock because, as far as she knew, their neighbour was a childless widow.

'Who are you?' she called. 'Surely you shouldn't be there?'

He ignored her challenge. 'You must be Larry's sister-in-law.'

'Yes, I am.' She continued brushing her clothes down, and was about to go inside when he said, 'Don't go in yet. We've scarcely begun to get to know each other.'

'I don't see any need to get to know you, and besides, I'm tired and thirsty.'

'Forgive me,' he said, edging along the fence so that they could have a closer look at each other. Anne guessed he was a good few years older than her. Late twenties, with light-brown hair and hazel eyes, a long thin nose and a weak chin.

'I should have introduced myself properly. I'm Keith Costain. I live in Chester. My sister who lives here will vouch for me and tell you I'm hard-working, honest, clean and dependable.'

Anne could not help laughing. 'I don't know why you think I need to be given a testimonial concerning your character. I'm not looking for a man-friend.'

'No? I forgot to add I'm not bad looking either, but you can see that for yourself.' His smile was cheeky and challenging but his confidence irritated Anne and her response was sharp and to the point.

'You forgot to mention that you're a lot older than me and fancy yourself.' She pushed the back door open wider. 'Ta-ra!' Anne went inside and closed the door behind her. She found a bottle of ginger beer in the larder, thinking she should have realised people would be gossiping about her moving in with Emily and Larry. She wondered just what Larry had told his neighbour, whose name she could not remember right now, about her and what she had told her brother.

He seemed an arrogant chappie and one to stay away from, even if his manner was a bit infectious. So very different from Andrew – she had to stop thinking about him in those terms. He was her brother… *her brother*. Anne felt that if she repeated it often enough she might come to believe it, but even so she was a little curious about Keith Costain; such as exactly how old was he, given that his sister appeared to be of a similar age to Larry?

She decided to put him out of her mind and went to see if any of the books in the case in the living room appealed to her as she had yet to join the library. There were several whodunnits and a couple of biographies but what caught her attention was an atlas of Great Britain. She took it from the shelf and returned with it to the kitchen table. She drank half of the ginger beer before opening the atlas and turning the pages to find Scotland.

She found Glasgow without any difficulty, searched for Greenock and circled it in pencil before searching for Cardross, finding it on the north side of the Firth of Clyde, so she circled that too. She decided to visit the library sometime soon to see what else she could find out about both places.

—

On one of her Wednesday afternoons off, Anne decided to have a day in Chester, so caught the train in. The station was a good walk from the city centre and it took her about a quarter of an hour to reach the cathedral and its gardens. She walked up into the famous covered rows which one reached by climbing steps up to a covered walkway. She gazed into a shop window filled with all manner of finery and fancy goods; it was as she descended the steps onto street level that she heard her name being called, and a few moments later she was confronted by her neighbour's brother, Keith.

'Hello Anne, fancy seeing you here,' he said. 'What brings you to Chester?'

'I'm looking for the library,' she replied.

'I can't say it's a building I'm in the habit of visiting,' he said, stroking his clean-shaven chin. 'But I can take you there.'

She was about to say that there was no need, then changed her mind, deciding it would be wiser to accept an offer from someone who must know the city well, and fell into step alongside him.

'Alright, you can show me where it is,' she said.

'It's on Northgate Street. Did you know that Chester still has part of its medieval walls and they have a number of gateways?'

'Of course. Everyone who has been to Chester would know that. And weren't there Roman walls before the medieval ones?'

'I know the Romans were here, but I can't say if the medieval walls were built on the foundations of the Roman ones.'

'That's all right,' she said cheerfully. 'Neither can I, although I suppose we could find out at the library if we were that interested.'

'I suppose so,' he said. 'And are you that interested?'

She shook her head. 'I'm after borrowing a good book about Scotland.'

'Why Scotland? Are you going on holiday there?'

'Not exactly a holiday.' She halted abruptly, wishing she had not said that.

'What does that mean?' His hazel eyes were curious. 'You're either going on holiday or not. Unless... Are you going after a job up there?'

'No!' She clamped her lips together firmly and walked on.

'You're a woman of mystery,' he said. 'You're not an undercover agent, are you?'

'Don't be daft!' She couldn't help but be amused by his teasing. 'You've been reading too many spy stories.'

He seemed to be enjoying himself. 'But it is true women are taking jobs from men these days.'

'If that were true, then all I can say is it's about time the good jobs were shared out between the sexes. It should be equal rights for all.' She tossed her hair back over her shoulder.

'You're quite the radical!'

'I'm not a red-hot fighter for women's rights, but I believe in equal pay for equal work. Now can we change the subject?'

'Can't take it?'

She turned and faced him. 'What's that supposed to mean?'

'Can't cope with an honest discussion?' Anne could see he had that look on his face again that seemed far too pleased with itself.

'For your information, all I wanted was for you to direct me to the library.'

'I've done better than that. Here it is.' Keith waved a hand in the direction of a fine-looking building.

'Thank you for your assistance,' she said primly. 'See you around.'

'I'm sure you will, and by then I'll have ferreted out your secret.' He grinned and strode off, whistling.

Thinking he was one of the most irritating people she had ever met, she went inside the library, though she soon put him out of her mind as she became engrossed in searching through the books in the British Isles section for ones on Scotland. There was a guide to the Trossachs and others on the Hebrides and various other areas, but Anne decided the one most likely to be helpful included Glasgow and the Firth of Clyde. She filled in the card the librarian gave her to join the library and left with the book under her arm before catching the train home.

She spent the evening turning the pages of her library book, admiring the photographs of some stunning scenery as well as attractive villages and towns, including Greenock, which the book explained had grown from a fishing village to be an important dock for trading on the Clyde. As for Cardross, that apparently had links with Robert the Bruce who died in his manor house there. She read carefully what was written about Greenock and Cardross and both now seemed so much more real to her that she was even more impatient than before to visit the land of her fathers.

It was only after she had closed the book and was making a jug of cocoa that she remembered what Keith Costain had said about ferreting out her secret. Did it matter whether he did or not? Emily or Larry might have already mentioned she was adopted and had Scottish connections; it was not as if Anne had anything to be ashamed of by his wanting to find out more about her Scottish roots. It was more just that she did not want *him* knowing her business. He was far too familiar for her liking already.

Chapter Fourteen

As the days grew longer, Anne would take herself out for walks down to Eastham Ferry and gaze across the river towards Liverpool. The urge to travel to Scotland was becoming irresistible and she often considered catching the bus into Birkenhead and taking the ferry across the Mersey to look into it properly. Then one day, on the shop's half-day closing, she found herself heading into the Exchange railway station in Liverpool and enquiring about the price of a return fare to Glasgow. To her own surprise, she emerged with a timetable and a train ticket to Glasgow on the Friday before the Whit Bank Holiday. It occurred to her that it would be almost a year since she and Andrew had been told the terrible news of their family connection. She wondered if happiness could ever be in their grasp and dearly hoped that her journey to Scotland would provide some hope for them. Anne remembered Andrew's words about travelling to Scotland himself but had stopped believing they would meet up.

When she returned home, it was to find Emily entertaining their neighbour Isabella Smith and her brother, Keith, who had dropped in and were partaking of tea and the butterfly cakes Anne had made that morning while Emily was doing a shift in the shop.

Anne was filled with excitement about her upcoming trip and blurted out her news. 'You'll never guess... I've bought my train ticket to Glasgow!'

'You're not still thinking of going to Scotland?' said Larry, lifting his head and staring at her. 'We might need you here. Poor Em's been suffering awfully with her legs. She's been doing too much.'

'But I've bought my ticket,' Anne said, 'and I can't get a refund.'

'What's money when Emily needs you?' said Isabella. 'After all, Larry has provided you with a roof over your head and you're not even proper family.'

Anne felt the blood rush to her cheeks. 'I don't see how that is any of your business!' she said.

'Now, no need to be hot-headed about it all. You're the one always talking about your Scottish family. We were only chatting,' Emily explained.

'I still don't think Mrs Smith has a right to express an opinion about my situation in the family.' Anne glared at Keith's sister and felt tricked, also realising that Keith must have known all along that she had a secret she didn't want to talk about.

However, she was surprised when Keith said diplomatically, 'It's obvious you three have matters to discuss. I think we'd better be going.'

He stood up, taking his sister's arm, guiding her to the door, though she did not look happy as the little cakes were quite delicious.

Anne wasn't sure she believed Keith possessed such tact and wondered what he was up to.

As soon as the two visitors had departed, Emily said, 'So who's going to have first say?'

'I've said what I felt needed saying,' Larry muttered. 'It was a shame that our dear neighbour had to put her spoke in.'

'You can say that again,' said Emily.

'I don't deny the truth of her comment,' Anne said in a tremulous voice. 'I'm not ungrateful and I know where my duty lies, so I won't be going to Scotland just yet. But I have enough money and I've promised Gordon I'll find out about the Anderson's ancestry. Emily, you must relax and allow me to take care of you and the cottage in the meantime instead of either of us doing so many stints in the shop. I'm sure Mrs Evans will appreciate working my hours and earning extra money.'

'I'm still not convinced you should go,' said Emily. 'You are only sixteen.'

'But I need to go,' said Anne. 'It was wanting to find out more about my ancestry that led me to go in search of Larry for you,' she added in a wheedling voice.

Larry seemed to mull this over. 'Mrs Evans was asking about some extra hours... I'll think about it.'

Anne decided to leave matters like that for now, so said no more, but went and topped up the teapot with boiling water. She was still determined to go to Scotland by hook or by crook. A thought occurred to her and she decided to drop a line to Albert, Gordon and Teddy that very evening.

As soon as she appeared downstairs, Emma started up the whole subject of Scotland again. Anne put on a jacket and hat. 'I'm going to post some letters. I won't be gone for long. I'm sure you'll cope without me,' she said pleasantly.

'Anyway, I think that Keith fancies you,' Emily said unexpectedly, changing the subject. 'He has a lot going for him. Not short of a bob or two, has a good job, his own place to live in Chester and isn't bad looking either.'

'I'm not that keen on him to be honest and I don't think his sister would like the idea,' Anne said. 'He seems a lot older than me.'

'What does it matter what she thinks?' said Emily, making a movement as if to brush their neighbour aside. 'You're getting older quickly and besides, if you get friendly with another chap it will take your mind off Andrew. No good will come of mooning over him any longer.'

'I agree with Anne,' Larry said. 'He is too old for her and she's a bit young to be thinking of marriage.'

Anne almost blurted out, 'I was sixteen last birthday!'

'Well I think he's a catch,' Emily continued, slightly miffed that her husband had taken Anne's side.

Anne thought she could feel a headache coming on. 'Can we drop this subject, please? I think I'll go for a walk. I need some fresh air and as I said I've some letters to post.' She left the house and walked swiftly towards the post box and then on to the Mersey.

As she approached the Eastham Ferry, Anne couldn't shake off the feeling that she was being followed. No longer able to resist looking over her shoulder, she gazed back and saw Keith a few feet away.

'What are you doing here?' she called.

'I thought you might need company.'

'Why?'

'I believe my sister upset you. She's the eldest in the family and has always had a big mouth, says just what she thinks.'

She considered what he said smacked of fraternal disloyalty and made no comment. 'I'm fine,' she said. 'I came out for a walk, so I can think.'

'I'll join you.'

There was something insistent in his manner that she didn't like. 'I'd prefer to be alone.'

He followed her, placing a hand on her arm, pulling her towards him. 'Surely a little friendly company wouldn't hurt?'

'I've said I wish to be left alone. Now let go of my arm!' She wrenched herself free and crossed the road to the waterfront. To her annoyance he followed he. She could scarcely believe the brazen nerve of the fellow. Making her way back to the village, she decided to go into the church and sit in one of the pews, trusting that he wouldn't take the liberty of following her there of all places and to her relief she was right. Anne bent her head in prayer and left ten minutes later. There was no sign of him, so she had a short walk before heading back to the cottage.

Neither Emily nor Larry brought up the subject of her trip to Scotland again when she returned. Fortunately, Emily dropped the subject of Keith too, but did go on about how lovely it would be if Anne met a local younger man and fell in love and decided to marry and lived close by, but also how nice it would be if they had children, whom Anne could bring to visit, which Emily thought might help make up for not having children of her own. Anne decided not to mention Andrew or Keith following her and his being a bit forward, so by the time Anne went to bed, she was even more determined to go to Scotland.

—

Keith continued to rile Anne by popping his head over the fence whenever he visited from Chester and Anne was in the garden.

'Why did you disappear into the church?' he asked in a self-assured manner, which irritated her. 'Is it because you felt in need of forgiveness?'

Anne didn't like the look in his eye when he said this. 'I'm entitled to sit quietly in prayer if it suits me,' she answered. 'Maybe it wouldn't do you any harm either. Perhaps it's you that needs to repent.' She remembered his grip on her arm that last time.

'Or perhaps,' he retorted, 'you consider yourself too young and are worried about your ability to have an adult conversation with me?'

'It's you that's childish,' she replied, annoyed all over again with his persistence.

'Perhaps it will do you good to have a mature man in your life. Besides, there's no harm in a few years' age gap between a man and woman.'

'I have no idea how old you are,' she said. 'But I reckon you are too old for me.' She did not wait for his response and went straight indoors.

Shortly after this incident, Emily informed her that Albert had written to them about his intention to visit. He gave no reason as to why he suddenly wished to visit his sisters and Anne could only smile, saying it would be nice to see him.

It was not the best of days, weather wise, when Albert arrived. More intermittent showers than sunny spells which meant they could not sit in the garden.

'So, to what do we owe this visit?' asked Emily, bluntly.

'I've heard through Gordon and Teddy that your rheumatism has been troublesome. They've also told me that you are intending to visit Scotland Whit week, Anne.'

Emily looked at Anne, but she remained silent.

'The upshot of things is that I know I have neglected you recently, Emily, and I'm sorry about missing the wedding, so I thought that some Welsh sea air might do you some good,' Albert said.

Emily beamed, delighted at this unexpected gift from her often selfish and sometimes gloomy elder brother.

'I can drive you and Larry back with me today,' he continued. 'He can stay with us for as long as he feels able to leave the shop. I thought you could stay for a week or longer if you like, Emily. See it as a belated wedding present from me and Gladys.'

'That's very thoughtful of you,' said Larry, turning to Anne with a smile. 'Now you'll be able to go up to Scotland without feeling guilty or worrying. It'll do us all good to have a break, although you'll have to beware of the midges in Scotland, Anne.'

'I doubt I'll be bothered by them where I'm going,' Anne said hopefully. 'Anyway, I can swat them away, unlike a certain other pest.'

'I hope you're not referring to Keith.' Emily frowned. 'You wouldn't believe it, Albert – here's a good catch who fancies her despite her youth and she's taken against him.'

Anne protested: 'I reckon he's at least fifteen years older than me.'

'Is he now? Then I agree that not only is he too old but you're too young to take on the responsibility of a husband and family. We missed out on our youth and having some fun because of the war. Emily, let the girl have some enjoyment before she settles down.'

Anne was grateful, if somewhat surprised by Albert taking her side against Emily. Maybe her big brother wasn't such a sour puss after all.

They all busied themselves for the next few hours. Larry decided that Anne would be able to manage the shop herself for a couple of days while he accompanied Emily to Rhyl, and hurried and excited goodbyes were exchanged later that day.

Anne had the house to herself as she made her final preparations for travelling to Scotland after the others had departed for Rhyl and spent the evening planning what she should take in her little suitcase. She imagined it would be a little colder up in Scotland and so took a warm jumper and her woolly stockings just in case. She listened to the wireless in the evenings and daydreamed about seeing Andrew again as she heard the romantic songs played on the radio.

She was on tenterhooks by the time Larry returned by train a couple of days later. Emily was already making friends amongst the guests at the hotel, which meant he had no qualms about leaving her. He told Anne that meant she was free to go to Scotland. That Friday, which was a glorious sunny day, Larry ferried Anne and her suitcase into his van to Birkenhead. He kissed her on the cheek and wished her luck but did not linger to see her off onto the ferry.

She felt excited to be travelling alone and thought about the women who had set out for distant parts of the Empire to join husbands or men they were engaged to. And what of those who had travelled to Flanders to care for the wounded soldiers during the Great War at great risk to their own lives?

Anne wasn't trying to compare herself to those women, but she did feel a sense of adventure and at least the natives spoke English where she was going, even if the accent might be difficult to understand. She also had some idea of the layout of Glasgow, Greenock and Cardross, having sent for maps which she now carried in her handbag. She had written to a guest house in Greenock town centre, not too far from the main library, and reserved a room for two nights with the possibility of staying a couple more and they had given her directions on how to get there from the railway station. The possibility that she might see Andrew in Greenock was becoming ever more real.

Once past Carlisle she knew herself to be close to the border and could not help thinking that soon she would be in the land that her two fathers had left for Liverpool. One she remembered with love and gratitude, and the little she knew of the other did not endear him to her. Perhaps if she had been born in Scotland there might have been a female relative who would have taken her in and cared for her; then she could have grown up knowing her natural father's family and Andrew and his sister, who died a year or so ago, but that would mean she would never have known the love of the Anderson family and that would have been a great loss.

When she disembarked at Glasgow Station, she soon realised that Glaswegians were just as friendly as

Liverpudlians when a woman took her by the arm and led her to the platform for the Greenock train. It was as she was about to board the train that she thought she recognised the face of a young man climbing into one of the carriages, but he was gone before she could get a proper look at him – could it have been Andrew? She could not rid herself of that moment of recognition, even when she was in conversation with a woman who turned out to be a native of Greenock and had once visited an aunt in Liverpool who had met her Scouser husband when he was training at an army camp in Scotland during the war.

Anne had no opportunity to look out for the young man she thought might be Andrew, because the woman, a Mrs McGuire, had her firmly in hand, having given herself the task of escorting Anne to the guest house on Roxburgh Street.

Her landlady was called Mrs McTavish and she welcomed her in the friendliest manner and told her that high tea would be ready at four o'clock. Once she had unpacked, Anne decided to have a walk before that and she set off to explore. It was still light as the daylight hours in Scotland were even longer than they were in Liverpool at this time of year.

She intended to go in search of the street where Liam Fraser had lived when he worked at the sugar factory up here, which she had been told when she went to the factory in Liverpool, and was glad of the street map in her handbag. According to Mrs McTavish, Ann Street was not too far away and the woman had told her a shortcut.

It took Anne longer than she had reckoned on to find the house on Ann Street and even before she reached it, she saw there was a young man waiting outside. Her pulse increased in recognition – Andrew. Marjorie must have told him of her plans. It had to have been him at the railway station – but even so she hesitated for a moment before taking a deep breath and approaching him.

He moved towards her as she came closer and hesitated briefly before taking her hands in his own. Andrew's face seemed to speak of a thousand things that he wanted to say but instead his eyes drank her in. Anne felt the same and it was a moment before she felt able to speak. Her heart was pounding as they faced each other.

'You know, I was hoping we'd bump into each other,' she said, a catch in her voice.

'You look all grown up,' said Andrew, his voice thick with emotion.

'Well, I'm a working girl and will be seventeen next birthday,' she said, unable to stop smiling.

'You've two or three years to go before catching up with me,' he said.

'That's not much,' she said.

He cocked his handsome head to one side. 'I've a confession to make. Marjorie and Gordon told me what day you were travelling and when she wrote to me I couldn't stop myself hoping we'd meet.'

'That's why you were on the same train!' It all made sense now.

'But you must have put some work into your enquiries to end up here too?' he asked.

'I did, and I enjoyed it so much that I'd like to be a detective. I wrote to Tate & Lyle and they dipped into their archives for me. Did you know that your father and my da both worked for the company ever since they were young?'

'No.' He paused, looking thoughtful. 'That I didn't know. Did they start work at the same time? Do you think they knew each other from Scotland?'

Anne agreed it might be possible.

'How long are you planning on being in Greenock? Marjorie also told me that you were going to Cardross to look up the Anderson relatives.'

'I am, so a couple of nights at most,' she replied. 'What about you, will you come back to Liverpool at all?'

She held her breath as she waited for his reply.

Andrew shook his dark head and said, 'My job is in London, Anne. I enjoy living down there. It's an interesting city and I've made friends.'

'Do you have a girlfriend?' she asked, her voice strained.

As he stared at her intently from his attractive face, he said, 'No, I've been far too busy to consider asking a girl out. Whereas I hear from Marjorie that you had a boyfriend for a short time. Is that true?'

Anne felt a blush warm her cheeks. 'Pete – he wasn't a boyfriend exactly, but he did make me laugh. I was very sad after Da died and I missed you awfully.'

Andrew smiled warmly. 'Anyone who can put a smile on your face is alright with me. Have you heard from him since?'

'No, really we were just chums. He wanted more and I couldn't think about anyone but you.'

Before he could make another comment, the front door opened to reveal an old woman standing in the doorway. They had both almost forgotten the reason they had come to Ann Street.

'Cannae help youse dearies?' she asked slowly in a strong accent.

'I hope so,' said Andrew. 'I'm trying to find out more about my father, Liam Fraser, who lived here before he went to Liverpool.' He held out a hand. 'I'm Andrew Fraser.'

The woman looked taken aback but she took his hand and shook it. 'That was where he went, is it? We moved in here straight after he left. Whisht, so he found another woman to take him on in Liverpool.'

'Yes, my mother was his second wife,' Andrew said in a friendly manner. 'She died and he married again. I know very little about his first wife and their son.'

'Mary Fraser died a short while before he went off to live in Liverpool. The child's grandmother took him back to Jura with her.'

Anne and Andrew exchanged glances. He addressed the woman again. 'Do you have a name and address for them?'

The woman hesitated. 'Perhaps you and your young lady might like to come inside while we talk.'

He thanked her and stepped over the threshold and Anne followed him, deciding that things appeared complicated enough without explaining that she was not his young lady.

They were led into a small but comfortable room to the rear of the house and told to sit down on a sofa. They did not exchange a word while their hostess bustled about fetching cups and saucers and other essentials. At last she handed them steaming cups of tea and sat down herself. 'I'm Mary Gillespie, by the way. Mrs,' she added. 'I presume Liam is dead, what with you coming all this way to find out about him.'

'Aye, he is that,' Andrew said. 'I know so little about Father and his family that I decided to have a go at finding out more.'

Anne watched him intently as Mrs Gillespie told him what she knew of Liam.

'He was not a native of Greenock,' she said, 'but was born in Antrim in Northern Ireland, though his family had Scottish blood. I believe his father was a doctor and wanted Liam to follow in his footsteps, but Liam wasn't cut out for the years of studying and left Ireland for Scotland in search of a job.'

'Do you know whereabouts in Antrim?' asked Andrew. 'And where exactly is Jura?'

'I don't have the address in Antrim,' she said. 'But Jura, where your brother went to live, is one of the Inner Hebridean islands. Famous for whisky and deer. It has a small population and is quite barren, I believe. Liam's wife, Helen grew up there and her mother's name was McDougal.'

'What is the boy's name?' asked Andrew. 'And how old would he be now?'

'Duncan, and he would be about twenty-five.'

'So not much older than me,' Andrew said, getting to his feet. 'Well, I won't take up any more of your time, Mrs Gillespie. No doubt your man will be coming in soon and wanting his supper.'

'He will that. He always goes for a walk before supper,' she said. 'I'll see you both out.'

Anne jumped up from the sofa, shook Mrs Gillespie's hand and thanked her for the tea before following Andrew outside.

'So, what next?' she asked after the door closed behind them.

He gazed down at her. 'You know where – Jura and Antrim for me and Cardross for you. It's been so good to see you, Anne.' For a moment, their eyes met and then he lifted his head and looked past her into the distance.

'It's good to see you, too. I've missed you,' she said softly. 'I still wish you'd said ta-ra before leaving.'

He reached out and took one of her hands. 'I explained on Boxing Day that I would have found it much harder to leave then. You must have guessed, Anne, that I'd grown fond of you and discovering you were my sister came as a terrible blow for the future I had in mind for us.'

Her heart gave a peculiar jump. 'We should have tried to talk things through.'

'How could I when you hadn't long left school and your parents didn't want me on the scene – and then to discover we were related, it was just too much,' he said earnestly.

She linked her slender fingers through his. 'So much has changed for both of us. Mother died a few months ago. I'm no longer living in Liverpool, but at Eastham on the Wirral with Emily and her new husband.'

'I know. Marjorie tells me everything because I'm always asking after you.'

'And I'm always asking after you. Tell me about your job. Is it going well in London?'

'I'm interested in people and what happens to them as well as sport and what's going on in the world. They send me out on a story to find out as much as I can and then I write it up as interestingly and excitingly or as amusingly as possible. Sometimes, I come up with an idea that I think would make a good article and put it to the editor – if he likes it, he gives me the go-ahead to write it.'

'How interesting – do you enjoy writing?'

He nodded. 'Right from my school days, when I used to make up stories. What about you?'

'When I worked in the jam factory, I found the work a bit repetitive, although it had its funny moments and I got along with the women I worked with. I miss them sometimes, although I quite like working in the shop and getting to know the customers and I don't mind house-work when it means I'm helping Emily out, as she did so much for me when I was growing up.'

'Oh Anne, so much has happened since we saw each other last.' He sighed heavily and a look of anguish flashed across his face. 'If only you being my sister wasn't true. I can't even begin to think of you like that, though God knows I have tried. Before that I'd hoped we might have married one day, had you wanted to...' His voice trailed away.

A tumult of emotions swept through Anne: joy at his loving words, quickly followed by the bleak realisation that their dreams could never be fulfilled. She desperately tried to cling on to some hope. 'I found my birth certifi-cate and it wasn't Liam who registered the birth but the midwife. I'm going to try and trace her to see what she can tell me about what happened when I was born.'

'Have you the birth certificate with you?' he asked hopefully.

She shook her head. They regarded each other for a moment and Anne was the first to speak. 'Right, we'll have to say goodbye for now and I wish you every success in your search. Hopefully, it won't be too long before we see each other again. I know it's difficult, but it would mean so much to me if we could at least keep in touch.'

He nodded. 'I want to hear about anything you might find out. We have to try.'

'I agree. Likewise, I'm interested to know how you get on with your search too and I would like your address in London, so that we might write to each other.'

He took a card from his breast pocket and handed it to her. 'You can reach me at either telephone number once I return to London and the address is on there too.'

She took a scrap of paper and pencil from her handbag and wrote Larry and Emily's address on it, including the shop telephone number, and gave it to him in return. He pocketed it and said, 'Good luck on your travels, Anne.'

Andrew's eyes searched the features that were so dear to him and he could not resist hugging her, planting a kiss on the top of her head as a parent might with a child. Anne clung to him, breathing in his particular smell and feeling the change in his embrace – Andrew was no longer the boy she had loved but a man. Conflicting emotions raced through her as they released each other and headed away in opposite directions.

Anne's thoughts were in confusion as she returned to the guest house. She felt as far away from knowing who she was as she had when she had found her birth certificate.

She and Mrs McTavish enjoyed a wonderful high tea when she returned to the guest house, which consisted of sandwiches filled with ham, some Scottish cheese and a delicious slab of Dundee cake. It didn't take her mind off the day's events, which were still whirling around her head as she climbed into bed that night. But two facts she knew for sure; the man she had regarded as her father for most of her life had been kind and had loved his children. Liam Fraser, however, had been inclined to leave other people to care for his offspring. Not only had he let his son be taken away by his grandmother, he'd also given his second daughter away. It was now up to her to discover the facts surrounding her birth. Once again, she felt in her bones there was a mystery to be solved.

Chapter Fifteen

Anne spent the following day visiting the sights of Greenock, such as the impressive Victoria Tower, and taking in the views over the Firth of Clyde. She had a cup of tea and a buttered oatcake at a cafe before heading for the waterfront and taking a walk along the bank of the Clyde, thinking of Andrew again. As she gazed at the seagoing vessels on the water, she wondered if he was on one of them and what kind of reception he would get on the Isle of Jura. Would he find out more information about his grandfather in Antrim from his half-brother, Duncan? She could not think of the old man as her own grandfather yet, because if she were to do so then she would have to accept the truth that Andrew was completely out of her reach. There could never be anything further of a romantic nature between them. She stared across the Firth to the northern shore, wondering what kind of welcome she would get from Hugh Anderson's brother who – as far as she was aware - still worked the family farm.

Greenock seemed a bustling industrious place and Anne decided she liked it very much. However, all the events from the day before had made her determined to head off to her adoptive father's old home in the morning, so she went to the railway station and bought a ticket for Cardross. After eating some fish and chips, Anne decided she had done enough for one day and turned back, before visiting the cinema and returning to the guest house later and telling her landlady of her plans over a cup of cocoa before having an early night.

The following day, she was up bright and early and arrived at the railway station in plenty of time for the Glasgow train and easily had enough time to make her connection for the Cardross train when she arrived there. She relaxed on a bench in the waiting area, watching people coming and going, listening to the chatter of the natives, yet unable to make sense of all that she heard; it was as if she were in a foreign country.

It was not long before she noticed on the Departures board that her train was waiting at the designated platform and she wasted no time in finding herself a window seat and making herself comfortable. She flicked through her copy of *People's Friend* and – not for the first time – considered its content very different from her own normal choice of reading material: *Woman's Own*. But the gentle homely short stories helped to while away the next forty minutes or so.

She left the station and realised that with a suitcase, it was a bit of a walk into the town centre, but there, she hoped she would be able to ask for directions to the Andersons' farm. Her first thought was to head for the library, but she was told by the rather stern librarian that if she'd asked for the farm, she would have left the train at the station before the one she did. Peering at her over her horn-rimmed spectacles. 'It would have been the easiest way to go,' added the librarian, 'but you could phone the farm from here. Miss Fiona is bound to be home and will come and pick you up. A cousin, are you?'

'Why d'you think that?' asked Anne.

'Because you've a look of her,' the librarian replied.

Anne was flabbergasted but managed to bite back the words *that's impossible!*

'I presume this is a surprise visit,' said the librarian. 'Otherwise Fiona or her uncle Donald would have arranged to pick you up from the station.'

Anne nodded speechlessly.

'You're looking pale? No doubt you're tired after your journey, having got up early to get here. Where have you come from, luvvie?'

Anne managed to regain the power of speech, 'Liverpool!'

'Och, you'll be one of Hugh's girls. I'd heard he'd had two lassies a while back – but nothing about them since.'

It occurred to Anne that one of the lassies that the librarian had heard about could have been Flora, the one whose nightdress had caught fire – maybe the letter informing of her tragic death had been lost in the post – so she just nodded.

Within a few minutes the librarian was on the phone, informing Fiona Anderson that her cousin from Liverpool had arrived and was waiting at the library to be picked up. Twenty minutes later a girl, still wearing an apron, entered the library like a whirlwind, coming to a halt a foot away from Anne.

'Oh, my word! You do look like me!' exclaimed Fiona, without preamble.

'It's true,' murmured Anne, scarcely able to believe that they could be so alike; the same-shaped nose, blue-grey eyes, dimpled chin and hair not quite the same shade of carroty-red but near enough, although not fashioned in the same style: Fiona's long hair was tied up in a ponytail. 'I'm Anne, so pleased to meet you.' It was the moment when she might, perhaps, have explained about being adopted, but somehow, she couldn't get the words out.

Fiona pleased her when she said, 'I'd forgotten what your name was.'

Anne had heard it said that lots of people had a doppel-ganger, but she just could not believe that this was a mere coincidence in this case. Something must have happened in the past that meant there was a blood tie between herself and Fiona – and most likely the answer lay up here in Scotland.

Fiona seized Anne by the shoulders and pulled her close to her, hugging her tightly. Anne was aware of the smell of baking and furniture polish. 'My goodness, you must have had a busy morning,' she commented.

'Too right I have.' Fiona hesitated a moment. 'Nothing special about that, but there is in having a visit from a cousin. I'm so pleased to meet you – and I'm sure Uncle Donald will be too – but we'd best not delay. He'll be in soon, expecting dinner on the table.'

A confused Anne picked up her suitcase and followed her outside. A light motor truck was parked outside which reminded Anne of the kind of vehicles that frequented the dock road in Liverpool. She had rarely been in a motor vehicle and was thoroughly excited. They climbed in and were off.

'So why didn't you write and tell us you were coming? Not that you aren't very welcome, of course,' asked Fiona.

'I didn't know who to write to and I certainly didn't know about you, and besides I wasn't absolutely certain my trip would come off as my sister Emily wasn't too well.' Anne paused. 'She has terrible pains in her joints.'

'Oh, that's awful,' said Fiona, with feeling.

'So, whose daughter are you?' asked Anne, liking her cousin immediately.

'The youngest brother Jamie's – he was killed in an accident on the farm a good while ago now. As for my mother, Catrina, she left before the war to visit her brother who had been very ill. He lived in Canada, and she couldn't stand life on the farm, whereas I love it.'

'Did she leave you after your father was killed?'

'No, before – on my eighth birthday. I'm now twenty-four.'

'How awful!'

'No need to pity me! I'm well used to it now, although it does hurt that she could leave me the way she did. I think she must be dead now because if she ever bothered to write to me the letters must have gone missing.'

'Does Uncle Donald have a wife?'

'Naw, he lives for the farm and says he's never seen the need for a wife – especially as he has me to cook and clean since Mother left, as well as the wireless to listen to and books from the library to read, and other farmers to discuss the beasts and crops and to complain about the government with.'

'You don't find it dull or lonely?'

'Occasionally, then I go to Helensburgh or even into Glasgow for a bit of life and the fancy shops, but I can't stand the noise and the crowds in the big city for too long.'

'Whereas I'm a city girl,' said Anne. 'I like the bustle, the department stores, cinemas and theatres; also, I enjoy living near the Mersey watching the boats come and go

– there's also dance halls where a girl can meet fellas, not that I've ever been to a dance hall.'

'We have dances in the country – generally in one of the barns or the church hall.'

'Have you got a fella?'

'Well, one of the lads who's a regular at all the dances – his name is Sandy – we've been out off and on for years. Trouble is Uncle Donald isn't keen on him because he's not from farming stock but an architect.'

Anne gave Fiona a sharp look. 'I bet the real reason is that he doesn't want to lose you. Who would look after him and the farmhouse if you were to get married? I know of this because of my sister Emily.'

'But sure, he'd have to fend for himself – and I couldn't let that happen. He's been good to me.'

Anne hesitated before saying, 'I know this might sound impertinent, but does he pay you?'

'I have a roof over my head and food in my stomach.'

Anne said, 'But surely you need some money for yourself?'

'On my birthday, Christmas and Easter he gives me thirty pounds a time and tells me to treat myself to something pretty.'

'That's quite a bit of money, so at least he does appreciate you,' said Anne, slanting a smile at Fiona. 'There's families in Liverpool living on less than two pounds a week.'

'It means a lot to me,' burst out Fiona. 'I save half of it. Grandma told me it's always a good thing to have something put away as one never knows what the future might hold. She was left to cope alone with the farm and her sons when she was in her forties.'

'Was she widowed?'

'No, Grandfather just took off on his travels; she said he had itchy feet and hadn't wanted to be tied down. It was his father who insisted he take on the farm with him being the eldest and he was persuaded to marry the daughter of the owner of the neighbouring farm, so the two farms could be worked as one.'

Anne was astounded. 'That sounds almost medieval. And it is funny that both your grandfather and your mother couldn't put down roots.'

'I've never thought of it that way, but yes, that's true.' Fiona looked thoughtful.

'Wouldn't you like to get married and have children and your own place?' Anne asked her, thinking that she would herself when she was older.

'I think about it occasionally.' Fiona paused and glanced sidelong at Anne. 'I suppose you have a boyfriend?'

'There was someone I really liked but things didn't work out.' Anne couldn't begin to imagine what the future would hold for Andrew and herself now she had met this girl who looked so like her, therefore she decided to say no more, aware that matters could get complicated if she were to tell the truth.

'Well, we're here,' said Fiona. 'Welcome to Paradise! Could you jump out and open the gate, please?'

Anne fumbled with the door handle and managed to open it; she looked before leaping as she spied all the mud on the ground and stepped down gingerly, tiptoeing over to the gate and unlatching it. She noticed a letter box was fastened to a nearby post.

Fiona called, 'Get right back and wait there until I'm through, then you can fasten it again.'

Anne did so and was glad she hadn't stayed where she was because a spray of mud flew up from the vehicle's tyres. She wasted no time climbing back into the truck, not wanting to be left behind to walk the rest of the way to the farmhouse across the muddy yard and ruin her best shoes. As they drew closer to the house, Anne realised that it must have been built a hundred years ago or more. It appeared to be constructed of granite and had bay windows with green painted sash frames and a hefty-looking door of the same colour set between two ground-floor windows. There were another two floors above, and the uppermost one had windows in the gabled roof.

'This is the rear of the house,' Fiona said, bringing the truck to a halt. 'We seldom use the front door.' She opened the vehicle's door, stepped down onto a brick pathway and walked swiftly up to the house, calling after Anne over her shoulder, 'Come on, don't be hanging back. You must be fair parched and longing for a cup of tea to relax with before Uncle Donald and the lads come in.'

'The lads?' asked Anne.

'The hired hands. They share the lodging built over the stables, but I cook their daytime meals for them; breakfast and dinner. They see to supper themselves.'

'It sounds a sensible arrangement.'

'It works well. I'm up early to cook Uncle Donald's breakfast, so I might as well cook theirs too,' Fiona said, pushing open the back door, leaving it ajar for Anne to enter as she went inside.

'What time is breakfast?' Anne asked, gazing about the large kitchen with interest, noting the good-sized table in the centre covered by a plain white tablecloth with cutlery and plates already in place.

'I generally serve the men and eat once they've finished,' Fiona said.

Anne presumed that she would be eating with Fiona and hoped the men wouldn't be long coming in as she was famished.

A quarter of an hour later Donald and the farmhands, Hector and Alistair, arrived.

'Uncle Donald, you'll never guess what's happened. This is Cousin Anne, Uncle Hugh's girl from Liverpool – she's come to visit!'

Donald was first at the large, square sink to quickly scrub his hands clean before drying them and reaching out to Anne, taking both her hands in his huge, work-worn ones and squeezing them gently as he gazed in wonder at her face. 'This is a marvellous surprise – I cannae get over how alike Fiona and ma mammy yer are.'

'It came as a shock to me, too, that I looked like Fiona, that is,' Anne said, scrutinizing his leathery, well-lined features amid which his wise, pale-blue eyes were set beneath a thatch of reddish-flaxen hair, atop of which was a tartan tam-o'-shanter with a green bobble. He had removed a well-worn tweed jacket and hung it on one of the pegs beside the door, revealing a Fair Isle pullover over a flannelette checked shirt tucked into dark-brown corduroy trousers splattered with mud. He had also taken off his boots and slipped his stockinged feet into a pair of leather slippers. She thought he couldn't be more different from his elder brother, Hugh, than peas were from string beans.

'I'll get the family album out and show you a photo of your grandma,' he said, and without further ado, he went over to the large dresser on the far wall and opened a cupboard from which he took out an album and brought it over to her.

Anne's arms sagged beneath the weight of it and she pressed it against her chest as she sat down on a nearby sofa that dipped in the middle. She opened it and the first photograph she came to was a sepia image of a couple dressed in what she guessed was late Victorian fashion.

'Yer grandparents, your grandmother, the lady that you look so alike was called Katherine. Graham was her maiden name,' said Donald, perching on the arm of the sofa.

And in that moment, as she gazed down at the couple, Anne could believe that they really were her grandparents: she could even see a likeness to Hugh in their faces, not just herself in the granny's features. *How strange!* she thought, turning the page over quickly to gaze down at a photograph of three boys in whose distinctive features she could trace Hugh and Uncle Donald; the third and smallest lad she presumed was Fiona's father, Jamie. There were photographs of more young men, but as they worked through the album, Donald could only remember the name of a distant cousin, Kyle, who had a twin sister called Heather. The family had moved to Glasgow and they had not heard from them since. There was also a photograph of Fiona's mother, Catrina, which Uncle Donald pointed out to her; she was pretty, just like her daughter.

'It is very sad that she went away.' Anne said.

'Och, I do not like to talk about her. It was a terrible business.' A dark look passed over his face and Anne thought he must still be angry, upset about Catrina leaving Fiona and his youngest brother, so decided to say no more.

By the time Anne reached the end of the album, she was convinced that Anderson blood must run in her veins. Somehow, in the past, there had been a mix-up, but what could possibly be the explanation?

Chapter Sixteen

For the rest of the day Anne toyed with increasingly improbable reasons for the likeness between herself, Fiona and her grandmother. Even as she carried on conversations with the girl and her Uncle Donald, her mind was busy wondering about her grandfather: was he dead or alive? Could he be the connection in some way? And if he were alive – where was he? After she was shown the guest room and retired for the night, her mind was still far too active for her to sleep right away, but eventually she dozed off, only to dream of Andrew. She awoke, knowing she was going to have to get in touch with him before too long, to tell him about her extraordinary physical resemblance to the Andersons. Surely there must be something she could uncover that would give certain proof that she wasn't his sister after all but a true member of the Anderson family? Then there would be nothing to prevent them getting together.

The result of all this would be a search to discover what had happened to Andrew's *real* baby sister. The answer to that must be in Liverpool, as perhaps would be the answer to who her own natural father was.

Anne felt so impatient to get at the truth she would have left the following morning, only she knew that wouldn't be kind or polite in the circumstances. She had only arrived yesterday. Even so, she wasted no time in composing a letter to Andrew at the address he had given her in London, so that her letter would be waiting for him when he arrived home.

It took her some time to get the wording of the letter to her satisfaction as she wanted to encourage him to join her in a search for the truth in Liverpool. But as soon as she had sealed the envelope, she immediately began to question if she was doing the right thing. There could be something she had not thought through properly, some fact that was crucial to the whole matter. What if her instincts were wrong and this was all just an incredible coincidence? Perhaps she should delay sending it?

Fortunately, she was not left alone to ponder on the matter for long due to Uncle Donald having decided to show her around the farm that morning. Come afternoon, Fiona was planning on driving her into Cardross to have a proper look around, but by the time Anne had seen the farm, admired cattle and cooed over ducklings and chicks, she was in no mood for much walking, so a leisurely walk along the main street was as much as she wanted. Fiona did drive slowly past St Peter's Seminary which, Fiona told her, was one of the best examples of modernist architecture in Scotland.

Anne attempted to look politely interested but she must have failed because Fiona said, 'I can see that doesn't interest you, but you'd be surprised at how many come to admire it.'

'I was hoping for a romantic old castle,' Anne said, wrinkling her nose.

'Well, we have Kilmahew Castle,' Fiona suggested. 'It was built in the sixteenth century and was in the Napier family for generations.' She paused. 'Then it fell into ruin and the estate was finally bought by the archdiocese of Glasgow. The castle was originally a four-storey turreted house which was altered over the years.'

'From the sound of it I'm reminded of a keep,' said Anne.

Fiona nodded. 'A lot of fighting went on between the various clans at that time. It's a few miles out of town to the north, if you want to see it?'

Anne nodded. 'Perhaps after that we can find a nice tea shop and have a cake and cuppa here in Cardross.'

'If we'd had the whole day, I'd have suggested Helensburgh – but we can go there tomorrow, if you've a mind to stay on a little longer?' Fiona paused. 'When were you going to leave for home?'

'Tomorrow, but I don't want to outstay my welcome,' Anne said.

Fiona beamed at her. 'You can stay as long as you like. It's a pleasure to have you.'

'Thank you, but I help to care for my sister Emily – she has rheumatism – so I'll only be able to stay a couple more days.'

Fiona looked disappointed. 'You'll have to come again, and we can make a real holiday of it.'

Anne said, 'That would be lovely. We could write or phone each other in the meantime. Shall we go and have cake and a cuppa now?'

There were a lot of cakes and scones to choose from in the smart tea rooms in the centre of the town. Anne decided on a tattie scone with jam and cream, only to discover that the tattie scone was more like a potato cake and expressed her surprise.

Fiona said, 'Surely you call potatoes "tatties" in England?'

'Of course, but I wasn't thinking,' Anne said. 'Anyway, it tastes perfectly okay with jam and cream on.'

'I can't wait to tell Uncle Donald. He'll split his sides laughing.'

Anne smiled reluctantly. 'It's not that funny.' But then she found herself laughing too as she munched the tattie scone, thinking that even a brick would taste nice with jam and cream on it. After a mouthful of tea, she reached for a slice of date and walnut cake which proved delicious. 'I'm eating like a horse.'

'Scottish air will do that; it must be agreeing with you,' Fiona said.

'My, this cake is delicious. I presume I can buy a whole loaf of this from the bakery?' she asked.

Fiona nodded.

'Great! I'll buy two – one for supper and one to take home for Emily and Larry to enjoy.'

'That's a good choice as it's one of Uncle Donald's favourites.' Fiona bit into the slice of chocolate gateau she had chosen and savoured every morsel. 'I love anything chocolatey.'

'Hmm, me too,' said Anne. 'But I thought I should sample the local delicacies first.'

'Oh yes, when in Rome! If I were to go to Liverpool, what should I eat there that the natives eat?'

'Why, scouse, of course, which is a sort of stew that mainly poor people used to eat, and was called lobscouse. Don't ask me why. Wet Nelly. They are the only two I can think of off the top of my head,' said Anne.

'I know what scouse is, but I've never heard of Wet Nelly.' Fiona chuckled at the name.

'It's a sort of pudding which is made with buttered bread, raisins, nutmeg and custard – although the one I had at a cafe when I went to Great Homer Street Market years ago with Emily tasted as if syrup and rum had been added. That made it richer, of course – and delicious.'

'I'd love to visit Liverpool one day,' said Fiona.

Anne said she would be more than welcome, and meant it. She had taken to her lookalike cousin immediately, crossing her fingers that she would be able to come clean about her true identity… or maybe she would be able to prove to Fiona that they were related by blood. 'You should get to know your Liverpool relatives – although we are rather scattered these days with Emily and I living on the Wirral and Albert and his wife in Rhyl. They run a hotel there. Gordon and Teddy and his wife Joan are still living in the family home in Liverpool.'

'But you could show me around?'

'Of course. Best if you come by motor if possible – be more convenient for visiting Rhyl, although there is a train.' Anne's teeth crunched into an oatcake.

'We'll have to be getting back soon,' Fiona said, having finished her chocolate gateau.

Anne nodded and within minutes she had finished eating and drained her teacup. Taking her purse from her handbag and picking up the bill, she went and paid it before going to the bakery and purchasing two date and walnut loaves.

By the time they arrived back at the farm, Anne was feeling pleasantly drowsy. She offered to help Fiona prepare the evening meal but was told she had done her share by providing the date and walnut cake. She was told she should sit in front of the fire and take it easy as she was on holiday, so that was what Anne did. She found it hard to shut her mind down, having realised that if Fiona did decide to visit Liverpool, it would be best to prepare the family for the likeness between herself and Fiona, and that meant she needed a close-up photograph of them together. Why hadn't she thought of taking one before now? Crazy not to have done so. She decided to ask her uncle to take a shot of them sitting on the sofa that evening if he was familiar with using a camera. Fortunately, she had not used up all the roll of film in Gordon's camera that afternoon and her Uncle Donald was able to use the camera. That done, she checked how many shots she had left for the trip to Helensburgh tomorrow, Donald having told her that there was a castle there, although only one tower remained of the original twelfth-century building, the rest having been demolished in the fifth century.

He added, 'What I find more interesting is that the town was originally named Millig, but after Sir James Colquhoun bought the land in the eighteenth century, he changed the name to Helensburgh after his wife, Lady Helen, who was the granddaughter of the sixteenth Earl of Sutherland.'

'I wonder how she felt about that,' mused Anne.

'Flattered I should imagine,' said Fiona, pausing in her knitting. 'You hear of folk being named after places such as Iona and Florence – but normally not the other way around. Uncle Donald,' she continued, 'you haven't mentioned the Highland Boundary Fault.' She paused, adding, 'It occasionally causes minor earthquakes in the area, Anne!'

'Earthquakes!' exclaimed Anne. 'You're joking!'

'No, it's the gospel truth,' said Donald. 'It's all down to what happened in the last Ice Age, which shaped the geography of the area – but they're nothing to worry about.'

'It does mean that you can see Lowland-like countryside and that of the Highlands not far away. In fact, Helensburgh is only a few miles from Loch Lomond,' Fiona said.

'I'd like to see it,' Anne said excitedly.

'Then you shall.' Fiona smiled, continuing with her knitting.

Anne began to hum the tune 'The Bonnie Banks o' Loch Lomond'.

And on that happy note her Uncle Donald stood up and went outside for a smoke of his pipe and Anne took out her map.

If Anne were to be asked what she enjoyed most about her outing the following day, she would have said seeing the exterior of the Hill House in Helensburgh, a very attractive building with a turret which conjured up all kinds of romantic possibilities in her mind. It had been designed by the famous architect Charles Mackintosh and his wife Margaret for Walter Blackie the publisher, earlier in the century. Unfortunately, the building was not open to the sightseeing public but Anne enjoyed walking along Loch Lomond, set among the lovely hills.

The following day was spent shopping in Cardross with Fiona, using up the last of her photographic film and buying several packets of shortbread as gifts for Emily and Larry. She also purchased some baccy for Uncle Donald's pipe and a silk scarf for Fiona as farewell gifts. They had been so kind and so welcoming to her; she wanted to say thank you in some small way.

When it came to take her leave of the two people she now thought of as family Anne felt rather full of emotion.

'I feel like I'm losing a friend,' Fiona said. 'Promise me you'll come again.'

'Yes, I will, and you must come to Liverpool,' replied Anne, delighted that they were planning to see each other again.

Fiona and her Uncle Donald drove her to the station for her train and Anne felt near to tears on the train journey back to Glasgow, but at least she could honestly say she had enjoyed herself, although she was now presented with a deeper mystery as to who she really was.

By the time she arrived in Liverpool after the long journey, Anne was exhausted. The voices of those she encountered, or simply overheard talking, sounded strange at first, but her ears soon adjusted to the accent of her birthplace and she began to feel at home once more. She made her way to James Street Station and caught the train that would take her to Eastham. As she found herself a window seat, she prayed that she wouldn't nod off and miss her stop. She thought about all she had to tell Emily and Larry and imagined their stunned expressions when she produced her photographs after they had been developed. Her arms and shoulders ached with the weight of her baggage as she left the train and walked home, and she wished she had been able to tell Larry what time she would be arriving so that he could bring her home in his van.

She dropped her bags in the hallway as she entered the house and let out a sigh. Emily paused halfway through knitting a row of purl as she entered the parlour.

'The wanderer has returned,' Anne said, flopping onto the sofa. 'Sorry, I'm so much later home than expected, but they wanted me to stay longer.'

'It doesn't matter. You've arrived safely, that's the main thing,' said Emily. 'So how was Scotland? Did you find our relatives?'

'I'll tell you after I've had a cuppa and a butty,' Anne said. 'You're going to be flabbergasted.' On those words, she went into the kitchen where she found Larry brewing a pot of tea.

He glanced over his shoulder at her and smiled. 'Have a good time?'

'Aye,' she said. 'Everything been all right here?'

He nodded.

Anne took her tea and a cheese sandwich and sat on the sofa, munching it hungrily while Emily and Larry stared at her. 'Well, flabbergast us, then?' said Emily.

'I'm the spitting image of Fiona Anderson and your grandmother,' Anne told them through a mouthful of food.

'What did you say?' Emily asked. 'I didn't catch that.'

Anne swallowed, took another swig of tea and after a few seconds, repeated her words.

Emily's jaw dropped. 'What d'you mean by that?'

'What I say – I'm the spitting image of your cousin Fiona and I look like your grandmother, Katherine, in an old photograph. So much so, it's impossible that we aren't related somehow.'

'Let's see this photo of Fiona, then.' Emily put her knitting down on the side table.

'I've yet to have the film developed,' replied Anne. 'I'll do it tomorrow.'

'Are you going to get in touch with Andrew Fraser about this?' her sister said.

'I've written him a letter, but I haven't sent it yet.'

'That's wise. There is no point giving him false hope by continuing to stir the pot until you know more. The sensible thing to do would be to find the midwife who delivered Andrew's mother's baby,' said Emily.

'And me!' said Anne. 'She could have delivered us both if we were in the same area.' This was the first time that Anne had thought of this possibility.

Larry said. 'The local GP will probably have known the names of the midwives in his patch, I should think.'

'There could be a register just like there is for state-registered nurses, if she was registered,' said Emily. 'You could ask at Central Library and they'll point you in the right direction. Although, there were women who acted as midwives who weren't registered in those days.'

'Oh great!' exclaimed Anne. 'It would just be my luck to have been delivered by one of them.'

'All of this seems to point to the possibility that there is some other story behind your birth. If so, I wonder who your mother really was and where she lived,' mused Emily.

'And who my real father is…' Anne said in a low voice.

'Well, one or the other of them would appear to be descended from my paternal grandmother or one of her relatives,' Emily said. 'Gordon might know Grandmother's maiden name, Anne.'

'I'm sure Uncle Donald told me it was Graham,' Anne said. 'I should have written it down.'

'Gordon will know. It's all so curious,' Emily said, shaking her head.

'Let's leave it for now,' suggested Larry. 'Tell us about your holiday, Anne.'

She told them all about her few days in Scotland, how wonderful the air and the countryside were and what an impressive area Cardross was. They all decided they must visit the farm and the surrounding area next summer. On that note, Anne realised her eyelids were drooping, so she decided to go to bed as she was tired out.

–

The following morning she awoke and as soon as she had her slippers and her dressing gown on, she searched in one of her drawers for the birth certificate and took it back to bed with her, carefully casting her eyes over it again and considering the name of the midwife again – Cissie Jamieson. She sighed and told herself there was no point lingering in bed as she was anxious to have the film developed, which would be the first step in trying to prove her identity. She also needed to go to Liverpool's Central Library, but breakfast first.

Emily and Larry must have smelled the bread toasting because they came downstairs as Anne was spreading marmalade on a buttered slice. 'You're up early,' said Emily.

'That's because I've a lot to do today,' Anne said. 'I need to go to Central Library. If that's all right with you, Larry? I'll make the time up later and do one of your shifts during the week. I want to see if I can find out more about the person who registered me or the Fraser baby. It was Cissie Jamieson, the midwife.'

'Alright, good luck with it,' he said.

Anne knew she was going to need it.

Anne went to Boots the Chemist in Liverpool first, and dropped off the film, then headed off to Liverpool's Central Library. Hurrying upstairs to the Reference, Records and Archives Department again, she once more explained to the librarian at the reception desk what she was searching for and within a short space of time he had provided her with an address to write to, in order to discover the names and addresses of registered midwives in Liverpool. It was called the Central Midwives Board. 'If you have no luck there,' he said, 'it might be worth your while to look in the *Kelly's Directory* for the year you're interested in as they list names, occupations and addresses, so you could find the woman you're searching for.'

Anne walked over to the shelves where the *Kelly's* were kept and passed a table where a man was seated, turning over the pages of a heavy-looking book. Anne felt as if the floor shifted beneath her feet. Taking a deep breath, she blinked several times before rubbing her eyes. Her vision cleared, and she realised that she wasn't imagining things – it was Andrew Fraser sitting there. Anne felt almost rooted to the spot and remained where she was until she felt more herself before crossing the space that divided them. She came to a halt beside the table and waited for him to notice her.

It wasn't until he reached the bottom of a page and turned it over that Andrew glanced up at her. He did a double-take before rising hurriedly to his feet, almost dropping his book in the process. He looked like he hardly believed it was her standing in front of him and said, 'How did you know I was here?'

'I didn't. How could I? It's sheer chance that I'm here now. You never mentioned that you were planning on coming to Liverpool.'

'I wasn't – but after meeting you in Scotland, I thought I'd drop in on Marjorie and Robbie.'

'But what are you doing here now?' she asked.

'I lost the bit of paper you'd written your new address on – although I knew I could have got in touch with Marjorie for it, so I decided to do some research into Mam's background while I was in Liverpool. I do have her marriage certificate, so I have her father's name but haven't been able to trace him. I do know the names of the two witnesses at the wedding; one could be the bridesmaid and the other might be Father's best man, who happens to be an Anderson.'

Anne sat down at the table. 'What's his first name?'

'Kyle. Does the name mean anything to you?'

She shook her head and then remembered Uncle Donald's mention of a cousin Kyle. 'There was mention of a cousin Kyle when I was in Scotland. When was the wedding?'

'August 1899.'

'I could ask Albert whether he remembers ever meeting a Kyle Anderson when he was a boy.'

'Thanks, that could help.' Andrew's smile took Anne's breath away and the two of them gazed in happy adoration of each other for a moment.

'How did you get on in Ireland and on the Isle of Jura?' she managed to ask when she was able to speak again.

'I met my half-brother, Duncan, who's a nice bloke. He has a job in the whisky refinery there and is engaged to a lass called Morag. He has no plans to ever move away from the island.'

'I bet he was amazed to meet you.'

'Duncan knew about me and Ruth, as apparently Father wrote the occasional letter enclosing a postal order on his birthday. He gave me Grandfather's address in Belfast but added that he was over here at some medical conference and they gave me the name of the hotel where he was staying, so I've written to him.'

'That's helpful, and at least your father didn't altogether forget his firstborn.'

'Apparently not. He was an odd one – one week up and the next down. You never knew where you were with him.'

Anne remembered the man who had stood and watched her outside the house. 'He came and watched me cleaning the step once. Da saw him off.' She took a deep breath. 'So, you never went to Ireland?'

'No, besides which Duncan showed me a newspaper cutting from the times of the Irish Civil War in the early twenties. It mentions my grandfather – turns out he was a bit of a hero for tending to the injured in a gun battle on the border.'

'You must feel proud.'

'Yes, I do, but I was even more made-up to discover he was still alive. His name is Dr William Fraser and he was delighted to hear from me. He wrote to me, saying he'd wanted Father to follow in his footsteps, but Liam didn't fancy the years of studying to be a doctor, so just walked out one day without saying where he was going.' Andrew slammed slut the street directory he'd been perusing.

'What did he have to say when you told him you were a journalist working in London?'

'He wanted to read some of my work.' Andrew smiled. 'Father was never interested.'

'I presume you told him your father is dead?'

'Of course. He was sad and shocked, but he told me something interesting, though.'

She sat down at the table. 'What, there's more?'

He nodded. 'Being a doctor, he had wondered if Father had some brain disorder. Apparently, even as a boy he'd suffered from mood swings. Unfortunately, it's only since the Great War there have been investigations into mental health because of the effects of shell shock on so many soldiers. Grandfather had blamed a fall Father had when he was only ten years old. He was swinging on a rope attached to the branch of a tree which snapped, and he fell a fair height and hit a log on the ground.'

'Did he ever try and find your father after he left?'

'Yeah, but it was difficult because there was a lot of unrest in Ireland, even then, with the Nationalists wanting Home Rule and people coming and going, and guards being placed on the border between North and South.'

'So, will you be seeing your grandfather?'

'Oh yes, he's coming over to Liverpool and plans to visit Father's grave before visiting me in London, as well as going to Jura to see Duncan later in the year, as he's got to get back to his practice to relieve the locum.' Andrew stood. 'How about going for a cuppa and you can tell me how you got on with the Andersons in Cardross?'

'OK. We could go to Cottle's Cafe on Dale Street.' She glanced at the street directory and saw that it was for 1898. 'I've things to tell you that will surprise you.'

'Can't wait,' he said, his eyes scanning her features.

'I suppose the Kyle you mentioned might not have been the head of the house,' she said, 'and that's why you haven't found him in there. It's not the same as the census which names everyone living at the same address.'

'But like I said, I have Mam's father's name and so guessed an approximate birth date for him. I can check church records for baptisms to find my Liverpudlian great-grandparents, but it'll take time.'

'The difficulty with that is that so many people were coming to Liverpool in search of work. You would need to know where they came from,' Anne said. 'There were lots of very rich people then, as well as loads of poor and abandoned children living on the streets. Have you ever read *Her Benny*?'

'No, but I've heard of it.'

'It was written during Victoria's reign, so I assume it gives a true picture of the times. It's about a brother and sister who are orphans – it's a real tear-jerker.'

'Tough times,' Andrew said.

'Yeah. No indoor plumbing, disease was rife and there were no votes for women.'

'Or education for poor kids.'

'Some were educated by the church and at home,' said Anne. 'And there were the ragged schools where the boys could learn a trade.'

'You've been researching the period.'

Anne nodded. 'I've grown interested in local history – ever since Gordon asked me to help him with finding out more about our ancestry. I also saw an exhibition of photographs of old Liverpool in the library and that had me hooked.'

They packed up their books and papers, left the library and walked in the direction of Dale Street until they reached Cottle's Cafe. They went inside and found a vacant table and sat down. A waitress came over a few minutes after they had perused the menu.

'What are you having?' Andrew asked.

'A couple of ham sandwiches and a slice of chocolate cake, as well as a pot of tea,' Anne said. 'I'm starving.'

Andrew ordered the same but asked for mustard on his sandwiches.

With that settled, he said, 'So, how did you get on at the Andersons' farm?'

'I was going to send you a letter, but I wrote it and then decided not to post it. I might as well tell you what I wrote now.' She paused. 'Fiona, a niece of my da's, looks very much like me. I had my Uncle Donald take a photograph of us together. I also discovered that I have a look of Da's mother. How's that for a mystery?' she said.

'I find it incredible,' he said, his hazel eyes alight as he leaned towards her across the table. 'I would like to see the photograph you mentioned.'

'The film is in Boots being processed, so we can go and see if it's ready before I return to Eastham,' she said.

'It seems too good to be true. I think we need more proof than just a likeness and a feeling.'

'I agree,' Anne said, reaching across the table and covering his hand with hers. 'I have the name of the midwife. It's Cissie Jamieson. She registered the birth of Jane Fraser, maybe because your mother died, and your father was in a state, grieving and worrying how he was going to cope. What I'd like to find out is who else was in the community having a baby at that time as well as your mother.' She paused. 'I know you were only a kid at the time, but do you remember anything about when your mother went into labour? I know there was a fire.'

He took a deep breath and closed his eyes and did not speak for several minutes, then he opened his eyes and said, 'I was only three and have only vague memories, but from what I was told, a fire broke out next door that evening and our house caught fire as well. The midwife assisted Mam out of our house. Father got me and Ruth out. I thought we'd all go to the hospital, but the midwife said that she had another mother in labour nearby, so was taking Mam with her, so she could keep her eye on both mothers.'

He gulped. 'It was the last time I saw Mam. A neighbour took us kids in, while Father hurried to remove our belongings. Then the fire brigade must have arrived and stopped them, saying it was too dangerous while they battled the fire. I had no idea where the midwife took Mam; it was only later I overheard Father telling the neighbour that the other mother in labour had digs above a pub near Anfield football ground and I realised Mam must have gone there. Everything was upside down the following day because we couldn't return home. Our house was unsafe and Father had to find us somewhere else to live, so we moved in temporarily with a mate of his mother's, in a house in Gill Street, then a house came up for rent and we moved into there and Father married Marjorie's sister. Before then he told us that Mam had died and so had the baby and that we had to be brave – he'd find us a new mother. I was told I yelled that I wanted the one I'd had and got a clout for saying it.'

Anne stared across at his flushed, anguished face and wanted to get up and give him a hug. He stared back at her and whispered, 'Don't cry.' It was only then that she realised her face was wet with tears.

'I can't help but feel for that poor broken-hearted boy and his sister,' she said, taking out a hanky and wiping her face. 'Where do we go from here?' she asked.

'We have to trace the midwife,' he said. 'She's the only one who knows the truth.'

'We might find out where she lives at the Sandon Hotel.'

'At least we know there were two mothers, your mother and the woman at the pub, so there must have been two babies born,' said Anne. 'The question is, did both babies survive or just the one?'

'We'll do what you say and start at the Sandon,' Andrew said, his attractive face now alight with excitement.

Anne sighed. 'I went there once but didn't have the courage to go in on my own. I meant to go another time but there was so much going on it slipped my mind'

'Well, you'll have my company now,' Andrew said.

'As much as I'd love your company,' she said wistfully, 'won't you be having to get back to work?'

Some of the light died in his eyes. 'I don't want to leave you alone to find out the truth; so much is riding on it for our future. I want to be there with you. Instead of returning to London this evening, I'll go back tomorrow morning. I can do some work on the train.'

She agreed, praying that the truth would be in their favour. 'So, do we start right away?'

'Of course. We have this afternoon,' he said. 'Eat up and let's get cracking.'

She bit into a ham sandwich. 'Do you know who your family doctor was when you were born?'

He shrugged. 'God only knows.'

'There's a thought,' Anne said. 'Now, if your mother had been a Catholic, I bet the midwife would have called out the local priest to give her the last rites.'

'She wasn't a Catholic, though.'

'A vicar then? If the midwife was religious and a baby was in danger of dying, she might get in touch with a minister if it was what the mother wanted.'

'We don't want a dead baby,' he said. 'Let's stick with visiting the Sandon Hotel which is still in business.'

'I wish you could stay for the whole week.'

'So do I – but I can't push my luck. I like my job and don't want to lose it.'

'Of course.' She gulped a mouthful of tea and then reached for her chocolate cake.

As soon as they had finished and paid the bill, Andrew helped her to her feet and gave her a hug.

'What was that for?' she asked.

'To thank you for giving us a glimmer of hope for a future together.'

Her cheeks turned a delicate pink and she licked the cake crumbs from round her mouth with the tip of her tongue. 'It's my pleasure. I know I'm only young, but I would like to spend the rest of my life with you.'

'Then that's our goal,' he said, and took hold of her hand. 'Let's go to the Sandon.'

Anne said, 'Before doing that, let's go to Boots and see if my photos are ready.'

Both were pleased when the shop assistant handed over a packet of photographs to Anne. They waited until they were sitting on the tram before looking at them. Andrew stared for what seemed like an age at the one of Anne and Fiona together before saying, 'It's incredible how alike you are.'

She agreed, adding, 'So, you agree with me even more so that there's a real hope that we can have a future together?'

He squeezed her hand and nodded. 'But let's hope we can find out more about your birth and that of my baby sister at the Sandon. It's a long shot but there just might be someone still around who can help us.'

Chapter Seventeen

Anne and Andrew stood outside Mitchell's Bakery across the road from the Sandon Hotel, staring at the partially white-tiled building. Andrew took her hand and they ran across the road. Fortunately, the pub was open, so they went inside, where the smell of beer and stale tobacco smoke caught in the back of their throats.

After scanning the large bar area, Andrew went over to the bar. 'We're trying to find some information regarding a baby, or maybe two, who might have been born here in 1913, the night of a big fire somewhere nearby.' The woman behind the bar appeared taken aback by the question.

'Bit before my time, chuck, and the previous landlady's dead. Ol' Stan might be able to help you, though. This has been his local for years and he was friendly with the landlady. You could give him a visit – he doesn't live far away.' She gave them directions and an address. They thanked her and left, crossing the road and heading up one of the streets on the other side of the road.

The house was a yellow-brick, two-up two-down terraced house on Viceroy Street. Andrew banged the knocker and somewhere nearby a dog barked, but it was a while before they heard footsteps approaching.

'Who's there? Friend or foe?'

'Friend!' answered Anne.

The door opened, and a craggy face appeared, topped by a mop of curling reddish-brown hair streaked with grey. 'I've no idea who you are,' he said, smiling. 'But the two of you look friendly enough. Otherwise I'd have turned the hosepipe on yer.' He opened the door wider and stood aside. 'Come through into the backyard,' he said. 'I'm just feeding me pigeons.'

Glancing at each other at this rather eccentric greeting, they stepped over the threshold and followed him across a small darkish room, then through a kitchen which had stairs going up to the left and a coal fire in the fireplace to the right. Straight ahead was a door that opened out onto a sunny backyard.

'So, what can I do for you?' he asked as he readied some bird feed in trays for the pigeons, who cooed and fluttered in many coups.

'We were told that you've been a regular at the Sandon Hotel for years and knew the former landlady,' said Anne.

'What of it?' he said, hand-feeding a pigeon some corn.

'We're trying to find the whereabouts of a baby that was born there in February 1913. In fact, we think there were two babies born the same night,' said Anne. 'We need to find the midwife.'

Stan looked thoughtful for a moment and then said, 'There was a Scots lass who was a barmaid at the Sandon Hotel.' Anne and Andrew exchanged glances. 'She got into trouble and gave birth there. Lived in one of the rooms upstairs. As for the midwife, Cissie, she's retired now, but still lives in the same house as she did then, and her daughter Jessie moved into a house on the same street as her mother after she married. It's Vienna Street.'

'You wouldn't have the house number?' Anne asked.

'As it happens, I do,' said Stan. 'Cissie gave me her daughter's address as well in case Cissie was at her house when I dropped by to see how she was getting on.' He scratched his head.

They thanked him, and Andrew gave him a thruppenny bit. 'Have a drink on me,' he said.

Stanley said, 'Ta, lad! Good luck.'

He saw them out and stood on the doorstep, clutching a pigeon and waving with his free hand.

'What a nice man,' said Anne.

'Yes, it was a bit of luck being given his name and address,' he said. 'I have to leave tomorrow. I can't put it off any longer, much as I'd like to stay with you.'

Anne forced a smile. 'It won't be as much fun without you,' she said. 'I'm going to miss you.'

'I'll miss you too,' he said, pulling her in and holding her tight against him. 'Anyway, on with the search. We must speak to Cissie Jamieson as soon as possible.'

Following Stanley's directions, they soon found the two-up, two-down house on Vienna Street and knocked on the door. There was no answer despite them knocking several times, so they went to the number of the daughter's house. Anne crossed her fingers and raised the knocker. Inside they heard the crying of a baby. Almost immediately the door opened, and a pretty young woman stood there with a toddler hanging onto her skirt and a baby in her arms. She stared at them. 'If you're selling anything, I can't afford it.'

'No, we're not tradespeople, and we're sorry to bother you, but we're looking for a midwife called Cissie Jamieson. A bloke called Stan, who lives on Viceroy

Street, suggested you might be able to help us if we got no answer at your mother's house.'

The woman's expression softened. 'Ah, how is Stan? We haven't seen him for a few weeks.'

'He seemed fine,' Andrew said. 'He was feeding his pigeons.'

'He loves those birds. Come on in,' said the woman. 'You'll have to excuse the mess but it's the kids. I can't be forever tidying up after them.'

They followed her through into the kitchen at the back, carefully avoiding a large empty cardboard box and a saucepan and wooden spoon, items which it looked like the children had been playing with. She waved them to a sofa. 'I'm Jessie, by the way. Mam's actually retired but she still gets called upon. Right now she's been called out to a birth on the next street, Number Thirty Venmore Street, as the doctor and the local registered midwife are out on another case.'

'I'm Anne and this is Andrew,' said Anne. 'We want to speak to your mother because I think she might have delivered me and possibly another baby girl in the Sandon Hotel in February 1913.'

Jessie frowned. 'My mam could be the person you're looking for, but I can't swear to it.'

Anne said reassuringly, 'We're just hoping she can help us find out what happened that night. I was adopted and we think there might have been a mix-up with another baby.'

Jessie frowned. She placed her baby on a rag rug and took a pencil and used envelope from the mantelpiece, dashing off an address before handing the envelope to Anne. 'I'm sure Mam'll help you if she can. She's got a marvellous memory for her age and she's still in touch with some of the mothers and babies that were in her care.'

They thanked her and left the house.

Andrew's expression was thoughtful. 'I really hope Cissie's willing to help us out.'

She squeezed his hand. 'I've a good feeling about her. I'm sure we're on the right track. I still can't get over the fact that my mother might have been Scottish and a barmaid.'

'Don't get ahead of yourself,' Andrew cautioned. 'We don't know anything for sure yet.'

'I know, but I can't help it. My mind is doing somersaults.'

'I understand. Are you thinking your mother might not be respectable if she worked behind a bar? Because lots of good people work in pubs,' Andrew said.

'My family wouldn't have approved of her,' Anne replied, 'but it wouldn't bother me. She must have been in desperate need of a job and lodgings so was prepared to take on the position. I suppose if the proprietor of the Sandon had been a man, she might have thought twice about taking on the job.'

Andrew nodded. 'Most likely if she is your mother then your father might have been a customer and got to know her better and took her out.'

'You could be right,' Anne said, and fell silent.

Andrew was quiet as well, paying attention to the number of houses as they walked up Venmore Street. As they passed number twenty-eight, suddenly they heard a scream followed by another, then another. Anne clutched

Andrew's arm. 'That's definitely the sound of a woman in trouble.'

'I think it came from inside number thirty,' said Andrew. 'Let's be quiet and listen.'

They froze and then another scream came, along with a gentle and confident voice saying, 'It won't be long now.'

'I bet that's Cissie,' said Anne, stopping outside the front door.

Andrew did not speak but noticed the door was slightly ajar. He knocked before pushing it wider and went inside. Anne followed him. Both paused as a woman who looked to be in her thirties came into the front room from the kitchen and stared at them. 'Who are you?' she asked.

Anne said, 'I'm Anne Anderson and this is Andrew Fraser. We need to talk to Cissie, but we are aware she has her hands full, so we'd like to wait here if you don't mind? And is there anything I can do to help?'

'You could make a pot of tea. It's my sister-in-law Rene up there in labour and I don't think she'll be much longer now, so she'll be ready for a cup of tea and so will Cissie. I'm Grace, by the way.'

A few minutes later they heard a baby cry and then shortly after that a voice called, 'Is that you, Doctor?'

'No, it's a young couple wanting to talk to you, Cissie,' answered Grace, hurrying up the stairs in the corner of the kitchen with a jug of hot water.

An elderly woman descended the stairs more slowly ten minutes later. 'What do you want?' she asked.

Anne did not reply immediately because she was pouring tea into five cups. She waited until she'd handed Cissie a cup of tea before hurrying upstairs with two cups of tea, leaving it to Andrew to begin to explain while she pushed open the bedroom door with her elbow and took in the tea. She admired the baby and offered her congratulations and then left the bedroom and went downstairs.

Andrew was sitting on the sofa and Cissie had settled herself in an easy chair with her cup of tea. Anne made herself comfortable on the sofa next to Andrew and faced the midwife.

Before Anne could speak, Andrew said, 'This is Anne Anderson, although she is believed to have been Jane Fraser when she was adopted by the Anderson family. We think she could possibly be the daughter of a Scottish woman who was working at the Sandon Hotel and who gave birth out of wedlock. If we're not mistaken, you're the midwife who delivered her there in February 1913.'

Anne could have sworn that the midwife appeared dismayed, even scared, when he paused. 'I am Andrew Fraser, older brother to the Fraser baby, daughter of Liam and Helen Fraser, who was in labour when a neighbouring house caught fire. It was the same night as Anne here was born. I had been told my sister had died with my mother.'

'We're hoping you can help us solve a mystery,' Anne said. 'I was handed over to a Hugh Anderson, whose young daughter Flora had died tragically when she was six or seven. I was brought up as a member of his family. The family believed I was the natural daughter of Liam and his second wife, but I didn't know this.' Anne paused and took a trembling breath. 'Andrew and I met a couple of years ago and grew to like each other a lot. I had been told my father was dead and that my mother had died in childbirth, so when I was told that I was Jane Fraser, it naturally came as a terrible shock to us both to be told we were brother and sister…' Anne's voice trailed off and tears rolled down her cheeks as she remembered that moment.

The midwife clicked her tongue against her teeth and shook her head.

'Andrew and I realised that if it were true that I was his sister, we had to accept that there couldn't ever be anything of a serious nature between us,' Anne continued. 'He went off to London and I remained in the Anderson home. A year or so has passed, so I decided to visit Scotland where both of our fathers had come from and, to cut a long story short, I discovered that I was the spitting image of Hugh Anderson's niece Fiona, as well as bearing a strong resemblance to a photograph of Hugh's mother. You will understand why I am so confused.'

'That's not surprising,' said Cissie. 'I suppose you want to ask me was there any chance of you and the Fraser girl having been mixed up and if so what happened to her?'

Anne nodded and glanced at Andrew. 'Our future happiness depends on it. Both sets of parents are dead now, so you don't have to worry about what they might say or do.'

Cissie took a deep breath and toyed with a button on her blouse. 'Blood will out,' she muttered under her breath. 'Your mother was a Miss Anne Graham, and she and the second Mrs Fraser both died giving birth within hours of each other. Jane was born first.' She hesitated. 'That both of the mothers died was tragic – Jane was a breech birth, which was difficult, and the woman helping me with Anne Graham hadn't washed her hands. I was furious about that lack of hygiene, but I couldn't cope alone. There is something you can't have guessed and that is that… there was another mother and child in this story.'

Anne and Andrew looked at each other in surprise.

'Please continue,' Andrew said. 'We're desperate to understand what happened.'

The midwife took another deep breath. 'A few hours before Jane was born, another woman called Lil had given birth to a daughter who was sadly stillborn. This woman had lost the sailor she loved at sea, and he was the father of her child, though they weren't married. She was heartbroken to lose her baby, but a woman's body is no respecter of broken hearts and as her milk had come in, I asked her to breastfeed your sister, Jane, Andrew, thinking it would not only benefit Jane but also comfort Lil, and in that short time Lil became very fond of her. Then you were born, Anne, and as your mother had died too, I gave you to Lil for her to feed as well, so she was wet nurse to both.'

Andrew made to speak, but Cissie held up her hand and said, 'Let me finish. The next day Mr Fraser came and told me that a couple he knew called the Andersons were going to have his baby daughter, Jane, as they had lost a daughter a few months earlier and the mother was in a terrible state, half out of her mind with grief. The father would be calling the following day to collect the baby.'

'My father, Hugh,' said Anne.

'That's right, but in the meantime, I explained the situation to Lil, the wet nurse, who wept and wailed at the loss of the babies until I could stand it no longer. Here was a heartbroken mother and a child that needed a mother's love… I told Lil that I would give you to Hugh Anderson as your mother was unmarried and, as far as I knew, your father didn't know anything about you.'

Anne could keep silent no longer. 'I'm hoping you're going to tell me that Lil kept Jane because she couldn't bear to be parted from her.'

Cissie nodded. 'As it was, what with Hugh Anderson never having set eyes on either baby, I didn't think it mattered which baby he took.'

Anne was so overcome with emotion that she burst into tears and it was some time before she could speak. 'So, Andrew's sister Jane went to live with Lil, and I went to the Andersons. Where are Lil and Jane now?'

'I could lie and say I have no idea because the Great War caused so much movement and disruption – but the truth of the matter is that Lil still keeps in touch with me every Christmas.'

Andrew reached out and grasped Annie's hand. 'Please tell us where they are.'

Cissie sighed heavily. 'You'll have to be patient. I must speak to Lil first. All these years they've been mother and daughter to each other. It will come as a tremendous shock to hear from you.'

'You mean Jane has no idea about what happened?' Andrew said.

'Lil told her the truth when she was old enough to understand, and both made a pact that only if her natural family came looking for her would Jane make contact with them. She and Lil are devoted to each other and both want to do what's best for the other.'

Anne felt all atremble. 'There are a c-couple of other questions I'd l-like to ask you,' she stammered.

'I suppose you want to know your father's name?'

'I'd like to know it, but I suspect my mother kept quiet about it.'

Cissie nodded. 'She did tell me that the father was a married man, and she hadn't told him about the baby – she didn't want him to know as she felt guilty about his wife and children.' Cissie paused, appearing to force down a lump in her throat. 'I thought the father had a right to know so he could take responsibility for his daughter.'

Tears glistened in Anne's eyes and her voice quivered as she said, 'But instead I was taken in by the Andersons by mistake.' She paused. 'Had my mother chosen a name for me?'

'Yes, you were Anne, after her,' said Cissie. 'She would have been made up to see the bonny lass you've grown into. You do have a look of her.'

'I suppose I'll never get to know who my natural father was now,' said Anne.

'But at least you and this young man can think about having a future together,' Cissie said brightly.

A smile lightened Anne's fine features and she said, 'I'll never be able to thank you enough. I suppose we'd better be on our way as we've taken up enough of your time.'

'I'm glad I was able to help you, and I'll drop Lil a line and let her know about your visit. If you give me your address, I'll pass it on to her if you like.'

Andrew handed her his card and Anne wrote her address on a scrap of paper and gave it to the midwife. Then they left, smiling with delight and their minds full of what they had been told.

Chapter Eighteen

Once outside Andrew swept Anne off her feet and kissed her passionately. 'I've been longing to do that for the past two years,' he said, lifting his head so they could draw breath.

'And I've wanted you to do it.' She laughed.

'Where next?' he asked. 'Mere Lane to speak to Gordon?'

She nodded, longing for him to kiss her again. 'Do we tell him and Teddy what we've discovered or wait until we meet your sister, Jane?'

'We'll tell them. There's no need to keep it secret now, is there? After all, they are already aware there's a possibility that you might be related to them in some way.'

Happily, Gordon was at the house, having dropped in on his way to deliver some fruit that he had picked up from the docks to a nearby wholesaler, and he and Teddy were in deep conversation. Apparently, Teddy had not gone into work that morning as his chest was bad and Gordon was going to put in extra hours doing his deliveries. Amy was playing with a doll, but immediately held up her arms to Anne when she entered the kitchen. Joan had just made a pot of tea, so fetched a couple more cups and filled them up for Anne and Andrew.

'To what do we owe the pleasure of this visit?' she asked. 'And where's he come from?' She pointed to Andrew.

'We've something to tell you,' Anne said, her excitement bubbling over. 'And to show you.' She dropped the packet of photos on the table. 'I also want to ask Gordon did he know that Da's mother's maiden name was Graham?'

Joan picked up the packet and took out the photos and began to look through them, only half-listening to the conversation.

Gordon said, 'I did, yes. Our grandmother's name was Katherine Graham. I found out some of this from Da. Surely you could have found that out yourself when you were up in Scotland?'

Anne's face was flushed with relief. 'I did but I wanted to check; as it was I had too much going on in my head. I thought that was the name that Uncle Donald had told me. Where there any more Grahams?'

'Grandma had a cousin who had twin daughters, but I don't know their names,' said Gordon. 'Albert might know.'

'But will he want to help me?'

'I could ask him for you,' Teddy said, looking slightly discomforted. 'Joan and I are to visit the hotel for a week. The fresh sea air will be good for me.'

'That's a turn up for the books,' Anne said. 'I thought you two were at daggers drawn still.'

'I think Mother's death has mellowed him,' Teddy said. 'And I think he's concerned I'll be next because of my chest.'

'What about Amy?' Anne asked, nursing the little girl. 'Are you taking her with you?'

Joan said hesitantly, 'I was going to ask you if you'd mind staying here for a week and looking after her? Gladys thinks it would give me a break that way. What do you say?'

'I could take her to Eastham. I'm sure Emily and Larry wouldn't mind.'

'All her things are here, though,' Joan said. 'Her cot and the like.'

Anne could understand her reasoning and said, 'It depends on what Larry says. I do work for him and I've already had quite a bit of time off.'

'We've thought of that. Surely our Emily could put a few hours in at the shop and I could give you a few bob to help towards your loss of wages?' Teddy said. 'I've still some money left that Mother gave me. So, what is it you were going to tell us?'

Joan interrupted by handing the photos to him. Gordon came and looked over his shoulder at them.

Anne wasted no time in telling them what she and Andrew had discovered that day. They were incredulous. Teddy said, 'Do you think Da had some idea of your real identity?'

'If he did, I can't see why he should pretend I was Andrew's sister. Anyway, sooner or later, I think we'll discover the whole truth. I'll put your suggestion to Emily and get back to you,' Anne said, adding, 'So, what do you think of the photo of me and Fiona?'

'I'm convinced you're related to us,' Gordon said.

Teddy agreed.

Shortly after that, she and Andrew left. Gordon went with them, saying he felt like a walk and would pop in and let Marjorie know what was happening, so Anne and Andrew headed for the stop to catch a tram to take them to Pier Head.

Once they boarded the D-tram, they went along Dale Street and passed the historic town hall with its balcony. Anne pointed to it. 'I'd enjoy standing on there and taking the salute when the soldiers from the King's Liverpool regiment march past when they return from duty abroad.'

'A proud moment for them and for Liverpool,' Andrew said. 'Although I'm glad I was too young to go and do my duty as some men did. I admire their courage but I think most didn't know what they were letting themselves in for – I'd be no good at taking orders and I'm not much of a fighter.'

Anne shivered. 'War's an abomination.'

He nodded. 'Shall we change the subject?'

Shortly after they arrived at the Pier Head and left the tram. For a few seconds, they stood looking up at the Liver Building towering against a clouded sky. 'Do you miss it when you are in London?' she asked.

'I sometimes find myself longing for the familiar sights and sounds of my childhood,' he said. 'But ship foghorns sound the same on the Thames as they do on the Mersey and there's Big Ben and the Houses of Parliament instead of the Liver Building, although its history is darker. I do miss the sound of the crowd roaring at Anfield and Goodison Park when a goal is scored for the home team. I'm still loyal to the Blues – and support the Reds against other teams.'

'What about food? Do you make yourself scouse or are you into jellied eels, which I believe the Cockneys like?'

'I still enjoy scouse with pickled beetroot or HP Sauce, especially on a cold, wet evening,' Andrew replied, adding, 'Let's go, we don't want to miss the ferry.'

She nodded in agreement and he seized her hand as they hurried towards the passenger entrance that led down to the boarding jetty. When they arrived, they saw that a queue had already formed and that a boat was already headed towards it. Andrew kept a tight grip on her hand as the gangway was lowered, and passengers left the ship. The people in the queue began to surge aboard the boat and Andrew and Anne clattered up the gangway, then up a stairway onto the top deck where they leaned against the side of the boat. They gazed down at the activity below, watching for the moment when the thick ropes were untied and the boat moved away from the landing stage.

Anne felt the deck tremble beneath her feet as the engines gained power, water foaming as the boat turned to make the journey across the Mersey to Birkenhead.

Around halfway into the crossing, they took a turn around the deck and Anne was aware of the sea breeze coming up from the estuary, toying with her hair, so that a strand whipped across her lips. Andrew reached over and moved it, tucking it behind her right ear before bending his head and planting a kiss on her mouth. His lips felt cool, she thought, as she returned his kiss; a kiss that was cut short by an ear-splitting scream.

They drew apart, glancing about for the source of the sound and caught the frantic, searching face of a girl who looked to be about twelve or thirteen years old, holding the hand of a boy little older than a toddler; his hair was jet black, he had almond-shaped eyes and tears were streaming down his face, washing away some of the dirt on it.

'What's wrong, sonny?' asked Anne.

'It's Mam,' the girl answered. 'She's gone over the side.'

Shocked by her words, the muscles in Anne's stomach clenched as Andrew drew her to the side of the boat. Their eyes searched anxiously in the water below and they saw, a few yards away from the vessel, a head bobbing up and the pale face of a woman staring up at the sky. She opened her mouth, but the wind whipped her words away as water splashed over her face.

The girl, who had hoisted herself up beside Anne, was clinging to the rail, sobbing, 'Please save her.'

Anne turned to Andrew, but there was no need for her to speak as he had already removed his jacket and was kicking off his shoes. She watched, speechlessly, as he climbed onto the rail. She looked about her for a lifebelt, spotted an orange and white one and removed it, aware of the rope attached to it, and threw it after Andrew as he dropped into the sea. She desperately prayed that both Andrew and the children's mother would survive as she went in search of a member of the crew with the two children clinging to her.

Within a few moments, they encountered one of the small group of crewmen emerging from a door accompanied by the oily stench of diesel. Guessing that he could be one of the ship's engineers, Anne grabbed him by the arm. 'Please, you've got to help us – the children's mother has fallen into the sea and my boyfriend has dived into the water to try and rescue her.'

The crewman immediately headed over to the rail and looked over the side. 'How long ago was this?' he asked.

'Just a few minutes, I'd say,' Anne said.

The man wiped a greasy hand over his jaw. 'Right, I need to tell the chief to set the engine in reverse and he'll also let the captain know what's happening.' He gazed at Anne. 'You need to find one of the deckhands. There's bound to be one or the other around.' He vanished into the bowels of the boat again.

Before doing as she was instructed, Anne went back to check on Andrew and the girl's mother. Fortunately, on the way, she saw a deckhand and other passengers gathered around with their heads bent over the side to see what was happening. Even as she explained to him what had taken place, she was aware of a change in the note of the engines and the sound of a bell tolling, while the passengers were looking alarmed as the noise level had risen. The deckhand appeared to have raised the alarm, so she hurried along the sides of the ship, hoisting herself up every now and again to search the surface of the Mersey. The children also wanted to try and see their mother, but Anne was getting far too tired to lift them up and down. She wished she knew more about the times of the tides and of the currents in the Mersey, worrying about Andrew being swept out to sea. Suddenly she spotted a flash of bright orange from Andrew's lifebelt as the boat changed direction and appeared to be approaching the pair in the water.

Anne could now make out that Andrew had managed to get the lifebelt over the woman's head and arms. He was holding onto a part of the lifebelt while swimming at the same time. She thought how brave and strong he was and felt so proud of him but also wished he was back by her side and not still in the dark and murky Mersey water.

Happily, within a short space of time Andrew and the children's mother were both brought aboard and the ferry quickly resumed its journey to Birkenhead. The children were reunited with their mother; not that she seemed at all interested in them but looked dazed and was shivering violently as a sailor wrapped a blanket around her. Andrew had already accepted one and wrapped it about himself.

It was only when Anne and Andrew were brought inside by one of the deckhands and they had a few moments alone in a corner of the saloon away from the other passengers and crew, that he explained to her that the woman had not wanted to be rescued. 'Between you and me, I think she's drugged up to the eyeballs. Opium probably,' Andrew said. 'The captain will need to notify the police and hopefully a doctor and an ambulance will be waiting when we disembark at Birkenhead.'

'The police must get in touch with the children's father,' said Anne, nibbling on her lower lip.

'Have they mentioned their father to you?' Andrew asked. 'The girl and the boy don't look like they have the same father and the little fellow looks like he may have Chinese blood.'

'No, they haven't said anything. Honestly, I think they are a bit traumatised.'

'This would make a great story for the paper. I wish I had my notebook and pencil handy.'

'You're always on duty. I have both in my handbag,' Anne said.

'Well, dig them out. I need to make some notes. Find out the kids' names for me as well.' He paused. 'The police are bound to want to talk to us,' Andrew added. 'And they'll ask the mother where they can get in touch with her husband.'

She nodded. 'You weren't half brave jumping into the water the way you did,' she said, admiration shining in her eyes.

'I was just trying to impress you,' he said, flushing.

'You're joking – there was no need for you to go to such lengths. You know already how I feel about you. I could kiss you again for being so brave.'

He smiled down at her. 'Don't let me stop you.'

She kissed him fervently.

He caught hold of her hand and toyed with her fingers. 'I really am glad you aren't my sister.'

'Me too,' she said.

'Hopefully, this Lil will agree to us meeting my sister, Jane.' His voice was filled with emotion.

She nodded. 'In the meantime, you need some dry clothes.'

'I'm sure the captain or the police can find me something dry to wear,' he said.

'The captain should have ordered someone to find you a change of clothes before now,' she said crossly.

'Naturally his first concern would be for the mother and her children, then his passengers and the ferry's timetable,' Andrew said.

'You're far too understanding,' she responded. 'I hope you don't catch your death of cold.'

'My teeth stopped chattering ages ago.' He squeezed her hand. 'But I like your concern for me.'

At that moment, the deckhand approached. 'Mr Fraser,' he said. 'The captain's compliments, sir. We've some clothes for you to change into – if you'll follow me to the captain's quarters, you'll be able to change there.'

Andrew grinned at Anne. 'Will you wait for me here?'

'Your young lady can come with you,' said the seaman. 'I'm presuming she's the lass who took care of the kiddies while their mother was in the water?'

'Yeah, that was me,' Anne said.

'The captain would like you to be present when the police come aboard and speak to them.'

'I wasn't present when the mother went overboard,' Anne said, slightly nervous about speaking to the police.

'The captain knows that – but the kiddies told you what happened.'

Anne nodded.

'There you are then,' said the seaman.

Anne said no more and followed him and Andrew out of the saloon and to the captain's quarters.

It was not long before the ferry moored up, and two policemen and a doctor boarded the boat immediately on arrival at the ferry port and were shown into the cabin where they were all waiting. It was soon proved that Anne's apprehension was unfounded because the officers of the law were polite and gentle with the children, as well as with Anne and Andrew. She hoped they would be the same with the children's mother. The woman was not very communicative but between her and her daughter they found out that the woman was an Irishwoman called Bridget, who was married but her husband was missing in Ireland, and that the children did not, indeed, share the same father. Mother and children shared two rooms in a house on Pitt Street with the boy's father and his Chinese grandmother. After the interview was over, Anne asked if they would kindly keep her informed about what happened to the children, who had told her their names were Mildred and Charlie, and their mother too. She and Andrew left the ship once he had changed into clean dry clothes and his own clothes had been wrapped up in layers of newspaper and tied up with string.

They made for the train station in Hamilton Square and took the Chester train which called at Eastham Rake. Both released sighs of relief once they were settled on a seat and the train was on its way.

'What a day it's been,' Anne said.

Andrew agreed, squeezing her hand as he added, 'It's had its good points.'

She nodded. 'Correct me if I'm wrong, though – isn't Pitt Street part of Chinatown?'

'Yeah, it is – and as I said earlier the boy is definitely part-Chinese. It could be that the mother has been smoking opium. It wouldn't surprise me if she was on the game – nor would it surprise me if the police raid the house and the children are put in an orphanage.'

Anne wondered what he meant by 'on the game' but did not ask and instead said, 'It's so sad for them. The girl wanted her mother saved, so she must be fond of her.'

'Most likely because she's the only mother she's ever known.'

'It makes you think, doesn't it?' Anne said.

'What does it make you think?' Andrew asked.

'I'm illegitimate just like those children,' Anne said darkly.

'You're not to blame; neither are the children.'

Anne did not deny it and she felt less depressed, thinking that she was more fortunate than the two children, whose mother had thrown herself into the drink whereas she had been adopted into a family who had cared for her. Still, her curiosity about her natural parents continued to burn.

Andrew's voice interrupted her thoughts. 'We know your father was married to someone else, but he and your mother must have fallen in love and could not fight their feelings.'

'There are so many "could haves" or "maybes".' Anne sighed.

'How about placing an advertisement in the *Echo* asking if anyone has knowledge of an Anne Graham? After all, it is read further afield than just Liverpool; there's the Wirral, Bootle, Crosby, Southport and North Wales.'

'It's a thought,' said Anne. 'Although I've asked Teddy to ask Albert if he remembers anything about an Anne Graham.'

'I've still got my contacts at the *Echo*,' Andrew said. 'Leave it with me and I'll have a word with the editor.'

Anne said, 'I'd rather you didn't. I doubt we'll hear anything after all this time. After all, she's dead now and it happened before the war.' She glanced out of the window. 'It won't be long before we reach Eastham now.'

'Good. I'm desperate for a drink – I swallowed a fair amount of oily water.'

'Do you believe she really wanted to commit suicide?'

'If she didn't, she was a bloody good actress,' he said grimly.

'She must have felt so desperate.'

'There's a lot of desperate people around since the war and the country is full of hungry and destitute people. But she should have given more thought to her kids before attempting to throw her life away,' said Andrew. 'Anyway, she'll get some help now and hopefully things will work out for her and the kids.'

'I hope so.' Anne sighed. 'I wonder if she has any family in Ireland?'

'I spoke to the policeman and he's going to let me know how matters go on,' he said.

Soon they left the bus and made their way to Larry and Emily's home. The couple could not conceal their surprise at the sight of Andrew.

'How come you're here?' asked Emily. 'I thought you were on your way back to London?'

'I thought I'd look in on Marjorie and Robbie on the way back from Scotland,' Andrew said. 'Anne and I met by accident in Central Library and so I decided I'd join her in her search for the midwife mentioned on the birth certificate.'

'Did you have any luck?' Larry asked.

Anne and Andrew sat down on the sofa and told them everything that had happened that day. Larry and Emily could hardly believe this new turn of events.

Chapter Nineteen

'So, you're a bit of a hero,' said Larry, studying Andrew intently.

He shrugged. 'I didn't feel like a hero.'

Emily changed the subject. 'It's a bit of a shock about this Anne Graham being your mother.'

'I wonder if Da saw much of her in Scotland,' Anne said. 'His mother and the twins' mother were cousins. They might have kept in touch and the Anne twin was given Hugh's address and looked him up.'

'Unmarried and pregnant, she might have been too ashamed to go back to her parents in Scotland,' said Emily.

'It's one of those weird coincidences,' Andrew said. 'I know from my job they do happen.'

'So, what next?' asked Emily. 'I presume you'll be returning to London, Andrew?'

'The day after tomorrow. I'm working on a story up here, so once I've finished with that, I'll have to go back. Hopefully, they'll like my story and print it and then I can sell it to the *Echo* as well. I'm already late, but at least I have a story in the bag, so have a good excuse.'

'Does that mean you want some more time off, Anne?' asked Larry.

She nodded. 'If you can spare me to look after Amy in Liverpool?'

'It would have been better if the child could have stayed here instead.' Emily frowned.

'But understandable that it's easier when everything she needs is in her own home,' said Larry, adding, 'We'll manage, Anne. Though I'm starting to wonder if you secretly aren't too fond of the greengrocer's life?'

'Don't be silly, it's fine,' she said, getting up and giving him a kiss on the cheek. 'You are a love.'

'These children whose mother you rescued,' Emily said. 'How can they be put in an orphanage if their mother and their father are still alive?'

'I should imagine the mother will be declared unfit,' Andrew said. 'But the boy could be placed with his father and grandmother.'

'There is a big age difference between the children,' Anne said. 'As for Mildred's father, he's missing somewhere in Ireland. Maybe that's the reason why her mother ended up the way she did.'

'She's been bringing up her daughter on her own until she met the boy's father and got hooked on opium,' said Andrew.

'And how would you know about such things?' said Emily sharply.

'I'm a newspaper reporter and I ask questions; besides we come across such things in our line of work,' he replied.

Larry said, 'Some women do have it tough and it's worse since the war.' He paused. 'Thinking about the name Graham – it's quite a common name in Scotland.'

'Besides which,' said Emily, 'if the twins' mother married, surely she'd have taken her husband's name?'

'Unless his surname was Graham too,' said Andrew.

Anne took the folder of photos out of her bag and handed them to Emily. 'Perhaps these might help you to decide.'

Larry placed his arm about Emily's waist, and they gazed at the photos together. When they had finished, they stared at Anne, having separated the photo of Anne and Fiona together from the others. They held it up.

Anne said, 'Me and Fiona.'

'I'm convinced,' said Larry.

'And me,' said Emily.

'Good,' Anne said.

'Anyway, I'm going to have to be going,' Andrew said. 'I've a lot to do.'

'I'll see you out,' Anne said.

Outside on the porch, she asked him, 'Will there be time for us to see each other tomorrow?'

'I'd like to see you, but I doubt I'll be able to as I need to finish my piece. I'll have to call in at the police station as well as the *Echo* offices. I need to know if any decision has been made about the kids and their mother's future before I can finish my story.'

Anne sighed. 'I'll be here all day, anyway, making up for taking more time off.'

'I'll tell Marjorie that Larry has agreed to you staying at Teddy and Joan's. She'll pass it on to Gordon who'll let them know,' Andrew said.

They kissed and parted and when she went back indoors, it was immediately obvious to Anne that Emily was worked up about her relationship with Andrew. 'Well, I never in all my born days heard such shenanigans. If you had any sense, Anne, you'd have nothing more to do with Andrew Fraser and consider a local boy as a future husband. You'd have a nice place to live in Cheshire and I'd be able to see you often. If you choose Andrew Fraser you'll be off to London and most likely we'll hardly ever see you.'

'I love Andrew – I've loved him since we met. We could marry straightaway, but I'm prepared to wait until Easter next year, even though, according to a new law that's recently been hitting the headlines, I could marry this year without permission from a guardian or parent at sixteen. As it is, Andrew most likely wants to meet his sister before getting married and I'd like to find out who my father is if possible.'

Emily sniffed. 'You want the moon and that's impossible. You might as well give up now.'

'I'm not a quitter, as you know,' Anne said, tilting her chin. 'Even if it means another journey to Scotland, I'll get to the truth. Fiona just might visit Liverpool soon and I'm sure she'll help me once I explain the situation. Anyway, I'm going to bed. I have to be up early in the morning and I need my sleep.'

Unfortunately, Anne had that much on her mind she lay awake for ages not only thinking over her day but also of her time in Scotland. As she drifted fitfully into sleep, Anne wished she could remember being held by her natural mother. She could still recall the feel of Hugh Anderson's sandpapery chin rubbing her petal-soft cheek; he used to call her a sweetheart. With that comforting thought of her adoptive father, she finally slept.

–

The following morning Anne wasted no time getting out her writing paper, pen and ink and writing a letter to Fiona.

Dear Fiona, she wrote and then sat for a while nibbling the end of her pen, thinking how to put into words that which she should have said when she was staying with them.

> *I must thank you again for making me so welcome. I really felt at home and wished I had made the journey years ago when Hugh was alive. There is something I need to tell you now, which I had great difficulty divulging while I was a guest in your home.*
>
> *I am not the person you thought I was. I don't know the full truth of who I am – Hugh Anderson and Sylvia adopted me when I was a baby to replace their youngest daughter, Flora, who had died in a tragic accident. It was not until I was fifteen years old that I was told that I was the daughter of a Scotsman from Greenock, Liam Fraser, whose first wife Mary had died after giving birth in Scotland to a boy, Duncan, who lives with his maternal grandmother on the Isle of Jura. To his Liverpudlian second wife, Helen, Liam had a son, Andrew, and a daughter, Ruth, and presumably could not cope with a baby after his wife died in childbirth having their third child. Anyway, he married for the third time to provide his two young children with a mother. I suppose he also wanted a housekeeper.*
>
> *I have recently learned that was not the true story of my origins. My mother was really a*

Scotswoman called Anne Graham who has some connection to Hugh's family in Scotland and is likely a second cousin. Could you speak to Uncle Donald and ask him if he knows anything about her? I believe her to have a twin sister, Mary. Also, I seem to remember a mention of a Kyle Anderson while I was staying with you, who could be the same man who was a witness at the wedding of Liam and his second wife Helen.

I would so appreciate it if you could help me, as well as forgive me for deceiving you.

Love, Anne Anderson xxx

She sealed the envelope, stamped it and then posted it.

-

Life settled down into its familiar routine while Anne listened out for the postman every morning. She had decided to wait until she heard from Fiona before getting in touch with Andrew again; as it was, she had a visit from the policeman, Sergeant Blakeman, whom she had spoken to on the ferry. She led him into the kitchen which was full of sunshine and made a pot of tea.

'Now, what have you to tell me about the children?' she asked, nudging a mug of tea across the table to him, as well as a plate of biscuits.

'The little boy's father has collected his son but does not want the girl or her mother back,' he said, reaching for a biscuit. 'The girl has been placed in the Seamen's Orphanage for the moment. The mother is in the Royal Infirmary. It could be that they'll end up in the workhouse.'

Anne shivered at the mention of the dreaded work-house. 'I wish there was something I could do to help Mildred. I was adopted and would like to give back some of what I was given. Perhaps I could visit her and take her out?'

'It's worth a try. I could put in a good word in for you,' he said. 'She's in the orphanage on Orphan Drive, the other side of Newsham Park. They don't know where the father is.'

'How sad!'

He nodded. 'It's a shame there doesn't seem to be any sign of the mother's family. When I was a lad, my mam told me that when her own mother died young, she left three boys and two daughters and that her aunties took the children in – one the boys and the other the two girls.'

'What about her father?'

'My grandfather was a sailor and whenever he came home from sea, my mam was allowed to stay with him, as was one of the boys. She would rush home to meet him as soon as his ship docked.'

'Your family sounds a very caring one,' said Anne.

'I think there are still a lot of families like Mam's – since the war, with so many men killed, family ties are even more important. Unfortunately, young Mildred doesn't know where her paternal grandmother lives now as the old woman moved after Mildred and her mother left her house. Bridget and Mildred lived with Bridget's relatives in Ireland while her father was at sea, so he joined them there, but when the Irish Civil War broke out in 1922, he insisted on Bridget and Mildred returning to his mother's house in Liverpool, while it's believed he got involved in the fighting in Ireland and was pronounced missing, presumed dead, a short while later. The war ended in 1923.' He sighed. 'Apparently, the two women didn't get on and Mildred's mother walked out, taking Mildred with her, and moved into a Chinaman's house when she got a job working in his laundry.' He paused. 'It would be a kind gesture if you kept in touch with Mildred; be like an aunt to her. Bridget would like to return to her family in Ireland.'

Anne agreed, liking the sound of that, and soon after the sergeant left, saying he would be in touch.

—

She did not have to wait long before receiving a letter from Sergeant Blakeman who suggested she meet him at the gates of the orphanage on Friday evening at six o'clock. This worked out well as Anne was staying over in Liverpool at Teddy and Joan's, who would be going to Rhyl the following day.

The rest of the day was lightened by the arrival of a letter from Andrew containing a wedding group photograph. Written on the back were the words:

Mam and Father's wedding day.

In his accompanying letter Andrew had also written:

I think Kyle Anderson is the only man besides Father wearing a kilt. It could be that the girl a few feet away is his twin sister, as she's wearing what looks to be similar tartan. Maybe it was through them that Father got to know Hugh Anderson rather than just from the lodge and working together at Tate & Lyle?

Anne stared down at the happy faces of the bride and groom and their wedding guests and picked out the man and woman, where Andrew had placed two tiny crosses; Kyle Anderson and his twin sister had a very noticeable similarity to each other. She read Andrew's letter again, her face breaking into a smile several times. She was already missing his kisses and the feel of his arms around her.

-

Friday dawned clear and dry, but the forecast was for the occasional shower so although it might be risky stepping out in a summer frock and just a cardigan, she decided to do so anyway, but she took a brolly with her just in case. She also carried a holdall containing everything she needed for a week looking after Amy at her old family home and she felt her heart lift, convinced it was going to be an interesting visit.

Teddy and Joan were pleased to see her when she arrived and she told them that she was going to visit the young girl whose mother Andrew had rescued from the Mersey.

Leaving her bag behind, Anne made her way to the orphanage, crossing the bridge over the boating lake in Newsham Park, and she was soon able to make out the orphanage through the trees at the edge of the park. She hurried across the road and noticed a man standing outside the gates who she soon realised was her policeman friend in plain clothes. They greeted one another and he led her to the entrance, pressing a bell at the side of the door. Within moments, they heard the noise of hurrying footsteps and the door was opened to them by a woman in a grey dress. After stating their business, they were ushered inside and led to an office where a middle-aged man sat behind a desk and a woman was seated in a chair to one side.

Sergeant Blakeman introduced Anne to the two people and explained that they were the guardians of the orphanage. They wasted no time getting down to the business of seeing for themselves if she was a fit person to take charge of one of their newest orphans for an outing. After a barrage of questions about who she was and where she lived, they quickly came to a decision and sent for Mildred.

The girl was escorted into the room by the same woman who had opened the front door and Anne smiled at the girl, who returned her smile shyly and wished Anne a good evening. It was arranged that Mildred could spend the next day with Anne between the hours of ten o'clock in the morning until four o'clock in the afternoon.

Anne agreed, also thinking that she would have charge of Amy from tomorrow, but she could put her in her pram and wheel her to Marjorie's, who would hopefully look after her until Anne returned with Mildred; she would check with Teddy and Joan that it would be alright for her to do this. It was her first day in charge after all.

The next morning, Saturday, Anne waved Teddy and Joan off to catch the train to Rhyl before heading off to Marjorie's, who was just about to go shopping. Marjorie was delighted to see Amy, who they all adored, and said she would happily take Amy with her to the shops and that she would see them both later.

Anne thanked her, walking with her as far as West Derby Road before they went their separate ways. A couple of hours later, Anne and Mildred arrived back at Marjorie's and the door was opened to them by Robbie, who welcomed them in. He sniffed. 'I can smell chips.'

Anne had bought two portions of fish from the chippy on the way, with a portion of chips to share between them all. 'That's right. Get out four plates and forks.'

Robbie wasted no time in doing so and, having heard the story of the rescue of Mildred's mother, he could not resist saying, 'Andrew's my big brother, yer know.'

'You're lucky,' said Mildred. 'I wish I had a brother like him.'

Marjorie had returned by this time and the four of them were soon digging in to plates of chips and half a piece of fish each, as well as slices of bread and butter. Anne fed Amy a rusk mashed in milk, which she ate with relish while sitting on Anne's knee at the table.

During the meal, Mildred and Robbie continued with their conversation, later sitting side by side on the sofa.

'You don't look like your big brother,' Mildred said.

'That's because we had different mothers,' he responded. 'I'm an orphan, too.'

Mildred shook a plait back over her shoulder and said, 'It's like me and Charlie, except we have different fathers, but his father is alive.'

He nodded. 'Where did you get the name Mildred from? I'm named after Robbie Burns who wrote "Auld Lang Syne" which is sung at Hogmanay in Scotland and in England on New Year's Eve.'

'I don't know, but I tell people I was named after the film star, Mildred Davis, because she's a favourite of Mam's, although she didn't become famous until after I was born.'

'Don't know the name,' he said.

She pulled a face. 'I bet you know Harold Lloyd, though?'

Robbie nodded. 'He's funny.'

She agreed. 'Well, Mildred Davis is his love interest in lots of his films.'

His face lit up. 'I know who you mean now. She's lovely.'

Anne said in a low voice to Marjorie, 'They seem to be getting on.'

Marjorie nodded. 'I suppose you heard what he said about Andrew being his brother?'

Anne nodded and Marjorie drew her chair closer to Anne. 'It's not true. My sister was already pregnant when she married Liam, but he wasn't the father and she told him so. He married her anyway, because he needed a mother for Andrew and Ruth. Besides which, she felt sorry for the kids.'

'So, neither he nor Andrew know the truth.'

'No. I decided it was best to keep it quiet. I know how much Robbie needs that connection.'

Anne said, 'I understand your reasoning. I suggest that you tell him soon. You don't want Robbie being deeply hurt if he were to learn the truth the way I did after you are gone, but you can trust me to keep quiet about it.' She ate a last chip and called across to Mildred, 'Time we were going if you want to go to the lantern slideshow at the Mission Hall on Lombard Street this afternoon.'

'Is there an entrance fee?' asked Marjorie.

Anne shrugged. 'I didn't see a mention of one but there could be a collection.'

Marjorie stood up. 'Then we'll come with you,' she said. 'It'll probably be worth tuppence and Robbie and I have just enjoyed a free lunch, thanks to you.'

'Oh good!' said Mildred, smiling at Robbie. 'It'll be interesting.'

The four of them set off for the Mission Hall chatting happily. Anne was dismayed to find that there was quite a queue to get in, but Marjorie said, 'It doesn't surprise me that there's a queue. Most here would love to go the flickers but can't afford it. A lantern slideshow is second best but better than nothing.'

Anne could only agree with her, hoping they would get inside, and how nice it would be for the young ones to enjoy it. She need not have worried as the queue moved quickly and they managed to get four seats, although on separate rows, one behind the other. The curtains were drawn and in no time at all, pictures were being projected onto a screen at the front of the hall. The first ones were colour-tinted pictures of historical scenes of battle. Anne reckoned they were of the Crimean War because there were pictures of female nurses caring for wounded soldiers and there was one of a nurse holding a lamp with the words 'Florence Nightingale' written at the bottom, followed by a rousing cheer from the audience for the lady whose name was known from one end of the British Isles to the other. Then there were black and white photographs of India with its ornate buildings as well as jungles and rivers with elephants and monkeys and a lone tiger in a cage. After that there were photographs of native people in Africa standing by their huts and the school and church built by the missionaries. They stood proudly in front of the new buildings with a group of

African children sitting on the ground in front of them. When the show came to an end there was a storm of applause before a collection was taken and a blessing given.

'That was interesting,' said Marjorie as they came out of the hall into the street. 'I'm glad we came. Imagine living in a country where tigers and elephants roam free.'

'I liked the monkeys,' Robbie said.

'Me too,' said Mildred.

'I remember when Da brought a monkey home which a sailor had sold him,' Anne said. 'We called him Mickey.'

'What happened to it?' asked Robbie.

'He didn't last long. Monkeys aren't really suitable pets for children. They have sharp teeth and clamber up the curtains. Mickey brought the curtain rail down once. Mother and Emily were furious and said he had to be got rid of. After that Da brought home a puppy who was much better behaved, so we called her Lady.'

'What kind of dog was she?' asked Robbie.

'She was a Labrador. We all loved her, and I cried when she died.'

'I'd have cried too,' Mildred said, slipping her hand into Anne's. 'We only ever had cats, though, to catch the mice. Grandmamma hated them. Sometimes we'd hear them scurrying behind the skirting board. I felt sorry for them.'

'Why, girl? They're vermin and spread diseases,' said Marjorie, pulling a face.

'They're only little,' Mildred answered.

'It's a good job they are,' said Marjorie. 'Imagine if they were the size of rats.'

Mildred shivered. 'I hate rats. I remember seeing one sneaking out of an empty building down by the docks and in Mam's cousin's cellar.'

'Enough of this talk,' said Anne. 'We'll walk across the park to the orphanage.'

'I don't want to go back,' Mildred said, pulling back from Anne with a mutinous expression.

'I know, love,' said Anne. 'But you have no choice and I promise I'll visit again. We can stop by the bandstand for a while and listen to the music if you promise to behave?'

Mildred sighed. 'I'll be good.'

Anne halted and gazed down at her. 'Promise?'

'I promise,' said Mildred. 'Cross my heart and hope to die, if I dare tell a lie.'

'That's good enough for me,' said Anne, pausing outside Marjorie's house. 'See you soon, Marj,' she called over her shoulder.

'Ta-ra,' Marjorie said. 'Thanks for your company.'

'Do I have to go in yet?' asked Robbie. 'I'd like to go with Anne and Mildred to the park and listen to the band.'

'All right, but be back by seven o'clock at the latest or there'll be no supper for you, my lad.'

'I'll make sure of it,' said Anne, and the three of them waved to Marjorie as they set off for the park.

Mildred and Robbie skipped ahead while Anne did her best to keep up with them and they could hear the music before they even reached the bandstand. They all enjoyed the oompah of the band, who played 'The Gay Hussars' and 'Rule Britannia' as well as many others which they all knew. Then, with reluctant feet, Mildred led Robbie and Anne across the road to the entrance of the Seamen's Orphanage.

The bell was answered this time by a young man with a mop of tawny hair, strong features and broad shoulders. Anne reckoned he was in his late twenties and that he looked vaguely familiar. She told him her business and left Mildred in his charge, saying she would be in touch about the next outing, unaware that he was staring intently after her.

Chapter Twenty

Anne could not get the fair-haired young man out of her mind. She could have sworn that she had never met him before, yet he seemed familiar, but she could not think why. Maybe the next time she went to the orphanage she would ask his name.

To her surprise she didn't have to wait until then, because the following day when she heard a rap on the door, she opened it with Amy in her arms to find him standing on the doorstep.

'What are you doing here?' he asked.

'I could ask you the same question,' she said, puzzled. 'I didn't give you this address, so you can't be here about Mildred.'

'I've come to see Hugh Anderson.'

She could not conceal her shock and her voice quivered when she said, 'You're a bit late. He died last year.'

He looked dismayed. 'That explains everything.'

'Such as what?' she asked. 'I'm Anne Anderson, his adopted daughter. Two of Hugh's sons live here still. Teddy and Gordon.'

He heaved a sigh. 'I've been trying to contact the family, but I didn't have enough information. My father and aunt were second cousins of Hugh's. After my father was killed at the Battle of Jutland, my Aunt Heather was so disturbed by his death that she had a nervous breakdown. She was in an asylum for years and I was able to find accommodation as a volunteer at the Seamen's Orphanage until I was old enough to be independent. I do have a job now as a delivery man and have my own place.'

'What's your name?' Anne asked.

'Kyle Anderson.'

Anne stared at him in astonishment. 'Was your father's name Kyle too?'

He nodded.

'Mystery solved,' she said, smiling. 'I saw a wedding photograph and your father was on it and so was his sister.'

'You did? They were twins and I think that was why she took the news of his death so badly during the Great War.' He paused. 'So, what now?'

Anne said, 'Come inside and have a cuppa and I'll see what we can do to help you. I'm here babysitting for Teddy and his wife while they're in Wales having a break.'

'Thank you,' he said. 'I'd like that. Mildred was telling me about you and the bloke who saved her mother's life. The family have had a tough time but they're not the only ones in these troubled days. What about your brothers and sisters? Are Emily and Albert married?'

'You remember them?'

'I never met them, but I remember them being mentioned by Father and my aunt. I was only a kid at the time. I'm twenty-seven now Father and Aunt Heather used to visit Hugh. My dad also used to see his old friend Liam Fraser while he was here; he'd been the best man at his wedding. My mam was a bit of an invalid and never went with them. She had her own friends and was bored when they talked of their childhood in Scotland, although it was a distant female relative from Scotland who would sit with her and me sometimes when they went out.'

Anne was fascinated by this information and wondered if it could have been Anne Graham who sat with them. She asked him if he could remember her name, but he could only remember that the woman had brought him sweets and that his mother had met her in a hospital where the woman had been a nurse. 'If you give me a little more time to think, I can check the diary I kept then and see what I wrote down.' Eventually Kyle told her why he had wanted to speak to Hugh. It was simply that he wanted to forge links to the family in Scotland so she told him about her visit to the farm in Cardross. He stayed for a couple of hours, also meeting Gordon when he arrived home. The three of them shared more memories and family knowledge before Gordon invited Kyle to go out for a pint with him. When Gordon returned a little while later, he was alone, but told her that they could expect more visits from Kyle, son of Kyle.

—

A week later, back in Eastham, when Teddy and Joan had returned after a few relaxing days in Rhyl, Anne sat up in bed and rubbed her blurry eyes as the rain lashed against the window and a dull light peeped through the curtains. *British summer time!* she thought. *Oh, why does it have to rain today of all days when I'm taking Mildred out?* She glanced at the clock on the bedside table and saw that it was later than she had intended on rising. Time to be up, washed, dressed and on her way to meet her new young friend at the station. Kyle had told her when he had visited Teddy and Joan's that because Mildred was a sensible girl, it would be OK for her to leave the orphanage on her own to meet up with Anne for their days out.

Larry was already up with the kettle on and was making toast. He turned to face her as she entered the sitting room, his face red from the heat of the fire. 'Good, you're up. I was going to give you a shout when the tea was ready.' He took the slice of toast from the toasting fork. 'Butter that, please, love,' he asked.

She did so and said, 'I'm late. I just hope Mildred hasn't arrived at the station yet. I had – stupid me – thought of taking her to Chester for the day but it's definitely not the weather for a trip on the Dee.'

'Save it for another time. She can come back here, have some lunch with us and if the rain doesn't ease off, the pair of you could go to the cinema in Chester instead. I'll treat you both.'

'That's really kind of you,' Anne said, pouring tea into three cups. She took a quick sip from one before putting on her coat.

She had not got far when a van drew up at the kerb near her. She looked inside at the front seat of the cab and a head popped out of the window which she recognised as Mildred.

'What are you doing there?' Anne asked in surprise.

'Climb in and all will be explained,' said Mildred. 'I'll move up.'

Anne wasted no time climbing into the van, trying not to squash Mildred, who was sitting alongside Kyle on the long front seat.

'This is unexpected,' Anne said, glancing across at him.

'I was at the orphanage yesterday and Mildred told me of your plans for today which I knew about, of course,' he said, 'so when I was picking up the van and saw the rain, I decided she might appreciate a lift this far.'

'That was kind of you,' said Anne. 'Anyway, due to the weather there's a change of plan. Now it's back to Emily and Larry's.'

'I've several deliveries this side of the Mersey, so I'll drop you there,' he said. 'It'll all be quicker once the tunnel under the Mersey is a reality.'

'It's been talked about long enough,' Anne said.

He agreed. 'And it should cut down the terrible traffic jams on the dock road.'

'I was up really early because I was so excited,' Mildred said, linking her arm through Anne's. 'I was so annoyed when I saw the rain because I thought you might decide not to take me to Chester.'

'It is a pity about the weather,' Anne said. 'But if the rain eases off we can go later today on the train or bus.'

Mildred said, 'Let's hope it does ease off. At least the rain makes the countryside lovely and green. I remember saying that to Mam and she said I wouldn't feel like that if I'd lived in Ireland like she did on the farm for years. Dublin's fine and she'd had a job there for a while. After my dad decided Mam and I had to go to Liverpool, she didn't want to come here, and they had this huge row. She was always going on about returning to Ireland to her mother's family, but she had no money. She got a job in a Chinese laundry, met Mr Chin, Charlie's dad, and we went to live with him and his mother. Then she stopped talking about going to Ireland for a while. Most probably because she took to the dream pipe.'

'It's sad your mother got herself hooked,' said Anne, presuming the pipe was used by the Chinese to smoke opium.

'I'd like to be able to take her back to Ireland one day,' Mildred said. 'But I wouldn't want to stay there for long. I love Liverpool.'

'Let's hope that'll come true,' Kyle said.

'Yeah, let's pray it will,' said Anne. 'We'd best get going. Larry and Emily will be wondering what has happened to me.'

When they arrived at the house, she asked Kyle in for a cuppa and to meet Emily, but he refused, saying he had to carry on with his deliveries. Before he left them, he dug into his trouser pocket and drew out some change. 'Have an ice cream on me if you make it to Chester,' he said.

Anne wouldn't have taken the money, only he insisted and she and Mildred thanked him and waved him off. The rain did cease eventually, giving way to sunny skies, so they decided to go to Chester in the end. They walked along the city walls for a while, eventually coming to a flight of steps that led them down to the Dee where Anne decided it was time to give their feet a rest and have an ice cream. They sat down on a bench not too far from a bandstand where day-trippers had already gathered as the band tuned up. 'You stay here,' said Anne, 'while I go for ice cream.'

'Will do,' Mildred said. 'I was just thinking Charlie would have loved this.'

'Do you miss him?' Anne asked.

'Yeah, but his grandma will see he's all right and he loves his dad.'

They listened to the band while they ate their ice creams and then went and queued up for the boat trip.

Anne thought how peaceful and pleasant it was as the boat glided between the trees and flower-scattered banks of the river and so different to crossing the Mersey on the ferry.

As it was, when Anne returned home with Mildred, it was to be surprised by the appearance of Andrew, who sprang up from the sofa as soon as she entered the sitting room. He crossed the floor and took her hands in his own. 'I'm so glad to see you. Larry told me you'd gone to Chester with Mildred. Did you enjoy yourselves?'

She nodded, unable to stop a huge smile spreading across her face, so delighted was she to see him. 'And I'm glad to see you, too, although I wasn't expecting to see you so soon.'

'I decided I couldn't stay away any longer when Marjorie wrote to me, telling us what Gordon had said about having had a visit from Kyle Anderson. Besides, I—'

'I was going to write and tell you this evening,' Anne interrupted, hoping he was not too annoyed with her for having delayed in sharing her news.

'She's been very busy,' Emily said.

'Did Marjorie tell you the Kyle at your father's wedding was his father – a sailor who was killed at the Battle of Jutland?' asked Anne.

'No, but I guessed he was his son when she said how old he looked.'

'Kyle gave me a lift here from the orphanage where he's a volunteer,' interrupted Mildred. 'Then he had to get on with his deliveries. His company has a motor van.'

There came a knock on the door and Larry went to see who was there. They all strained their ears to distinguish who he was speaking to and shortly after he entered the room with Kyle.

'I was just on my way back to the depot and was passing, so thought I'd pop in and see if Mildred wanted a lift back to the orphanage,' he said, addressing the girl.

Mildred said, 'Yes, please. I had a lovely day and we enjoyed an ice cream thanks to you.'

'My pleasure,' he said, regarding Andrew, who was silently appraising this new addition to the gathering.

'Let me introduce you two,' Anne said, having noticed the way the two men were weighing each other up. 'Andrew, this is Kyle Anderson. We met at the orphanage where Mildred was taken the day you rescued her mother.'

'I spent a short time there myself as an orphan,' Kyle said. 'Now I help out when I can.' He held out a hand to Andrew, who took it, and they shook hands firmly.

'I believe that our fathers were friends and that your father was the best man at my parents' wedding,' Andrew said.

'Yes.' Kyle nodded. 'That is my understanding too; it's a small world so they say.'

'That was a bit of luck that you were at the same orphanage as Mildred,' said Andrew, sitting on the sofa next to Anne and the young girl.

'It's almost as if fate intended us all to meet,' agreed Kyle.

'How is your mother, Mildred?'

'She's still in hospital but making a good recovery,' said the girl. 'Kyle took me to see her.'

'Has Kyle, by any chance, been able to help us at all in other ways?' Andrew asked, looking meaningfully at Anne, and she wondered what he was getting at.

'Not much so far,' said Kyle. 'Next time I'll bring my diary, although I did have a glance at it and I had written down a couple of names of women who used to keep my mother company when Dad and Aunt Heather visited Cousin Hugh. I believe they might be of help. One was a Mary Graham and her friend. They had been in service together nursing during the war and had decided not to return to Scotland.'

'Did you have any other information about them?' asked Andrew.

Kyle creased his brow in thought. 'They had worked in a temporary hospital in a school, nursing wounded soldiers. Mary came from the same part of Glasgow as Dad; her mother had been visiting Glasgow and met her husband there and the families knew each other. They always brought me sweets or a lollipop. I've a feeling she and Mary had a sweet shop. I don't know where she lived or her proper name. I just called her the Sweetie Lady.'

'I presume you don't know what happened to her?' Andrew asked.

'No. Mam was a Liverpudlian and she met Dad in Liverpool when he was a merchant seaman and his ship docked in Liverpool. This was before he joined the Royal Navy when war broke out. Mam was always a bit of an invalid, so Aunt Heather came to Liverpool because she missed Dad but also to help Mam after I was born. Mam died before Dad and Aunt Heather was put in the asylum for a while after he was killed, but due to the treatment she had, she lost some of her memory. I went to the Seamen's Orphanage and she died while she was in the asylum.' He looked downcast. 'Sorry I can't help you more.'

'You've given us something to go on,' Anne said. 'Hopefully, I'll hear from Fiona or Uncle Donald soon with the name I need.'

Kyle glanced at the clock on the mantelpiece. 'I'd better get going. Are you ready, Mildred?'

She nodded and thanked Anne and the family for tea.

Anne saw them out, promising Mildred that she would see her again soon.

Chapter Twenty One

Once Kyle and Mildred had left, Anne cooked bacon and eggs for her and Andrew and they caught up on each other's news. Emily and Larry had already eaten.

'Perhaps we could meet up tomorrow and have a visit to Everton Library, like old times?' Andrew suggested.

'That would be grand,' Anne agreed enthusiastically.

'No, you can't,' Emily cut in. 'I need you here and Larry will need you in the shop during the week.'

'Of course,' said Anne, knowing that she had neglected her duties long enough, but her heart sank all the same.

'We could meet there in the evening, then,' Andrew said. 'On weekdays the library doesn't close until eight o'clock. We could go to the flickers afterwards.'

With that settled they finished their meal and soon afterwards Andrew left to catch the train to Liverpool where he was staying with Marjorie and Robbie.

The whole of the following day was spent working in the shop, tidying shelves and refilling the wooden containers with potatoes of various kinds, such as King Edwards, Lincolns and the local Cheshire spuds as well as carrots and turnips. It was only late in the afternoon that Larry told Anne she could go at four o'clock. She reached the library approximately an hour later and found Andrew there already. It was fun having a look at the new books that were on the shelves and discussing what they wanted to read next, and Anne was reminded of how much had happened between them since their first meeting. Andrew suggested they went and had something to eat at Marjorie's before going to the Olympia Cinema on West Derby Road, which had been converted from a theatre to a picture house.

Steamboat Bill, Jr. starring Buster Keaton was showing, so he treated Marjorie and Robbie as well, certain they would enjoy the film.

Andrew saw Anne onto the train afterwards, saying, 'I'm getting impatient not hearing from Cissie about Lil.' He paused. 'I'd also like to go and speak to Mildred's mother myself, to see how she's doing.'

'She's in the Liverpool Infirmary in Pembroke Place. I'd like to go with you, but I don't see how I have the time. Emily and Larry have made it clear they want me to knuckle down in the shop,' Anne said.

'That's all right,' he said. 'I'll go on my own. I do have an interest in her recovery.'

'So do I, for Mildred's sake,' Anne said, and went on to tell him what the little girl had told her about her Irish relatives and her English grandmother.

Andrew said, 'I'll go tomorrow and let you know how I get on. I need a happy ending for my story.'

She nodded. 'I feel all bubbly inside. What I need now is Fiona or Uncle Donald to write and tell me anything more they know about Anne Graham and her twin.'

Andrew held her in a tight embrace. 'I feel like we are getting closer to the truth.'

'I hope so… Here's my train. See you soon.' They shared a lingering kiss and Anne felt her heart increase its beat.

-

The following day, Andrew stood across the road from the Royal Infirmary, which was a red-brick building built in late-Victorian times. The original infirmary had been erected in the eighteenth century on the site where St George's Hall was now situated, during a time when disease was rife in the overcrowded and unhygienic streets of Liverpool as people poured into the town in search of work, especially those from Ireland.

Andrew found Mildred's mother on a ward that seemed to go on forever – it was so long, with tall windows that were too high up for anyone to see what was going on in the outside world. The woman whom he had last seen as a bedraggled, wild-eyed and soaking-wet bundle of rags was sitting up in bed, gazing into space, as if oblivious to the visitors at other patients' bedsides.

Andrew drew up a chair next to her bed. Slowly, Mildred's mother turned her head in his direction as he placed a couple of magazines and a bar of chocolate on the bedcovers in front of her.

'Do you remember me?' he asked.

The woman did not reply immediately but stared at him and after a moment replied, 'How could I forget the man who saved my worthless life?'

'Mildred doesn't believe you're worthless,' he said.

'What do you know about my Mildred?' she responded, a nerve twitching at the corner of her left eye.

'I saw her the other evening. She wants you to be able to return to your family in Ireland.'

'Why?' She reached out towards the chocolate and a magazine then hesitated.

'It's alright,' Andrew said. 'They are for you… Mildred can't care for you any longer by herself. If you can tell me the name of your mother and her address in Ireland, we can get in touch with her.'

Her eyes brightened. 'I'd like to see me Mam again.'

'Then help me find her,' he said.

'I can't afford the ferry fare.' A tear trickled down the woman's cheek.

Andrew put a hand over hers. 'I'll sort that out. What's your name and that of your mother – and where did you come from in Ireland?'

'My name's Bridget Martin. My husband is Joseph Martin but he's missing after an ambush during the Irish Civil War and I can only believe he'd dead after all this time. My mammy's name is Sarah O'Donnell and she's a widow. I was born in Co. Cork and before coming to Liverpool I had a job in Dublin, but Mammy and some of my sisters and cousins moved to my granddaddy's farm in Co. Cork and so did I with my daughter. Joe joined us there, but he wasn't pleased, and he had many an argument with the menfolk.' She paused. 'But what about my Charlie?'

'He's with his dad and grandmother.'

She sighed. 'They love him and will hang on to him.'

'I'll see what I can do for you and Mildred about going to Ireland,' Andrew said, rejoicing at the thought of the copy he would write at the happy ending he could see on the horizon, even if it was only on the printed page.

He stayed only a short while longer and then hurried away, desperate to get writing and to see Anne. When he told her what he had learnt, she said, 'I could speak to Sergeant Blakeman again. I'm sure if I explained the situation to him, he could talk to his superior about the situation and they could then get in touch with their opposite number in Cork to speak to this Sarah O'Donnell. We need to tell her that her daughter and granddaughter need a home.'

Andrew agreed that made sense, although he would have liked to be more involved himself. He kissed Anne. 'I should have trusted that you would have worked out a sensible plan. You're such a caring person.'

'Well I know that you have to return to London,' she said. 'Anyway, I can ask Kyle to help Bridget and Mildred if they need a man's helping hand.'

Andrew held her off at arm's length. 'You're not getting too fond of this Kyle fellow, are you?'

She twinkled up at him. 'I can't believe you're jealous.'

'I'm not jealous.' Anne thought his expression said otherwise. 'I don't have cause to be, do I?'

'Of course not! Kyle's a nice man and he's family, that's all. It's you who makes my heart go pitter-patter and whose kisses I long for when you're away.'

'I'm glad to hear it.' He drew her close again and kissed her passionately until her knees gave way and she had to cling to him to stay upright.

'It's time we found Jane,' he said, when they came up for breath. He slid his hands down her arms and, taking one of her hands in his, held it firmly. 'Let's go and catch the train to Eastham.'

When they arrived back at the house, there was a letter waiting for Anne with a Scottish postmark. She wasted no time in slicing the envelope open and saw that it was from Fiona in Cardross. Her eyes scanned it quickly.

'What does it say?' asked Emily.

She went back to the beginning and began reading it again, more slowly this time. 'Uncle Donald says that his mother's maiden name was Graham and that there were two Annes in the family, a mother and her daughter. In fact, the daughter, Anne, was one of two sisters; her twin was called Mary. Well, that agrees with what Kyle told us. Twin Anne left Scotland in 1912 and Mary left shortly after, hoping she could find her twin. She joined the auxiliary nurses with a friend after war broke out. Apparently, they eventually heard from Mary at the end of the war when she wrote to them and told them not to worry about her. She was perfectly fine, but had not found her sister, Anne. She and a friend had settled down in Liverpool and had earlier in the war met up with Kyle Anderson senior and his second cousin Hugh and opened a shop called Miss Tillymint's Sweet Treats.'

'What a quaint name,' Emily said.

'I'm sure I've seen it somewhere,' said Andrew. 'I wonder if they ever advertised in the *Echo* back then?'

Anne thought of her conversation with Kyle and his mention of the 'Sweetie Lady'. 'See if you can find out?' Anne said.

'I will,' he said, 'as I'm sure it's likely this is the same Anne Graham Mary was looking for and who died in childbirth.' He frowned. 'It sounds like Hugh never met Anne Graham. Otherwise, he'd have told Mary.'

'Unless he met her whilst she was working in the Sandon and didn't like mentioning it to Mary, who'd tell her parents and they'd be ashamed of their daughter working as a barmaid,' said Anne, before adding excitedly, 'Fiona also says she's planning on coming down to Liverpool and would like to stay with us, if that's all right, Emily?'

'Of course. We can't say no when she put herself out for you so generously when you were up in Scotland,' said Emily. 'Besides, she's my cousin and I'd like to get to know her.'

'That's settled,' Anne said. 'She can share my room and no doubt she'll want to meet the rest of the family, so can divide her time between us. I'd been planning to visit Albert at some point, so I can take her for a couple of nights then come back and she can stay on longer with them if she'd like to. I'll answer her letter later and tell her all about Kyle Anderson too, or I suppose I could phone her if Larry doesn't mind. Now, I'm making cocoa and then Andrew and I will take ours out in the garden as we've a lot to discuss.'

Anne led the way out of the house and sat on the bench in the garden, asking Andrew, 'Are you warm enough out here?'

He seemed to hesitate for a moment. 'Maybe this is now the right time to ask… Will we get married next Easter?'

'Yes, please. I'll be seventeen then.' Anne felt almost delirious with happiness. 'Will we get engaged first?'

'Of course. We'll let people know our intentions. Let's meet in Liverpool tomorrow and choose a ring before I return to London.'

She wriggled with pleasure. 'Life can only get better.'

Chapter Twenty Two

After Andrew had gone, Anne told Emily and Larry of she and Andrew's engagement.

'An engagement!' Emily said. 'Congratulations. I presume you're both sure of your feelings?'

'I've never been surer of anything else,' Anne said with fervour.

'You know,' said Emily, 'I'm warming to Andrew, partly because Larry likes him, and he's convinced me that I'm wasting my time foisting someone else on you.'

'Can I have the time off please, Larry?' Anne pleaded.

'Of course you can, and congratulations on your engagement. When do you think you'll get married? You're still only sixteen.'

'Next Easter Saturday. I'll be seventeen then. You probably have read in the *Echo* that the age of consent is being increased to sixteen this year after it being fourteen for years. I wish I didn't need Albert's permission for me to marry before I'm twenty-one. But hopefully I'll be able to persuade him. Then I'll move south with Andrew. Of course, I'll miss you both and I must say I've appreciated you providing me with a home and work.' Anne choked on the words and, getting up, flung her arms around Emily first and then Larry.

'We'll miss you, too,' he said gruffly.

Emily had tears in her eyes and could not speak, only returning Anne's hug.

It was not long before the three of them had control of their emotions and Anne went and made three cups of cocoa before they went up to bed.

She was up early the following morning, choosing her prettiest and best frock to wear, yellow with white spots, as well as a cream cloche hat with a yellow ribbon and cream gloves. She had a handbag to match, which held her purse, a small phial of perfume, a lipstick and a compact.

'You remind me of a daffodil,' Emily said. 'A touch of spring in August. No wonder he wants to marry you.'

'See you later,' Anne said, fluttering her fingers at her. 'Ta-ra!'

There was a spring in her step as she made her way to the railway station and she could not stop smiling. As she sat in a carriage, gazing out of the window at the passing scene of fields, trees and gardens in their late summer colours, she thought about London and sharing an apartment with Andrew.

She thought of them having children and the idea was somewhat alarming. Was she ready for such responsibility? She guessed she was going to have to wait and see. Before that, there was the wedding to arrange and a honeymoon, which surely Andrew would sort out. Albert was the fly in the ointment but these things were some way off, and for now she must concentrate on finding out if Cissie had heard anything from the wet nurse, Lil. It would make Andrew's day if his sister could be at their wedding.

Suddenly, she came back to the present and, looking out of the window, realised they were at Port Sunlight station. There were still several more stops to go before

Hamilton Square and then under the Mersey to Liverpool. She felt a thrill of excitement, thinking of meeting Andrew and choosing their engagement ring. Her mind was filled with images of diamonds, rubies and sapphires, but of course, her choice would depend on how much Andrew could afford.

He was waiting for her outside Central Station, near Lewis's department store. Anne's heart felt it would explode with love when she saw his eyes light up at the sight of her as they hurried towards each other. He seized her hand and drew it through his arm as he led her across Ranelagh Street and then through Cases Street to Addlestones, the jeweller on Elliot Street. They stood gazing at the beautiful rings in the window and it did not take Anne long to decide which one she liked as her eyes kept coming back to a ring that made her think of a flower. It had a large garnet at its centre surrounded by smaller ones; she tried to avoid looking at the price, but she needn't have worried as Andrew didn't bat an eyelid at the price tag, suggesting instead they go inside and ask to try it on. Disappointingly, when they did, it turned out to be too big, but the shop assistant said they could fit it to her size, and it would be ready in a few hours time. He measured her finger for her ring size, Andrew handed over a deposit and they left the shop and headed for lunch at the Berkley Cafe on Church Street. Over the meal, she talked to him about contacting Cissie to find out whether she had heard from Lil, as well as bringing up the subject of what they should do if Albert refused to give his consent, knowing they would need to book the church soon if she was to have her wedding on Easter Saturday 1930.

'I'd like to marry sooner but that that would be a perfect date, even more so if we have brilliant weather and my sister could be there,' Andrew said. He also suggested that they spend Christmas together and that she should come down to London.

Anne had mixed feelings about the London part. 'Surely it would be more sensible for you to come to Liverpool with both our families being up here?'

'You're right,' he replied with a smile. 'London can wait. As long as we're together.'

After coffee, they returned to the jeweller and collected Anne's engagement ring, which now fitted perfectly, then they said goodbye at Lime Street Station and she saw him onto the train with a kiss and a wave.

Afterwards, as she walked along Lime Street, she suddenly felt rather depressed, although every time she glanced at her engagement ring her spirits rose. Even so, she was in no mood to return to Larry and Emily's just yet. She wished she knew Lil's surname, then she could have gone to Central Library and looked her address up in the street directories. The mystery of who her father was, which remained unsolved, nagged away at her, and it was at that moment she decided to visit Cissie instead of writing to her. She wasted no time in catching a tram to take her along Breckfield Road North opposite the Mere Lane cinema. She crossed the road and walked the short distance to Cissie's house.

Anne did not receive the warm welcome from the midwife that she had expected, and it was not long before she found out why.

'I went to visit Lil a little while ago and had every intention of telling them all about your visit,' Cissie began, after settling Anne with a cup of tea at her kitchen table. 'Lil told me she is ill and I was shocked to see the change in her. When Jane was out of the room, Lil told me that she has a terminal illness, but is keeping it from Jane for as long as possible because she does not want her to worry about just how serious her condition is.'

'Did you try to persuade her to tell Jane?' Anne asked, feeling unsettled at this new development and very sorry for Lil.

'Oh, I did try, very hard. Jane has a right to know, but Lil refused and said I was not to tell Jane or she would never speak to me again.' Cissie sighed over her teacup. 'I just didn't think it was the right moment to mention Jane's brother was searching for her. They have enough on their plate.'

Anne could understand Cissie's reasoning, even though she felt certain that Andrew wouldn't. Most likely he would consider it reason enough to step in and assist Jane, but she decided to leave matters as they were for now.

On arriving back at the house in Eastham, Anne flaunted her engagement ring under Emily's nose. 'What do you think?'

Emily took hold of Anne's left hand and said, 'It's very pretty. I hope you'll both be very happy, and you'd better invite us to visit you often after you're married. I've never been to London. But you'd better not forget to speak to Albert about your intention to marry and ask for his consent when you go with Fiona to Rhyl.'

'Will do,' sighed Anne. She hugged Emily and then told her and Larry of her visit to Cissie's.

'It's a difficult situation,' said Emily.

'I think Cissie isn't thinking straight,' Larry said. 'I would have thought it makes more sense for Andrew to step in at this point. Surely if Lil is dying, it should be a comfort to her to know that Jane's natural brother, and you too, Anne, are there to support Jane after Lil passes away.'

Emily agreed. 'They both need to know they're not alone.'

'You're right. I'll get in touch with Andrew today. Larry, could I use the telephone in the shop? I have a card he gave me with a telephone number I can ring.'

'You're going to telephone his newspaper?' said Larry.

'Yes. They'll know where he is, and I can ask that he call me back from a telephone box as soon as possible as it's urgent.'

As it was, Andrew returned Anne's call within a couple of hours. Her heart fluttered as Andrew's voice said clearly but in an anxious note, 'Anne, is that you? Are you alright?'

'Yes, I'm fine, but apparently Lil, Jane's adoptive mother, is terminally ill. She doesn't want Jane knowing the truth about her illness and has made Cissie swear not to tell her, which means she won't tell her about our search for her and won't give me the address.'

'That's crazy. I could help them.'

'I agree, that's why I wanted to tell you right away.'

'We need to persuade Cissie to give us that address.' His voice had an urgency to it.

'I doubt she'll break her word to Lil,' said Anne, 'but I have thought that Cissie's daughter could be of help to us.'

'That's a good idea. She might have some advice for us,' he said. 'I'll be up again to see you as soon as I can. In the meantime, you visit the daughter.'

Anne thought the daughter's name was Jessie and said she would go and see her as soon as possible. Just then Larry called her as there was a queue of customers, so she blew kisses down the mouthpiece and said, 'I must go, love, take care.'

'Love you,' he said.

She echoed his words and replaced the receiver.

Anne decided to visit the orphanage that evening in the hopes of seeing Kyle and was fortunate enough to find him there, so told him of the plan to help reunite Mildred and Bridget with their family in Ireland.

'I think it's a good idea,' he said. 'Have you spoken to the police?'

'Sergeant Blakeman? I think he'll agree that it's better than the workhouse.'

'Are you going to take Mildred out and tell her that Andrew has visited her mother and how you both want to help them?'

'If I can.' Anne added, 'While I remember, can I have your address?'

He nodded and wrote it on a slip of paper and handed it to her. 'I'll go with you to the office and explain the situation to the guardians and see what they have to say. I'd like to help in any way I can,' said Kyle.

They explained the plan to contact Mildred's family in Ireland, which the guardians approved. Mildred was called in to the office and told the news about Andrew having seen her mother and of the plan to contact her grandmother in Ireland.

The young girl was almost overcome by tears. 'Now all the fighting is over, it should be perfectly safe for us to go to Ireland. Maybe we can find out more about Daddy.'

'You've something to look forward to now,' Anne told her, though when Mildred smiled in return, Anne thought the girl's smile had not truly reached her eyes.

'Is there something the matter?' she asked.

Mildred looked at her feet. 'I'll miss Liverpool – and you, Andrew and Kyle too.'

Anne reassured her that they would write to her, but she understood how the girl was feeling. Mildred had faced so many trials in her young life already.

–

The following morning while working in the shop, Anne received a telephone call from Fiona, saying she would be catching a Glasgow train the following Saturday morning and would appreciate it if Anne could meet her at Liverpool Exchange railway station. Anne asked the time of the train and whether Fiona definitely wanted to visit Albert in Rhyl.

'Of course,' said Fiona. 'I've already been in touch with him.'

Fiona continued to explain her plans and Anne was surprised about Fiona arranging the visit to Rhyl by herself, but as she had lots of other business to think about she told Fiona how much she was looking forward to seeing her again and said goodbye. Anne then immediately telephoned the orphanage asking for a message to be passed on to Kyle and Mildred that she was going to be unavailable for at least a fortnight as she had a visitor coming from Scotland.

Fiona would be staying at least a fortnight or so in Wales, she'd said, but Anne had explained that she could only stay with her for a couple of nights. To her relief, Andrew arrived later that evening, and as she greeted him at the doorway, she told him all about Fiona's visit and the planned trip to Rhyl, and that Kyle had been roped in to help with the plan for Mildred and her mother, Bridget.

'He wrote and told me that he is planning on taking Bridget and her mother back to Ireland,' Anne told him.

'You seem to have been having a very busy time,' said Andrew. 'I would have liked to accompany Mildred and her mother in order to follow the story through, but in the circumstances, Kyle's the best choice we have and I'm hoping that between him and Mildred, they'll come up with a decent ending for my story.' He held her in front of him and gazed into her eyes.

In a low voice, she said, 'I'm glad you can see it that way. I thought you might be cross with me. I know how important this story is to you.' She toyed with a button on his jacket. 'You might be best leaving the story where they sail away from Liverpool, back home to Ireland.'

'Why?' he asked. 'I thought Mildred and Bridget returning to the bosom of the family was a perfect ending.'

'I'm not so sure it's entirely what Mildred wants. She's half-English, remember — and her English father went missing over there and could be dead.'

'But she wouldn't remember him, would she? So how can she miss him?'

'Believe me, you can miss a person or something even if your memory of them is only vague,' whispered Anne. 'You never met Jane, but you want to help her.'

'Mam gave her life for her. I know it's what she'd want.'

Before they could say anything more, they were interrupted by Emily asking what was keeping Anne, and who was at the door.

She called, 'It's Andrew. We're just discussing things.'

'Bring him in,' said Larry.

Anne and Andrew went into the sitting room, where Larry greeted Andrew with a shake of his hand and congratulated him on his engagement. 'Anne has been telling me about your sister, Jane. Have you decided what you are going to do about all of it?'

'Reassure her and her mother, Lil, that I have no intention of coming between them,' said Andrew.

'You need to discover her whereabouts first,' Emily said.

'We're hoping Cissie's daughter, Jessie, can help us there. It mightn't be only the mothers who keep in touch,' said Andrew. 'I thought I'd nip and see her in the morning. I'm staying at Marjorie's, so it won't take me long to get there.'

Anne said, 'I'll come over in the afternoon as its half-day closing. It's a while since I've seen Marjorie.'

'Good idea,' said Andrew. 'We could go to the flickers later if it all works out the way we want.'

Decisions made, Anne made hot drinks, and not long after Andrew made his excuses and left, saying that he would see Anne at Marjorie's.

The following day, after spending the morning serving in the shop, Anne made lunch for the three of them before changing and leaving to catch the train to Liverpool, then the tram to West Derby Road. She could scarcely believe how swiftly the time had passed since she had last seen Marjorie. As it turned out, Marjorie was at work, but Robbie was home as it was half-term and the next day was Duck Apple Night, as Halloween was known in Liverpool, where many households would carry out the tradition of trying to take a bite from one of many apples placed in a basinful of cold water. Andrew was also there. He looked up from the newspaper he was reading, his serious expression relaxing when he saw her.

Immediately Anne asked how he had got on at Jessie's.

He smiled and put aside the newspaper. 'Despite her mother having told her to keep quiet about Lil and Jane's whereabouts, she agreed with me that I should see them and offer any assistance I can.'

'Did she tell you where they live?' Anne asked.

'Aughton Street in Ormskirk. They moved there to live with Lil's great-aunt, who was becoming feeble,' he said. 'The old woman died a while ago and Lil inherited her cottage where she and Jane have lived ever since. Jane works in a florist's shop and Lil worked in a bakery until ill health forced her to give up her job.'

'So, when are we going?' asked Anne excitedly.

'There's no time like the present,' he said, getting to his feet.

They took their leave of Robbie and boarded the tram to take them to the station in Liverpool where they would catch another train to Ormskirk. It was getting on for four o'clock by the time they arrived there and asked for directions to Aughton Street.

Andrew led the way up the short path to the front door and banged the knocker. There came the sound of hurrying footsteps and the door was flung open to reveal a young woman who appeared to be of a similar age to Anne. For several moments none of them spoke or made a move as the girl and Andrew took in each other's faces, which had a distinct family resemblance. Anne held her breath, waiting for Andrew to say something, and at last, he stepped forward and took the girl's hand.

'You must be Jane,' he said. 'I can't express how pleased I am to meet you. I'm Andrew Fraser, your brother.'

The girl lifted her hands to her mouth, gasping in shock. 'How did you find me?' she asked, her voice catching on a sob.

'I've found you thanks to this young lady here,' he said, nudging Anne. 'This is my fiancée, Anne Anderson, and in her search to find the identity of her natural mother, we've managed to trace you.'

'I can scarcely believe this is happening,' Jane said in a tremulous voice. 'I knew of the exchange of the babies and have often wondered about the Fraser family. But you must come inside, we can't be talking on the doorstep when there is so much to say.'

They all sat in the small kitchen of the cottage as Andrew continued explaining. 'Father told us you had died along with Mother at your birth. It was only years later that I was to discover this was not the truth and by then I'd met Anne and we had fallen in love. You can imagine just what a shock it was for both of us to learn that Anne was believed to be my baby sister. I had to move to London out of temptation's way because my feelings towards her were far from brotherly and it seemed there was no hope for our future together at all. It was only when Anne visited some relations of her adopted family in Scotland that she discovered what a remarkable resemblance she bore to two of them. Anne felt there must be more to the story than we'd been told. She did some more digging and managed to track down Cissie, the midwife who told us the truth about the fate of those babies; how you'd been intended for adoption by the Anderson family but that Lil had felt such a strong bond with you that she couldn't bear to be parted from you. The rest you know…'

'Fate must have a hand in all this because of the timing of your discovery,' said Jane. 'I'm needed here. Mam is ill, and I can't leave her.'

'We know Lil is ill. We've come to help you both and we'd like to meet her.'

Jane led the way into the front room where Lil was in bed, propped up by several pillows. Her wispy hair was neatly brushed and her almost translucent skin had little colour in it, though she was wearing a touch of lipstick. About her shoulders was a pale-pink lacy bed jacket and around her neck hung a silver cross on a chain. She gazed at the three of them uncertainly. 'I heard talking and was wondering what was going on,' she said faintly.

'Mam, this is Andrew Fraser and his fiancée, Anne Anderson,' introduced Jane, and then proceeded to tell her mother Andrew's story.

Far from being upset, as Cissie had thought she might be, Lil gave a weak smile. 'I was foolish to swear Cissie to silence as if I'd be able to keep things from Jane, and I also always hoped that one day you would come to find us,' she said faintly.

Andrew perched on the side of the bed and covered Lil's hand with his own. 'I so much wanted to meet you and Jane,' he said. 'I also came to see if there's any way in which I can help you both, seeing as we're family. Besides which, Anne is hoping you might be able to help with any information you might have about her real mother to add to the little that Cissie was able to tell her.'

Lil looked thoughtful and then said to Jane, 'Fetch me my little treasure box from upstairs, lovey.'

Jane left the room and was back within a short time. Lil opened the small wooden box inlaid with fancy carvings and removed a necklace consisting of an amethyst amulet on a silver chain. 'This was Anne Graham's. I met her while both of us were pregnant but had no idea we'd give birth around the same time. We were both on our own in the world and we met outside a pawnshop on Breck Road; she needed some ready cash and was going to pawn this necklace. I took a fancy to it and offered to buy it from her. She had been working in the local pub but had managed to get herself in the family way. We got to know each other quite well and I promised that I would do what I could for her baby if anything happened to her. As it happened, I was able to help keep her baby alive by breastfeeding it after losing my little one and after Anne died.' Lil held out the necklace to Anne. 'She'd want you to have it,' she said.

Anne hesitated only a moment before taking the necklace, thanking Lil while Andrew helped with fastening it around her neck. Lil stared up at her. 'It looks lovely on you,' she said. 'Your mother would be delighted to see you wearing it.'

Anne's fingers touched the amethyst, and the thought that her mother had worn this very same one brought her closer to the woman she had never known and who had given her own life for hers. 'Did she ever mention my father to you?' she asked Lil.

'Only to say he was a married man with children and she had broken off the relationship because she felt guilty about his children.' Lil's voice had weakened to almost a whisper and now her head drooped onto her chest as her eyes closed.

For an awful moment, Anne thought Lil had passed away, but Jane was calm and said, 'Let's go back into the kitchen and have a cuppa. Mam's exhausted herself and needs to rest.'

Andrew and Anne followed Jane out of the parlour. 'So, what next?' Jane asked, pouring tea into three china cups and pushing the milk jug and sugar basin in their direction across the table.

'I'll keep in touch and I'll visit as often as I can,' Andrew said, taking out his card and giving it to her.

'In between his visits, I'll come and see you too,' said Anne, 'and you're welcome to visit me if you can manage a trip to Eastham on the Wirral, or we could meet in Liverpool and have a coffee in the Kardomah.' She paused. 'Although, I doubt we'll be able to see each other this next fortnight or so as a cousin from Scotland is coming to stay.'

Jane smiled and hugged herself. 'It's all so exciting. If only Mam was not so ill.'

The three of them talked a while longer. Andrew spoke about Marjorie and Robbie, as well as Duncan, their half-brother up on the Isle of Jura, and their grandfather in Northern Ireland, before returning to front room where Lil had now woken up. Jane placed a tray in front of her and Lil reached for the cup of tea and took several gulps before reaching for a jam tart.

'We'll leave you for now, Lil,' said Andrew. 'Hopefully it won't be too long before I can see you again. Jane will tell you what we discussed.'

Lil beamed at him. 'I'm so glad you found us. My lovely girl is going to need your help during the next few months.'

He bent over the bed and kissed Lil's forehead. 'God bless you,' he said gruffly.

Anne said her own farewell and Jane saw them out with tears in her eyes. They both hugged her, and Jane stood watching them at the gate until they were out of sight.

Chapter Twenty Three

Anne stood on the platform as the Glasgow train pulled into the station and it wasn't long before she heard her name being called. Looking along the length of the platform, she spotted Fiona stepping down from the train and began to walk towards her.

'How lovely to see you,' Fiona said. 'But my, you're a deep one with all of your secrets.'

Anne hugged her, delighted to see Fiona again. 'I'm sorry, but I never found the right moment to explain things to you. Did you have a good journey?'

'Fine. I'm looking forward to hearing more of your story and about what you've found out since.'

'I'll tell you everything, but first you should know I've arranged with Albert for us to go to Rhyl,' said Anne. 'I wrote and told you about Kyle Anderson. He is going to pop over to Eastham this evening to meet you as he's going to Ireland in a day or two with Mildred and her mother.'

Fiona linked her arm through Anne's. 'I'm feeling nervous about meeting all my kinsfolk.'

'There's no need for nerves. They will all love you. I like your kilt by the way, is that the Anderson tartan?'

'Aye. I only wear it for special occasions.'

'That's a nice tweed jacket you're wearing, too,' Anne said.

'It was my mother's. She didn't take it with her when she left, so I decided to wear it because it's so warm.'

'And there's no need to feel nervous about Kyle, he's a love and so easy to talk to. You'll get on like a house on fire. Mind you, he and Andrew didn't hit it off straight-away.'

'Perhaps they were both a bit jealous of each other. How is your search for your mother and father going?'

Anne smiled. 'I met Jane, Andrew's sister, and the wet nurse who fed me. She told me a bit about my mother, Anne Graham. You mentioned that her twin sister, Mary, came to Liverpool in search of my mother and I'd like to find her and the woman who accompanied her. If I could discover the whereabouts of the sweet shop – Miss Tillymint's Sweet Treats – that would be great.'

'All that talk of sweets makes me think of Edinburgh Rock,' Fiona said, wistfully. 'I remember Dad loved that and used to send away for it. He kept most of it for himself, saying it would ruin my teeth. He had false ones.'

'I wonder if he sent all the way to Liverpool for it?' Anne said.

'Unlikely,' Fiona said. 'It's produced in Scotland. There's still half a box of rock in a cupboard in his old bedroom. I couldn't bring myself to eat it and neither could I throw it away because it held such a strong memory of him for me.'

'I can understand that,' Anne said, suddenly recalling the small suitcase of Hugh's which Albert had taken and which she wanted to have a look inside of. 'Anyway, let's go back to Eastham. You must be starving after your journey.'

'I'm longing for a cup of tea,' said Fiona, keeping pace with her.

In no time at all they were on the Wirral and Anne was telling Fiona a little about the places they passed through on their way. When they arrived at their station they left the train and walked home through the village.

'It's a pretty place,' said Fiona.

Anne agreed and pointed out the church. 'Andrew and I are planning on having our wedding there next Easter if Albert will give his permission.'

'So, Andrew's the one?' Fiona said.

'He is,' Anne said. 'Unfortunately, you can't meet him yet as he's back in London.'

'Do you think absence makes the heart grow fonder?'

'We miss each other that's for sure,' Anne said.

Fiona sighed. 'I'm hoping Sandy will miss me enough to follow me down here and propose. If only he and Uncle Donald could tolerate each other.'

'What have they got against each other?'

'Uncle Donald won't talk about it and Sandy just says it was a falling out with his father years ago.' Fiona paused. 'It would help if I knew what the quarrel was about and then I could try and reason with Uncle Donald.' She sighed. 'Anyway, I'm not going to let it spoil my holiday.'

'No, you shouldn't,' said Anne, leading the way across the road to the house. As she opened the front gate, she caught the sound of voices coming from the back garden, so the two of them walked around to the back of the house. There they found Emily having a conversation with Keith, who was leaning on the fence in his usual self-confident way. He spotted the two girls before Emily did and called to Anne over her shoulder, 'I believe congrat-ulations are in order.'

She thanked him, warily, and introduced Fiona to him and Emily.

Keith smiled and said, 'How about my showing you Chester while you're here, Miss Anderson? Is it all right if I call you by your first name, Fiona?'

Fiona returned his smile. 'I suppose so, and do I call you Keith?'

'Of course, I'd like us to be friends,' he said.

Anne thought that Keith was being quite forward and exchanged glances with Emily, who clearly thought the same thing. 'I'll put the kettle on. Fiona is desperate for a cuppa.'

'I'll come inside with you. I'm looking forward to getting to know my young cousin,' said Emily.

'See you again, Fiona,' called Keith, before vanishing back inside his sister's home.

'He's a fast worker,' Fiona said once inside the kitchen, but was laughing as she said it. 'But he's not bad looking either.'

'Don't be fooled by his looks,' Anne said.

Emily interrupted, 'Anne dear, just because you didn't get along with Keith, don't spoil Fiona's opportunity to enjoy Chester in his company.'

Anne put the kettle on and kept her lips firmly closed, thinking that maybe having a few hours in another bloke's company could be just what Fiona needed, but anyone other than Keith would be preferable; she still didn't trust him fully, despite his congratulations.

Emily showed Fiona into the sitting room and began to bombard her with questions about her home and her family which Fiona fielded good-naturedly. When Anne returned with the tea tray, Fiona had produced a tin of shortbread from her large handbag and was handing it to Emily. 'Just a small present for you.'

'How thoughtful, and just the perfect biscuit to have with a cup of tea,' Emily said, opening the tin and passing it around.

'I love shortbread,' Anne said. 'They make it in the biscuit factory, not far from where I used to work, although they don't quite match up to this one,' she added, biting into her piece.

'I brought some Dundee cake as well,' Fiona said. 'I made that myself.'

'Shall we save that for this evening?' said Emily. 'Anne could make custard to go with it.'

'Suits me,' Anne said. 'As soon as we've finished our tea, I'll show Fiona to the spare bedroom.'

After they had finished, Anne took Fiona's case and showed her upstairs. Fiona's face lit up and she exclaimed with pleasure as she entered the neat little bedroom. 'What a lovely bright room!' She crossed to the window and looked out. 'I can see part of the garden and into the neighbour's one. Is that where Keith lives?'

'No,' answered Anne. 'He has an apartment in Chester and it's his sister who lives next door.'

'He knows Chester well, then,' Fiona said cheerfully. 'I can imagine his apartment will be classy.'

Anne shrugged. 'I've never seen it. It will be all show and no substance like him.'

'Oh! You sound like you don't care for him very much,' Fiona inquired as she placed her suitcase on the bed, opened it and removed a few items of clothing and her toiletry bag. 'What is it you have against him?'

'He's too full of himself.'

'Has he reason to be? Does he have a good job?'

'So I've been told,' Anne replied. 'I think I heard he's an accountant. Are you really considering going with him to Chester? What would Sandy think?'

'I think it could be a good thing if he was jealous. Maybe it would push him into realising if he doesn't make a stand against Uncle Donald and ask me to marry him, then he'll lose me.' Fiona thrust out her chin determinedly.

'I think you should consider it more carefully. I'm not sure Keith is much of a gentleman. Don't say you weren't warned!' She left Fiona to unpack the rest of her things and went into her own bedroom to change.

–

The girls went downstairs to find that Larry had come in from the shop, and that Kyle Anderson had also arrived and was invited to stay for the evening meal. Anne and Emily left the two men to talk to Fiona while they prepared the tea.

It was Kyle who brought up the topic of Miss Tillymint over their meal and told Anne that he had met Marjorie and Gordon in Newsham Park when he was on his way to the orphanage. They were both watching Robbie play football and he'd joined them. While they had been talking, he had mentioned Mary Graham and the sweet shop and to his surprise, Marjorie thought she remembered it and had told him its whereabouts. It turned out not to be far from West Derby Road, and she recalled it from when she was a young girl and was taken on a special trip to buy a twist of sherbet every now and then, although it had different owners then.

'So, where exactly is it?' asked Anne.

'On the corner of Whitefield and Belmont Road,' he said.

She felt a surge of excitement.

The conversation moved on to another subject in the headlines that was worrying Larry and that was the collapse of the London Stock Exchange following the financial crash on America's Wall Street. Larry told them many people had been ruined around the world and tough times could lie ahead, which ended the evening on a sober note.

The next day Anne was allowed time off to take Fiona to visit Teddy, Joan and Amy in Liverpool and Gordon planned to drop in during his lunch hour. Anne was intending to go to go and see if the sweet shop was still in business, leaving Fiona to spend more time with the family – Fiona received a warm welcome on their arrival, but Anne only stayed a short time before making her excuses.

When Anne arrived at the shop she was delighted to find it was still open; a bell tinkled as she entered Miss Tillymint's Sweet Treats. The interior was small and dim but smelled deliciously of mints, pear drops, chocolate and all manner of sugary confections. On the wall behind the counter were shelves of glass bottles containing boiled sweets in all the colours of the rainbow and Anne immediately spotted a jar of her own favourites.

'Excuse me,' she said, clearing her throat a little. 'Could I have a quarter of the Barker & Dobson chocolate dragees?'

The woman behind the counter was bent over but she looked up and stared at Anne. Her grey eyes were sharp in her lined face, which was topped by Marcel-waved greying brown hair. She spoke with a faint Scottish accent.

'Yes, dearie. Let me get those for you.'

As Anne watched her weigh out the sweets in a metal pan on a set of scales, she asked her where in Scotland she was from. 'Because I was up in Scotland not so long ago visiting family. I went to Greenock, Loch Lomond, Helenburgh and Cardross.'

The woman straightened up. 'My friend who owned the shop with me had cousins who lived in the Cardross area. It's a small world.'

'You can say that again,' Anne said. 'What was your friend's name?'

'Mary Graham, but she died some time ago.'

Anne's heart sank a little, feeling sad that the woman who had most likely been her aunt was dead. 'Why did you leave Scotland and come to Liverpool?' she asked, taking the bag of sweets and handing over the money for them.

'Mary wanted to trace the twin sister she had fallen out with. Her name was Anne and she'd stormed out of the family home after a row and they'd never heard from her after that.'

'Did Mary find her?'

'No, despite getting in touch with relatives down here, she was unable to trace her. She decided not to return to Scotland and when war broke out. The pair of us joined the auxiliary nursing corps and ended up working in a hospital here in Liverpool right up until the end of the war.'

Anne remembered hearing that a school close to her old home had been used as a hospital at one time. She had the idea of asking whether Miss Tillymint had a photograph of Mary and did so. She received an odd look in return and had to think up a reason for asking in a hurry. 'I just thought if she was looking for her twin, who I presume is identical, then I might recognise her, having lived in Liverpool all my life.'

Miss Tillymint smiled. 'Now there's a thought, although it's too late now for Mary.'

'Is it too late for the rest of their family, though?' asked Anne, feeling slightly guilty, knowing that if this was the right Anne, she had long since passed away. Anne hoped Anne had been united with her twin in Heaven.

'If you'll wait a moment,' Miss Tillymint said. 'I'll go and get one.'

She did not have to wait long before Miss Tillymint reappeared with a sepia-tinted photograph in her hand. She handed it to Anne, who gazed down at two young women in nurse's uniforms. One was clearly the woman on the other side of the counter and the other had to be Mary Graham. As Anne bent forward to have a clearer look at the photograph, the amulet that Lil had given her dangled in front of her open coat.

Miss Tillymint's eyes widened. 'Where did you get that?' she asked, touching the amulet lightly.

'I was given it by a friend of my mother. I believe it was made in Scotland.'

'I've seen one the same – or very like it. What was your mother's name, dearie?'

Anne could feel her heart beating fast. She took a deep breath. 'I believe it to be Anne Graham,' she said breathlessly. 'I never knew her. She died after giving birth to me.'

Miss Tillymint sagged against the counter. 'You're not having me on, are ye?'

'No. Kyle Anderson told me about Mary and your sweet shop. I'm so glad you were able to show me a photo of her and I'm sorry for being secretive. I wanted to be sure first before saying anything.'

'Of course, I understand. Anne and Mary would be roughly the same age as you in that photo,' Miss Tillymint said.

Anne nodded, gazing down at the photo again. 'I'll be seventeen next February. I was adopted,' she added. 'It's only recently I discovered who my birth mother was.'

They talked for a while longer before Anne brought the conversation to an end by asking for a quarter of pear drops. She promised to call again with an invitation to her wedding and then left.

It was only later that she realised that she had not mentioned Hugh. She had been told she could keep the photo of Mary, thrilled that she now had a good idea of her own mother's appearance.

Anne showed the photo around when she arrived back at Teddy's, to everyone's great excitement, and soon after she and Fiona left and returned to Eastham.

'So, what sweets did you buy?' Emily asked as soon as they were indoors and Anne had removed her coat and hat.

Anne bent down and picked up a note which she'd found on the doormat. She handed it to Fiona. 'It's addressed to you and has Keith's name on the back.'

Fiona slipped the note into the pocket of her dress. Anne handed Emily the bag of pear drops. She and Fiona had already consumed all the dragees on the journey home.

They were glad to put their feet up and filled Larry and Emily in on all the day's events. Emily listened with interest as she sucked on a pear drop noisily, before crunching and swallowing it. 'It's a good thing that they had their own business like that and didn't need a man to manage their affairs. I was recently reading an article about women's progress and where their struggle for freedom takes them.'

'Well, it took Miss Tillymint from Scotland to Liverpool and being her own boss,' said Anne. 'She's quite nice looking and hasn't lost her Scottish accent. She and Mary had been nurses in a hospital in a school towards the end of the war. I wondered if they could have been at Loraine Street School? I have vague memories of being told that during the war, the school was closed for lessons and wounded American soldiers were housed in the building.'

Emily said, 'You're right. I'd forgotten about it until you mentioned it, Anne. There was another article with the headline "Do you need a servant?" There's such a shortage that the government is talking about training more girls for the job.'

'They haven't got a hope,' Anne said. 'Girls don't want to slave away for the upper classes these days when they can be paid more for working in a factory.'

'Some factories could close down because of all the financial uncertainty,' said Larry.

'And some of the upper classes mightn't be able to afford to hire servants if they've invested in stocks and shares,' Emily said. 'The British stock market has been badly affected by what's happened in America.'

'Is there anything in what Miss Tillymint told you that will help you find out who your father was?' asked Fiona.

Anne said, 'I don't know. I've other things to think about right now – such as our trip to Rhyl tomorrow. I need to pack a few things.'

'I need to sort out a few things to take, too,' said Fiona. 'It shouldn't take me long.' She patted the letter in her pocket. 'Keith has suggested picking me up at seven and taking me to Chester to see a film and to show me around the city afterwards.'

Anne pushed down the urge to tell Fiona not to go, because she could see the girl's mind was made up.

Chapter Twenty Four

The following morning was a fine clear early November day, although it was much colder than of late, but at least it was not foggy. Larry had already lit the fire and the kettle had boiled when Anne came downstairs. She made a pot of tea and some porridge and went upstairs to wake up their guest to tell her that breakfast was ready. Fiona was already awake and getting dressed.

'I'll be down in five minutes,' she said.

'Good. We don't want to miss the connection at Chester. How was your evening with Keith?' asked Anne, who had been in bed by the time Fiona had arrived home.

'The least said about that the better,' Fiona said stiffly.

Anne said, 'That sounds as if you didn't enjoy yourself.'

'That's an understatement, but I'd better get ready instead of standing here chatting.'

Anne thought she'd let Fiona get ready and try to find out what had happened on their journey to Rhyl; it sounded like her worst suspicions had been right.

—

As soon as they crossed the border into Wales, Anne said, 'So, what was the film like?'

'It was a talkie and quite scary, directed by Alfred Hitchcock and called *Blackmail*.'

'Did Keith take you for a meal afterwards?' Anne asked softly.

Fiona gazed about the carriage which they had to themselves. 'I just knew you'd bring him up again.'

'Well, of course I'm curious, so tell me what happened? Was it a fancy restaurant?'

'He took me to his apartment which was quite classy and said he was going to cook dinner for me – but then he made improper advances, so while he was pouring drinks, I escaped.' Fiona shuddered. 'I think he wanted to get me drunk and I hardly ever drink alcohol. I'm glad I'm going to Rhyl and when I return, I'll go and stay with Teddy, so there's no chance of my seeing Keith again.' She paused. 'I'm sorry I didn't listen to you. You were right about him.'

'That's alright,' said Anne. 'He seems charming but he's a bit of a cad. Maybe you'll be better off with your Sandy?'

'If only he'd stand up to Uncle Donald… but I don't want to think about that now.'

'I hope you and Sandy will sort your difficulties out and can both come to my wedding,' Anne said.

Fiona huffed, folded her arms across her breasts and fell silent as she gazed out of the window.

Anne took out her library book and began to read.

Albert was at the station to meet them in a large Wolseley. He greeted them with a hug and a kiss. 'It's marvellous to see you both,' he said, taking their baggage and stowing it in the boot. He helped Fiona into the front passenger seat and Anne climbed into the back.

She sat quietly, listening to Albert and Fiona's conversation, which was all about the running of the hotel, and she concluded the place was doing well.

The hotel was not too far from the station and when the car drew up outside the cream and pale-green façade, Anne climbed out of the car and remembered how Sylvia had approved of Albert and how he had gone up in the world. Looking at the impressive building she couldn't help but agree.

'When was the hotel built?' Anne asked. 'It's larger than I thought it would be.'

'It's wonderful,' said Fiona. 'I can't wait to see inside.'

'It was built during the Edwardian period,' Albert replied, removing their baggage from the boot. 'There are photographs of its early days on the walls inside; the guests find them fascinating.'

'You should put on an Edwardian evening where guests and staff can dress up in the style of the times, and there can be dancing and other entertainments of the period,' suggested Fiona.

'It was very rundown when we bought it and we've spent a fortune on doing it up,' he said. 'We need it to start making some real money for us now.'

'Make it a Christmas charity event, say for the RLI, seeing as Rhyl is a seaside place; you'll get a good crowd who'll pay a fair price for the tickets,' Fiona said. 'You can take out your expenses but most of the profit can go to the charity. You'll make a good name for yourself as well as useful contacts. Such an event will be a great advertisement for the hotel.'

'Lifeboats are a good cause,' said Anne. 'But how did you come up with such an idea living in the back of beyond, Fiona?'

'Winter is the time when we can't be out in the fresh air so much, so there's plenty of get-togethers going on,' she answered mildly. 'In Scotland, we make a big fuss of Hogmanay and Burns Night, so that's when there's money to be made and charity dos are popular.'

Anne could understand that but thought from Fiona and Albert's conversation that it was clear they must have been in touch quite frequently. Why hadn't Fiona told her more about them being in touch? Anne gazed about her at how bright and clean the area was and she was about to ask after Gladys when she appeared, coming down the stairway that curved up and out of sight to the upper floors.

'You've arrived,' cried Gladys, descending the stairs with her arms outstretched.

Anne leaned towards her and felt compelled to kiss her powdered cheek. 'You're looking well, Gladys,' she said.

'So are you.' Gladys held her at arms' length. 'Is that due to life going your way at last?'

'Then you've heard that Andrew and I are engaged?'

Gladys nodded.

'But did you know,' Anne continued, 'that we've also traced the real Jane Fraser and I now know the identity of my mother?' She was aware that Albert's expression had changed, and he was looking stern.

'I think it's very exciting,' Fiona said. 'And Anne Graham being your mother explains our resemblance to each other and to Grandmother perfectly.'

'It's good to have that sorted out,' Albert agreed. 'Now there's no need for any more detective work, Anne. You know who you are. But we need to discuss this engagement of yours.'

'I couldn't agree more,' said Anne. 'I only wish I knew the identity of my natural father,' she added. 'Despite him never being able to match up to the man who adopted me.'

'Let's not stir up sad memories when we have so much to celebrate,' said Albert, seemingly keen to change the subject.

'Don't worry, I'm not going to rattle on about it,' Anne said. 'Did you know that Gordon plans on getting married next year too?'

'We did hear that he'll be moving out of Teddy and Joan's,' Gladys said.

'Joan writes to you?' exclaimed Anne.

Gladys's carefully pencilled eyebrow elevated towards her forehead. 'Our husbands are brothers, so why shouldn't she? She's thinking of taking in a lodger when Gordon leaves, or moving somewhere smaller.'

'That doesn't surprise me,' Anne said. 'She'll miss his money.'

'It's possible he mightn't have a job by the time he gets married,' Albert said. 'The country's economy is in a mess.'

'Larry was saying something of the sort last evening,' Anne said. 'Trade's going to be affected which means shipping and the docks will be in trouble. Marjorie works for Nelson's Jam Factory. I should imagine she'll still keep her job, as soft fruits grow over here, and people will always want jam!

She gazed at Albert. 'You've grown a moustache, big brother. Why?' As the words slipped out, she saw an expression in his eyes that she had not seen for a while and she realised that she had not called him brother for a long time.

He drew her hand through his arm, saying, 'Let's go to our private quarters and we can have a good natter and a cuppa.'

—

No sooner were Anne and Albert settled on a sofa inside the cosy living room on the top floor, with its view over the rooftops towards a glistening horizon, than tea was poured. A couple of plates of sandwiches and cakes were set on an occasional table and Gladys and Fiona left them alone to talk. The sash window was open, and shouts and cries of enjoyment could be heard coming from the fairground on the breeze that fluttered through the curtains.

'So, how does Emily feel about your marrying Andrew Fraser and moving to London?' Albert asked.

'We'll miss each other, but she does have Larry,' Anne said, staring at him, fascinated by his moustache. He was staring at her now as if waiting for her to say something more. 'I do need your permission to marry next Easter. I hope you'll be generous enough to agree and give me away.' She paused but he did not reply, so she changed the subject. 'So, you and Gladys seem taken with Fiona. Did you start keeping in touch after my visit there?'

'She got in touch with us.' Slowly, he said, 'I wrote to her when you told me she was coming to Liverpool. She wrote back, saying she needed to get away as she felt she was being taken for granted at home by her boyfriend. I suggested she come here for a long stay as business is quiet in the winter and she could do a little work for us here at the hotel.'

'I see,' said Anne slowly. 'There's something else I wanted to ask you about – Dad's small suitcase. I'd like a look through the things inside. I'd like to know if there was any other paperwork to do with my birth and adoption.'

'I think it was left in the old house,' Albert said, quite evasively she thought, as he gazed at a point above her head. 'Ask Teddy.'

Anne knew he was lying, remembering him carrying it out when he had left for Rhyl at one time. Suspicious about his reasons for denial, she allowed the subject to drop but was determined to find the suitcase and have a look inside before she went home. She changed the subject. 'Thinking of Fiona, why did she go off with Gladys instead of staying with us and having a chat with you? I thought the aim of her coming here was to get to know you better.'

Albert looked relieved. 'Gladys will have more to do with Fiona and wants her to take some of the hotel house-keeping off her shoulders. She's going to stay here and work in the hotel for a while.'

Anne thought of Uncle Donald and Sandy worrying about Fiona when she did not return, although perhaps after a while of life in the hotel, she would tire of running around after people and being ordered about by Gladys; she'd be swapping one kind of drudgery for another. Still, Anne wondered whether she should get in touch with Uncle Donald as Fiona was meant to be her guest and not Albert's. Perhaps it would be best if she phoned Larry and Emily to ask their thoughts on the situation and maybe Emily could phone Uncle Donald. She had great faith in Larry's common sense and having made that decision, she said, 'Would you mind if I went out now and had a walk on the front for some sea air? I might have a look around the fair, too.'

Albert said, 'Perhaps Fiona would like to go with you? We can go and find her, and I can show you to your bedroom at the same time.'

'I'd like that,' she lied, wondering what it was her brother was keeping from her.

They left the room and went in search of Fiona and Gladys, whom they found in a twin-bedded room on the third floor. 'I thought you girls would like to be together,' Gladys said, turning to face Anne squarely. 'Fiona's just been telling me about Miss Tillymint's sweet shop and the Graham twins.'

'What's this about the Graham twins?' Albert asked, his voice ending on a higher note than usual.

Anne stared at him. 'Did you ever meet them?'

'No, but I remember Mother and Da talking about them years ago before the war. Da thought he'd recognised one of the sisters coming out of the post office on Breck Road, but she had crossed the road and was lost in the crowds going to the football match before he could catch up with her.'

'I don't suppose he recognised which one it was, did he?' Anne asked.

'Not that I remember,' Albert said, sitting on one of the beds. 'I wasn't that interested, but if they were identical twins he wouldn't have been able to tell the difference, would he?'

'I suppose not,' Anne said. 'Anyway, I came up here to ask if Fiona wanted to go for a walk to the seafront.' She glanced at Fiona.

Fiona stared at Gladys. 'Do you need me?'

Gladys said, 'Go and have some fresh air. It'll do you good. We can talk some more later.'

The two girls went off towards the seafront and the attractions, both silent until they came in sight of the sea.

'I suppose you're wondering what Gladys and I can have to talk about?' said Fiona.

'I already know. Albert told me because I was curious about you going off with Gladys instead of staying to talk to him. I can't understand why you didn't mention it to me.' Anne held her face up to the sun, which had a hint of warmth despite the time of year, and took a deep breath. 'I wouldn't mind staying a bit longer myself, but I've had enough time off and need to pull my weight.'

'Shame,' said Fiona. 'But no doubt there'll be another opportunity for us to spend time together.'

Anne stared at her. 'No doubt. Shall we go on the beach now and walk along the water's edge?' There was a bad atmosphere between them now, Anne thought. All the secrecy around Fiona coming here and no one telling her what was going on had made her feel cross with her.

'The water will be freezing,' Fiona said.

'We don't have to go in, just get close enough to watch the waves.' Seagulls wheeled overhead, screeching raucously, and Anne's mind drifted back to her conversation with Albert and how he had not answered her request for his consent to her marriage to Andrew.

Anne was brought back to the present by a shout from Fiona warning her that a big wave was coming. Anne stepped back swiftly but even so, her shoes still got wet. They made their way back to the hotel as the sky was starting to cloud over and the wind was even chillier than earlier.

Gladys was on reception and, after asking if they'd enjoyed themselves, she suggested Fiona join her, so she could instruct her in the role of receptionist. Albert was nowhere to be seen and Gladys told them that he had gone to a meeting with some members of the Rotary Club. Anne had the perfect excuse to go upstairs and, having been shown earlier where their bedroom was, she changed her shoes and stockings and made her way to the couple's private rooms. It did not take her long to spot Hugh's case on top of a wardrobe and, with difficulty, she managed to get it down by herself. She was fortunate enough to discover a large envelope with 'Da's' written on it. She glanced only briefly at the papers and letters inside before returning the case to the top of the wardrobe and stuffing the envelope down the front of her dress. Then she left the bedroom hastily and returned to the bedroom she shared with Fiona, placing the envelope under the possessions in her holdall.

That evening Anne sat in the guest's lounge, drinking a glass of dandelion and burdock, reading her book and people-watching. Two men and two women sat at a table playing cards and two middle-aged women were knitting and talking in low voices. There was also a good-looking lone male with a moustache and slicked-back dark hair that glistened with pomade beneath the light from a floor lamp behind his easy chair. He was smoking a cheroot while reading a newspaper.

As if sensing her eyes upon him, he lifted his head and glanced in her direction. He smiled. Embarrassed by being caught out staring at him, Anne lowered her gaze to the open pages of her library book before shortly feeling a hand on her shoulder.

It was Fiona who said, 'Interesting book?'

'Yes, it's a murder mystery set on the French Riviera.'

'I bet the weather is hotter there than here,' Fiona said.

'According to the British detective it's too hot – "blistering".' Anne placed a finger between the pages of the book to mark her place and found herself saying the thing that had been bothering her all day. 'I can't understand you wanting to work for Gladys and Albert. It looks to me that you'll be nothing more than a glorified housekeeper.'

Fiona looked shocked. 'You've stayed at the farm. You must see the difference between there and here? Gladys appreciates me already. She told me she had a younger cousin who she was very fond of, who I remind her of. The cousin died of influenza during the epidemic towards the end of the war and she still misses her.'

'It's the first time I've heard of a cousin. Perhaps she sees you as a sort of replacement?'

'I thought of that myself but I doubt I'd lose by it if I stayed on here longer than I first thought of doing. They have no children, so they might see me as someone worth encouraging to take over the hotel in the future.'

'You mean when they're getting too old to do any of the work themselves?'

Fiona stared at Anne. 'I don't understand why you're being so nasty about me working for them.'

'It's been kept so secret. Neither you nor they have mentioned it to me or any of the family in Liverpool, never mind Uncle Donald or Sandy.'

'Uncle Donald and Sandy will know soon enough if they miss me and can be bothered to get in touch. Anyway, I don't see how it's any of your business. You kept being adopted a secret from me and Uncle Donald when we first met.' Fiona took a deep breath. 'Anyway, I was that fed up of them and my life, I felt desperate and had to do something to make them sit up.' Fiona looked sincere and so unhappy. 'I like life in the country, but it's hard on the farm and no one ever shows me any appreciation.'

It was at that point that Anne made up her mind not to interfere for the moment.

Fiona stared at her. 'Nothing else to say?'

Anne shook her head. 'It's your life. You're right, I should mind my own business.'

Fiona smiled in a conciliatory fashion. 'I want us to remain friends and I just have to try this. The surroundings are a lot more tasteful than the farmhouse and I could do with a bit of glamour in my life. You know what people say – a change is as good as a rest. And with that in mind – who's this person coming over?'

Anne glanced at the man who was the focus of Fiona's attention and saw that he was the one she had been staring at earlier. 'I haven't the foggiest,' she said.

'Tall, dark and handsome,' murmured Fiona. 'Shall we introduce ourselves?'

The man stopped a foot or so away from them. 'Good evening, ladies!' he said with the smallest of bows. 'May I introduce myself? I am Michael Lancaster, travelling salesman of textiles, the best of bedlinen and tableware.'

'You have a wooly back accent, which means you're from up in Lancashire,' Anne said thoughtlessly.

His handsome features changed. 'And you're a Scouser, if I'm not mistaken.'

'I'm a Liverpudlian,' said Anne cheerfully. 'I'm Anne Anderson and this is my cousin, Fiona, from Scotland.'

'Am I right in thinking, ladies, that you are related to the owner of this establishment?'

'You are indeed, Mr Lancaster,' Fiona answered. 'And I will be working here for a while, although Anne will be returning to the Wirral where she now lives.'

'I'll be leaving tomorrow,' said Mr Lancaster. 'But I'll be back in a week or so.'

'So, am I to presume this hotel is one of your regular stopovers?' questioned Fiona.

'It certainly is,' he replied. 'So, I look forward to seeing you next time I'm here.' Mr Lancaster inclined his gleaming dark head.

While this exchange had been going on between the man and Fiona, Anne had settled herself comfortably with her book again, despite still listening to what they were saying. She thought of Uncle Donald and Sandy and hoped they would put a spoke in the polished Mr Lancaster's plans because she did not trust him. She could only hope Fiona had learnt her lesson from the incident with Keith, though she seemed all too keen to make friends with men she barely knew – Fiona must be desperate for a bit of excitement, she thought. Surely Albert and Gladys would keep an eye on her to see she came to no harm?

Chapter Twenty Five

Anne was glad to arrive home at Eastham, having felt on edge in case Albert discovered the envelope was missing, guessing he would immediately suspect her of having taken it. She had resisted taking it out on the train, wanting to be alone when she read what was inside. She had brought up the subject again of having his permission for her to marry Andrew next Easter, but he had replied that he needed more time to think about it. She had only just managed to control her temper.

Fiona had seemed happy when they had parted and was excitedly looking forward to helping at the hotel. Anne still had her reservations, knowing that the shine could easily come off life with Albert and Gladys, but Fiona surely had to find that out for herself.

That night, she wasted no time in emptying the contents of the brown envelope onto her bed. There were some photographs, so she removed them first and set them aside as she looked through it all. Eventually, she found a studio portrait of a young girl whom she took to be the young sister, Janet, who had died of pneumonia. Then she came to a photo of two young women – one was Fiona's mother, Catrina, who she recognised from the photograph album Uncle Donald had shown her, and the other was either Anne Graham or Mary, and there was a young man who reminded her of Hugh and in the background was an ocean liner. Her heart began to beat faster and her hand shook as she turned it over and read the inscription on the back with names, the place and the date the photograph was taken. This told her that it was likely to have been the day Fiona's mother had departed for Canada and she wondered why Catrina had never written to her daughter. The other girl was indeed Anne Graham. She could only think that they had asked a passer-by to take the photograph, but what were Hugh and Anne doing together and this photo in his stuff. She took a deep breath as she searched for an unused envelope amongst the various papers, and placed the photo inside the one she found, and tucked it safely inside her handbag.

Most of the letters appeared to be from his mother and brothers in Scotland, telling him their latest news and asking after him and his family, although there were others there too; the odd one from the Graham cousins, including Anne and Mary's mother, asking if Anne had been in touch with him, as well as Kyle Anderson senior, and a man called Alex Murray. There were even a couple from Catrina in Canada. It was obvious that the family had attempted to keep in touch with Hugh. There were also a few letters from Albert when he was in the army.

She was about to begin her exploration of the businesslike documents when the bedroom door opened. Immediately Anne threw the eiderdown over the clutter on the bed and closed her eyes, pretending to be resting.

Emily called out, 'Are you all right?'

'Just tired,' Anne said.

'Good night, God bless,' Emily said, closing the door.

Anne breathed a sigh of relief and picked up the top document which appeared to be Sylvia's will. She could not resist reading it and then re-reading it because this one mentioned her as Sylvia's adopted daughter and as one of the beneficiaries. This meant Albert had kept money from her and she felt anger boiling inside her. Only when she calmed down slightly did she ask herself why he'd cheated her out of an inheritance. Could it simply be because he needed as much money as he could lay his hands on for the hotel? Or did he believe she had no right to it because she was adopted? Or could there be a deeper reason? She knew that she was going to have to confront him about the matter soon because surely this would give her some leverage when it came to him agreeing to consent to her marriage. She turned back to the other letters and removed the ones from Alex Murray, with postmarks from both Glasgow in the earlier ones and Edinburgh in the later ones, and there was an Edinburgh address.

Taking them in order she began to read and it was obvious from the tone of the letters that they had been close friends, closer even than Hugh and his brothers, although there had been a time when obviously Donald had spent time with them. It was fishing that had caused a rift between Alex and Donald due to Alex having caught a trout called the Big Un; they had laid bets on who would catch it. Apparently, Alex had caught it when the brothers had been away, and Donald had called him a cheat, accusing him of using a worm which was not allowed in fly-fishing. Alex had denied it. Hugh had accepted his word, but Donald had not, and it had marred the friendship. Anne thought how silly it was to fall out over a fish, but then men did take sport seriously. Still, it was a pathetic reason and, she thought, unworthy of Donald. Girls had occasionally been mentioned, one of them being Anne Graham. In later letters Anne Graham figured more frequently and Anne was astounded to discover that there had been a relationship between Hugh and Anne. It was clear from the letters between Hugh and Alex that Anne's parents had wholly disapproved of the liaison between them because they were second cousins. Eventually Hugh had left Scotland for Liverpool, not only in search of work but to try and forget Anne. There the trail had ended, and Hugh settled in the city, and having given up all hope of marrying Anne, had made a marriage of convenience. She came across a letter between Hugh and Alex, in which Alex referred to the fact that several years later Anne had arrived in Liverpool and she and Hugh had come face to face in the pub where she worked and after that they had met regularly.

Anne continued to read with growing excitement – was it possible that her adoptive father was her natural father? If that was so, did it mean he had known she was his daughter when he had taken her, despite having been told that she was Jane Fraser? Her head was buzzing, and she knew that she would need positive proof that Hugh was her natural father before rejoicing.

She decided to write to Alex Murray at the address at the top of the letter in the hope that he could tell her more. She posted her letter the following morning, then tried to put it to the back of her mind.

Chapter Twenty Six

A week later, Emily told Anne that there had been a phone call from Uncle Donald, saying that he was coming down from Scotland and bringing two guests from Canada with him. They would only be in Eastham for a short time as they were desperate to speak to Fiona, so would be going on to Rhyl.

Anne was flabbergasted. Having been through Hugh's papers, the only conclusion she could come to concerning the visitors from Canada was that one of them must be Fiona's mother. 'Did you tell Uncle Donald that Fiona is in Rhyl staying with Albert?' she said.

'I didn't have to,' Emily said. 'She'd written to him.'

Anne mulled this over while she made herself a cup of tea and a slice of toast before going to work in the shop. Once there she told Larry about her suspicions regarding one of the guests from Canada, as well as what was going on in Rhyl concerning Fiona. He seemed more amused than shocked. 'Well, Albert and Gladys are in for a shock and no doubt so is Fiona. As Robbie Burns wrote, "The best laid schemes o' mice and men"…' He paused. 'I can't quite remember how the rest goes, but he's saying things don't always go right.'

Anne could only agree with him and await the arrival of Uncle Donald and his guests. They arrived just before tea-time. Anne immediately recognized Fiona's mother from the photograph but was stunned when she introduced the young man with her as her son Ranald. He had a shock of wiry black hair and brown eyes like his mother's, though his strong features and a square, chiselled jaw bore a marked resemblance to the Anderson family.

Larry suggested that they stay overnight and on the morrow motor to Rhyl to see Fiona there.

Anne said, 'I'd love to go with you so I can see Fiona's expression when she sets eyes on her mother and brother. But I've had enough time off already.' She glanced at Larry as she spoke.

He sighed. 'You go. I understand how you feel.'

Anne jumped to her feet and kissed him. 'You're the most wonderful brother-in-law ever!' She decided to give up her bed to Catrina and sleep on the sofa. Donald and Ranald could share the spare room.

'There's no need for the soft-soap,' Larry said, but looked gratified all the same.

'It will be a pleasure to have your company,' Fiona's mother, Catrina, said.

–

The following morning Catrina, Ranald and Anne set out for Rhyl in Donald's car. Anne and Ranald sat in the front and Catrina in the rear. Donald had said the journey from Scotland had tired him out and so he would wait and see Fiona another day. Anne could scarcely believe what Donald had said and she began to wonder if she had been mistaken about his character when in Scotland. Anne and Ranald talked intermittently about the weather and the landscape as well as Ontario and Nova Scotia; the latter was where Catrina and her son had moved to after the death of her brother, preferring to be on the east coast rather than the west, so far away from Scotland.

'It was then I began to get an urge to visit the old country,' Ranald said. 'Isn't that a fact, Mom? Although I was born in Canada I knew my ancestry was back in Scotland. Mom told me she had left the family farm because she hated the life, but I sensed she wasn't being honest with me – especially when she appeared reasonably content living on my uncle's farm. After he died, though, my aunt sold the farm and she and her daughters moved to the Pacific coast nearer to where her sister lived, but Mom didn't want to be so far from the old country, so we settled in Halifax on Nova Scotia. Actually, there's another Liverpool further down the coast from where we lived.'

Anne was interested in all Ranald had to say but mostly she wanted to know if he had discovered what his mother had been keeping from him. 'When you arrived in Scotland, what was it like? Did you find answers to the questions you had about your mother and what she might not be telling you?'

He glanced over his shoulder at his mother and saw that she had dozed off. Even so, he lowered his voice. 'She told me that her husband, supposedly my father Jamie, had died, and it was true that he had done so, but I discovered that his death didn't occur until *after* Mom had left Scotland. She didn't know he was dead until a while after he died. Uncle Donald had written to her shortly after Jamie died but she did not receive his letter because of the move. His letter had been redirected to my aunt's new address on the Pacific coast. She redirected it to Nova Scotia, but all this took time.'

'How did Uncle Donald greet the pair of you when you turned up at the farm in Scotland?'

'With open arms,' Ranald said.

'You do surprise me,' she said. 'I thought he had no time for your mother.'

'That was to disguise how he actually felt about her.' Ranald gulped. 'Brace yourself as what I'm going to tell you will come as a bit of a shock.' He hesitated before taking a deep breath, and carried on. 'The fact is, Uncle Donald is my father and not Jamie. When I pressed Mom, she came clean – I think it had been preying on her mind. Over the last few years she has felt a strong need to come back and make things right, if she could, with her daughter Fiona.'

Anne could barely believe it, then remembered Uncle Donald's face as he'd looked at the photograph of Catrina.

'Donald... I mean Dad... and my Mom grew very fond of each other after his brother Jamie married her and brought her to live on the farm. Their feelings became something they couldn't ignore and despite both trying to suppress their emotions, their feelings overcame them when they were alone one time. After that she knew she had to get away from the farm, so she made visiting her sick brother in Canada her excuse, leaving her daughter behind with Jamie, believing that she was a bad wife and mother and that she was doing them all a favour by taking herself out of their lives. It was only after she left that she realised she was pregnant with me.'

'How could she be so sure that you were Uncle Donald's child?' asked a stunned Anne.

'Because her husband had been away at an agricultural show for a while before.'

'So, what will happen now? Will you and your mother be settling in Scotland?' Anne asked.

'You bet! Mom's just praying that Fiona will forgive her when she tells her the whole story. Mom did write to her, but Fiona never replied.'

Anne prayed that Fiona would find it in her heart to forgive her mother and Donald. She had suffered without a mother's love. Would this change Fiona's plans to stay on at the hotel?

Anne could feel the tension in the car growing as they got closer to their destination. There was a real possibility that Fiona would reject her mother and Anne could only hope that she would give Catrina a chance to explain.

–

The car had barely drawn to a halt outside the hotel when Fiona and Albert emerged from the entrance. As Ranald assisted his mother from the car, Anne, who had already climbed out, was aware of Albert drawing in his breath with a hiss. She stared at him, wondering if he recognised the woman, and if so then he realised his plans to have Fiona working at the hotel could come to naught, then Anne's gaze passed on to Fiona's face. It was clear that Fiona recognised her mother and to say that she received a tremendous shock would have been an understatement because a moment later she slid to the ground in a dead faint. Albert barely had the chance to move before Ranald and his mother hurried to Fiona's side.

Fiona was only unconscious for a short time before her eyelids fluttered open and she looked up at her mother, and then her gaze took in Ranald's face too. 'Mother?

271

What is going on? Who is this?' she asked in a voice barely above a whisper.

'Fiona, I'm sorry to have given you such a fright. This is your half-brother, Ranald,' she said.

Fiona's brow puckered. 'I don't have a half-brother! What is happening?' Suddenly she glanced over his shoulder and saw Anne. 'Anne, what are you doing here? I thought you went back to Emily and Larry's.'

'I did but I'm back here in Rhyl with Ranald and your mother,' Anne responded, moving towards her. 'First, let's get you off the ground and inside before you catch a chill.'

'Are you sure I'm not dreaming?' Fiona said. 'How can Mum be here? She's dead – and that lad, he can't be my half-brother. And where's Uncle Donald?'

'Back home with Emily and Larry,' said Anne. 'It surprised me, too, that he stayed behind. I thought his reason of being tired after the journey from Scotland was a feeble reason.'

Before she could say any more, Albert stepped forward and helped Ranald and his mother hoist Fiona to her feet. 'She's confused,' he said. 'That doesn't surprise me, Aunt Catrina.'

'I can do all the explaining that's necessary, Albert,' said Fiona's mother tightly. 'But not out here and only to my daughter.'

'You two know each other?' Anne said.

'Of course,' she said with a sniff. 'He was hanging around when Anne and Hugh waved me off on the liner to Canada. My brother had been at death's door and I'd been wanting to visit him for a while but never had the money or the opportunity. Fortunately, he was fighting back and was improving, so Donald gave me the money for my fare, so off I went.'

Catrina placed a trembling hand on her daughter's pale cheek. 'I'm truly sorry for giving you such a shock and for all the distress I've caused you. Please forgive me.'

'You're asking a lot,' said Fiona, struggling to remain upright. Her three helpers almost dropped her in their haste to help her. 'This is ridiculous,' she said. 'I'm quite able to stand. Let go of me. Mother, you've been gone for ages and never wrote to me.' Slowly, Fiona made her way, slightly wobbly, to the entrance and through the doors, closely followed by her mother, Ranald, Anne and Albert. Fiona went over to a sofa in the reception area and sat down, placing her head in her hands. Gladys came from behind and sat next to her, putting an arm about her shoulders.

'What's wrong, dear?'

It was Albert who said, 'She's had a shock, Gladys. Her mother and her half-brother, who she didn't know existed, have just turned up along with Anne.'

Gladys glanced at the figures clustered around her husband. 'I don't understand. I thought her mother was dead.'

Fiona lifted her head. 'I just presumed it when the years went by and we heard nothing from her.'

'So, what's her excuse?' Gladys asked.

'I don't see how that's any of your business,' Catrina said coldly. 'And I did write to her. I can only believe Jamie picked up the letter first. Read it and didn't give it to her but destroyed it.'

'Why should Dad have done that?' said Fiona hotly. 'You're just making excuses when he's not here to defend himself.'

'You have every right to be angry with me,' said Catrina, composing herself. 'Only please give me the opportunity to explain in private?'

'I think that makes sense,' Anne said. 'Perhaps you should take your mother up to your room, Fiona?'

Fiona did not respond straightaway and then she rose from the sofa and said, 'Come this way.'

Albert made to protest by standing in their way, but Gladys drew him back.

Anne would have loved to listen in on Fiona and Catrina's conversation but knew this was one of those moments when it would be a mistake to intrude. No doubt she would discover later some of what passed between mother and daughter, and she could question Fiona's mother about the matter, which was close to her own heart. In the meantime, she would ask Ranald whether he would like to go with her for a walk. He'd probably be ready for some fresh air and exercise after the journey.

It was as she thought, and soon they were making their way along the seafront, though neither had spoken since leaving the hotel. Now Ranald said, 'Jeez, I never thought Fiona would pass out like that. I didn't think I looked so scary.'

'Of course you don't, it was just the shock. You heard Fiona – she had come to believe her mother was dead. Much easier than believing she had just deserted her.'

'Hopefully, once Fiona knows the truth that Mom and Donald had fallen for each other, she'll understand that Mom had to stay away,' he said.

Anne said, 'Let's hope so, but it will still take some getting used to.'

Ranald nodded and thanked her for making him feel welcome. He and Anne walked some more, enjoying the fresh air before returning to the hotel where they found Catrina, Fiona, Albert and Gladys waiting for their return.

It far from settled what Fiona would do with her future now her mother had returned, but whatever had passed between mother and daughter in private had gone some way to ease Fiona's anger and resentment at Catrina. Maybe time would be the healer, Anne thought.

As the day drew on and the time came for Anne to return to Eastham, it became obvious to her that Fiona was not going to be rushed into making any hasty decisions. Catrina and Ranald decided to stay on in Rhyl and before Anne left Fiona drew her aside and told her some of what her mother had said. 'She told me that she had written to me explaining about her and Uncle Donald falling in love and that her staying away was because of that. She did eventually write to me and tell me about it, but I never received her letter. Dad must have picked it up, recognised her writing and read it. Naturally, he was furious and confronted Donald, but he never forgave them, and Donald believes he couldn't get it out of his mind so he lost his powers of concentration and that was what caused the accident that killed Dad. Donald blamed himself and thought he didn't deserve to be happy, so he didn't tell Mum straightaway about Jamie's death and ask her and Ranald to come home, but eventually time worked its healing and he wrote to her. She believes he stayed behind at Emily's because he was worked up about facing me and didn't want to meet here at the hotel. We've grown close over the years and he didn't want to lose my affection, believing him to be a cad and would never forgive him. She said that he'd never really recovered completely from the early death of his sister, Janet, but that I'd gone some way to fill the space that her death had left. It's partly the reason why he's hesitated to agree to Sandy and I getting married, but now things have changed, who's to say what might happen next?'

Anne took a deep breath and said, 'He's suffered from a lot of pent-up emotion over the years. You need to forgive him.'

Fiona nodded. 'I know, but it won't happen immediately.'

'So, what will you do now?'

'Pray,' she said simply.

Anne was not completely satisfied about Donald's reason for not agreeing to Fiona marrying Sandy. What about his antagonism towards Sandy's father?

She had no more time to think about that because Albert was calling her to take her to the railway station. She kissed Fiona and said she'd see her soon. After saying her further goodbyes, she went outside and climbed in the car where Albert was already waiting.

Anne soon realised that he wanted to discuss matters to do with Fiona. 'Gladys and I had our hearts set on Fiona staying on at the hotel and becoming a long-term member of the staff,' he said. 'We both like her and she has some good ideas to make the business a roaring success. Her mother has no right to expect her to simply fall in with her plans and return to Scotland after disappearing the way she did.'

'Whatever Catrina told Fiona, it must have satisfied her. You don't think it was rather selfless of Catrina to leave the man and daughter she loved behind? She knew how hurtful and divisive it would be if her husband had discovered that his wife and brother were in love and carrying on behind his back if she had stayed.'

'They should have been stronger-willed and kept their distance,' said Albert, his hands tightening on the steering wheel. 'It must run in the family.'

'What d'you mean by that?' asked Anne.

Albert's face was set in a look of disapproval and when he answered she sensed he was still holding something back. 'Grandfather Anderson left Grandma and went off on his travels, leaving her to cope with the farm and the boys on her own. I know Uncle Donald didn't go wandering but he was weak-willed.'

'You don't know what you're talking about,' Anne said. 'You've only just met Uncle Donald. I got to know him quite well on the farm, and I can tell you there's nothing weak about him.' She paused, deciding that now was the time to mention Hugh and Sylvia's wills and other stuff she had read and tell him that he owed it to her to right matters by giving his consent for her to marry Andrew next Easter. She waited until he parked at the railway station.

'I've a bone to pick with you, Albert,' she said in a rush. 'I took some papers from Da's suitcase which you wouldn't allow me to look at before you came here for the first time. You lied to me when you said it was in the family home.'

The colour drained from his face. 'You had no right to go stealing private papers.'

Anne stared at him with a disgusted expression. 'I had every right because a number of those papers referred to me. You did not give me all the money due to me in Da's will and nothing from Sylvia's will. I knew there should have been more from Da because he had spoken of it to me. I've also read the letters from his friend Alex and I'm pretty sure that my mother is Anne Graham. You knew that she and Da were close because Fiona's mother mentioned you hanging around when Anne and Hugh saw her off to Canada.'

'I knew even before that,' said Albert through gritted teeth. 'I saw them together in the Sandon and could tell there was something between them by the way they behaved, and him a married man! I asked the landlady was he often there flirting with her and she said they were obviously very fond of each other. Disgusting! I don't know how I managed to keep my mouth shut and not tell Mother.'

'Sylvia and Da's marriage was not a love match!'

'They had five children!' Albert blurted out.

'So what! You and Gladys have none, but you love each other, don't you?'

He agreed that they did and that it was just hard luck that they hadn't had children. She thought he was about to say something else, but his voice trailed off.

'So,' said Anne. 'Are you going to give me your consent to my marrying Andrew next Easter?'

'I suppose so, as long as I can give you away and you keep your mouth shut about the wills,' said Albert.

'Agreed.' Anne stretched out a hand and they shook.

He kissed her cheek and she went to catch the train.

Anne was exhausted by the time she arrived home, but she bucked up as soon as she set eyes on Andrew sitting on the sofa drinking a cup of tea. Immediately he set the cup and saucer down on the floor and jumped up to greet her, both almost falling into each other's arms.

'I'm so glad to see you,' Anne said.

'Me too,' whispered Andrew against her ear.

Emily came in from the kitchen followed by a stranger whom she introduced as Alex Murray. Anne gasped and then shook hands with him. He said, 'You wanted to see me, Anne?'

She nodded. 'Thank you for coming. Maybe we can talk privately later.'

He nodded and they all sat down and listened while Anne explained what had happened in Rhyl and how Fiona had taken the stunning news about her mother, half-brother and Donald. All the while Andrew kept his arm around her reassuringly.

'Where is Donald?' asked Anne.

'He's gone for a walk,' Larry said. 'I offered to go with him, but he said he'd like to be alone to think.'

'Was this before Mr Murray arrived?' Anne asked.

Emily nodded. 'I wish he'd come back. It's cold and dark out there now.'

Alex said, 'Has Fiona has made no decision yet about her plans for the future in light of the revelations?'

Anne said, 'Not yet. She's been working there and had considered staying for a while if it suited her. Albert and Gladys were keen for her to do so.'

'But what about Sandy?' asked Alex.

His question took her by surprise, and she stared at him, flabbergasted.

'I'm Sandy's father,' he said.

'I see,' said Anne, the excitement she had felt at seeing him growing. 'And where's Sandy?'

'I should hope he's talking to Fiona by now,' Alex said.

'I think it's possible her prayer's been answered then,' said Anne, leaning towards him.

Suddenly Alex stiffened. 'That jewellery you have around your neck. Where did you get it from, Anne?' he asked.

'I was told it belonged to my mother.'

'Come over here and let me see it properly,' he said.

She moved closer and he peered at the amulet and Anne saw some of the colour drain from his face. 'It's very like one that Hugh bought for his little sister for her birthday, but she died before he could give it to her. I remember because it had been such a sad time and the three brothers had all been tremendously upset. Hugh had been even more so because he had not been able to give it to her in time.'

'How sad,' whispered Anne.

Alex shook his head. 'It seemed to take Donald the longest to get over it according to Hugh.'

Anne took a deep breath and turned to face Andrew. 'Shall we go for a walk and catch up? I've something important to tell you.'

He nodded, taking her hand, and they excused themselves as they went into the hall for their coats.

They decided to walk to Eastham Ferry. Andrew held her tightly around her waist. 'I wish we could get married now, then I could take you to London with me.' He leaned in and kissed her. 'I've really, really missed you.'

'I've missed you, too,' she said, returning his kiss. 'But as much as I'd like us to get married sooner, Albert has agreed to us marrying next Easter, so I think we should stick to the original plan.'

Andrew's face lit up. 'That's marvellous. How did you persuade him? And you don't mind moving south?'

'I'll miss good ol' Liverpool,' she said. 'But I accept that we need to live where your job is, and we can always come back to visit the family.' She sighed, then added, 'I suppose I blackmailed Albert into agreeing.' Anne paused.

He stared at her expectantly. 'Go on?'

'I told him I'd read the wills and letters and I had a feeling he had known all along that Hugh was my natural father and Anne Graham was my mother.' Anne's voice broke. When she found her voice, she took a photograph from her pocket and handed it to him. 'Show Lil this picture of Mary, which I was given by Miss Tillymint. My mother was supposedly her spitting image. If Lil sees this picture, she'll know if Anne Graham, my mother, was her twin. Although I do actually have a picture of Anne and Hugh, but you'll have to wait to see that one.'

Andrew peered at the photo but could barely make out the features. 'Do you think Hugh knew he was your father?'

Anne shrugged, full of emotion. They both looked at each other.

'It will be thrilling for you if she positively identifies her,' he said.

'Yes,' she said. 'And it was through Kyle and Marjorie that I found the sweet shop.'

'Kyle,' muttered Andrew. 'I was wondering when his name would crop up. I suppose he'll turn up while I'm here too?'

'I doubt it. He's still in Ireland with Mildred and Bridget. I had a letter from him saying that they have found the farm and he gave me an address. I'll write to Mildred when I get a moment, like I promised.'

'Will he be staying there?'

'I presume he'll be back for Gordon and Marjorie's wedding.'

'Pity. I'd have been happier if he was off the scene,' said Andrew.

'You've no need to worry about Kyle,' Anne said, squeezing his hand tightly. 'I feel towards him as I would a brother, whereas I could never feel sisterly towards you – you're the one I want to marry.' She looped her arms about his neck and kissed him.

'We can look forward to our honeymoon knowing he won't be on the scene,' Andrew said, his eyes aglow with desire.

'Where shall we go for our honeymoon?' she asked. 'Somewhere romantic.'

'Sorry, Paris and the Mediterranean are out of my price bracket. We could go to the Isle of Wight and hopefully being together will be romantic enough.'

'That would be wonderful – I've never been there before. I think islands are romantic places,' Anne murmured. 'I remember in the past, standing on the jetty watching the ships and the occasional ocean liner thinking if I'd been a boy I'd have gone to sea.'

'I've to go back to London for work tomorrow afternoon, but will you come with me to see Jane and Lil early tomorrow morning?'

Anne agreed.

He escorted her back to the house, and they were just in time to see a taxi drive away. They kissed and he hurried off to catch his train.

When Anne went inside the house it was to find that Alex had left but had promised to ring her and arrange for them to have dinner at his hotel in Chester to have that conversation about Hugh.

Chapter Twenty Seven

The following morning dawned frosty and bright, which meant wrapping up warmly. Anne decided to wear a woollen dog-tooth checked skirt with matching jacket, coupled with a tan-coloured jumper and a fox fur collar. On her head was a brown cloche hat trimmed with an orange flower. Sheer stockings and her brown strapped shoes with a Louis heel completed her ensemble.

She arrived at Exchange station in Liverpool at eight o'clock in the morning and she was delighted to see that Andrew was already waiting at the newsagent's booth. She saw his eyes light up as she approached and held out both hands to him. He took them and drew her to him, kissing her lightly on the lips. 'Did you remember the other photograph?'

She nodded. 'I'll show it to you on the train.'

Andrew said, 'I think we should hurry to the platform. It's a good half an hour wait if we miss the train.'

He strode in the direction of the ticket barrier and she fell in step beside him. 'I bought you a ticket,' said Andrew, taking her hand. 'I thought it would save time.'

She thanked him and soon they were sitting comfortably in a carriage on the Ormskirk train. She asked him about the article he had to finish and he told her that he had needed to do a bit more research for it, which had meant spending a couple of days in the National Army Museum in London. 'The photograph?' he said.

She produced it and he stared at it intently. 'When you think of it, this was taken before the war.'

'And now they're both dead and the world has changed so much,' she said.

She returned the photo to her handbag. It was only later when they were walking past the clock tower in Ormskirk that Andrew said, 'It was good that Alex Murray responded to your letter.'

'I think we should invite him to our wedding as long as Sandy and Fiona make up.'

Andrew agreed.

'The time will soon pass. Once Christmas is over, it will fly.' Anne added, 'Though, Christmas won't be much fun for Jane with Lil so ill. We need to consider them in our plans for Christmas.'

Andrew agreed and soon after they left the train and were making their way up the short path to Jane's front door and were rapping the knocker. There came the sound of hurrying footsteps and the door was flung open to reveal Jane.

Andrew stepped forward and took Jane's hand. 'How's Lil?'

'Not so good,' Jane answered, her voice a little shaky.

She led the way into the front room where Lil was in bed, propped up by several pillows. Anne thought her collarbones appeared sharper and her face paler and more angular. Andrew sat in a chair placed next to her bed while Anne and Jane perched on the small sofa.

'I'm so glad you were able to get here again so soon,' Lil said faintly. 'I dared to hope that you would before I went to meet my maker. Jane is a thoughtful and determined young lady, telling me that I've months ahead of me, but I'm a realist and know I've little time left. I'm at peace now, knowing my lovely girl is not alone in this world.'

'You can trust that she'll be safe with us,' Andrew said.

'I do trust you,' Lil said. 'It means everything to me that she has such a good person for a brother.'

'Lil, Anne and I would like to show you a photograph.' He indicated to Anne to come forward and she took the photograph from her pocket and handed it to Andrew. He leaned closer to Lil so she could see it.

'My!' she exclaimed. 'Is that Anne Graham in the photo? It's almost like yesterday looking at her.'

Andrew and Anne looked at each other, their eyes shining with excitement despite the sad situation that Lil was in.

'It is Anne, and do you recognise the man she is with?' asked Anne.

'I can't quite see him,' Lil said weakly. 'If only he wasn't wearing that straw boater.' Lil's head then slipped back onto the pillow and they could see the effort had tired her out.

'Let's go and make a pot of tea,' said Jane.

The two girls left Andrew with Lil and it was ten minutes or so before he joined them in the kitchen. 'She roused for a bit but now she's gone to sleep,' he said.

Soon Andrew and Anne had to leave and return to Liverpool.

–

On the way back, Anne was subdued. 'It's been proven beyond doubt that Anne Graham is my mother, but I still don't know for certain that Hugh is my natural father.'

'It does seem like there is no question they knew each other, but we can't be sure they were lovers.'

'I feel it must be the case. I found letters from Alex Murray and in them he mentions that Da and my mother were in contact after seeing each other in the pub where she worked.' Anne also told Andrew more about Sylvia's will and her father's and Albert withholding all her inheritance from her. 'I really think it was because he needed the money for the hotel. Although, he seems convinced that Hugh had betrayed his mother with Anne.'

'Lil asked me to be one of the executors of her will,' Andrew said. 'She told me she doesn't quite trust solicitors.'

Anne thought how there was another certain executor that she didn't trust either. She felt her stomach fluttering with excitement. Hugh and Anne Graham had been in a relationship in Scotland before they were forced apart according to his letters by her parents. Then Hugh met her in Liverpool and told Alex Murray about it. Could it really be true that Hugh was Anne's married lover and her own natural father, or was it just that they met up because they were second cousins? If that was the reason, then who was her natural father?

Anne was lost in her own thoughts as they hurried to Lime Street Station. She kissed Andrew three times, not wanting to let him go. He responded to her kisses but then released her, saying they would be there all afternoon if she didn't let him go. Afterwards Anne felt a bit low, so she decided to catch the tram to West Derby Road and see Robbie and Marjorie.

Marjorie was pleased to see her and excitedly told her that she and Gordon had decided to bring their wedding plans forward and would be marrying just before Christmas.

'We were thinking of it being a quiet affair,' Marjorie said. 'We don't want a big fuss and see no reason to wait any longer. I have no other family and I'm content to have just you and Andrew, Robbie, Emily and Larry and Teddy and Joan. I would like Andrew to give me away.'

'I'm sure he'll say yes,' said Anne. 'What about asking Jane to the wedding as she's one of the family now?'

'If you think she'd like to come,' Marjorie said.

'You aren't asking Albert and Gladys?' Anne asked, adding that Albert had given his consent for her to marry Andrew and wanted to give her away.

'Gordon doesn't want them,' said Marjorie. 'He thinks they're more concerned about the business and making money than the family. It would cost them to close the hotel, and besides, now they've your wedding to look forward to — and don't forget Albert didn't tell his family about him and Gladys getting married or invite them to his wedding. So, if you get in touch with Albert, tell him that our wedding will be a quiet affair, please? We're just having our wedding breakfast here in the house.'

Anne nodded and after a cup of tea and a couple of jam tarts she left and headed back into town. She noticed that *The Singing Fool* with Al Jolson was on at the Trocadero. It was a super luxurious picture palace built seven years earlier in 1922 and had an enormous Wurlitzer organ. The film was a mixture of silent action and talkie with musical numbers and two of the songs were already popular: 'I'm Sitting on Top of the World' and 'Sonny Boy'. She would have liked to go and see it but decided she didn't have time. She thought how the talkies would put some musicians out of work, although there were still dance halls and the theatre and the music hall on Bold Street for them to play in. She remembered Hugh telling her that John Braham, the famous tenor, had performed there in Victorian times. He also remembered Adele Astaire and her brother Fred dancing at the Empire theatre this century. Anne had asked who John Braham was. She'd never heard of him and had been told he was Jewish and born in London. His real surname was Abraham and he became world famous and sang opera.

Anne crossed the road and went up Ranelagh Street to Central Station to catch the train to Eastham. She knew that she must let Albert know about Gordon and Marjorie's wedding plans and also confirm hers and Andrew's wedding date with the vicar in Eastham.

When she arrived home, Anne decided to go and see the vicar and, once the date was definitely set, she would write and let people know about it. She wrote to Jane rather than telephoning the florist's where she worked, then to Albert as well as Fiona, and she also sent a brief letter to Kyle and Mildred addressed to the farm. By the time Anne got to bed that evening she had writer's cramp, but all the letters were in envelopes and addressed. She just needed to go to the post office for some stamps the next day.

—

Within a few days, she had received several replies that contained surprises.

Albert's letter to Anne was brief and to the point; he made no mention of Gordon and Marjorie's wedding but said he looked forward to seeing Anne on her birthday.

In the meantime, she decided to concentrate on more important matters, such as visiting Jane next weekend. Jane had replied to her letter with the news that a neighbour was going to sit with Lil for Marjorie and Gordon's wedding. Fiona had written to say she and her mother were getting on better now, having come to an understanding, and that Ranald would be driving their mother back to Eastham next week. Fiona herself would be returning with Sandy and she would tell Anne all that had happened when she saw her.

The following day Anne was surprised and delighted to receive a visit from Kyle and Mildred. 'I have to be back at work tomorrow,' he said, 'so when Mildred got your letter, the family in Ireland decided she might as well return with me as long as you write to them, saying she arrived safely and that she didn't lose the wedding present they had sent for you.'

Anne said in an astonished voice, 'A gift! I'm more than happy to do so and to thank them for their wedding present.' Mildred told her it was Irish linen, and Anne was bowled over by their generosity. 'My wedding isn't until next Easter, though. It's Marjorie and Gordon who are getting married soon.'

'It doesn't matter,' Mildred said. 'They wanted to say thanks to you and Andrew for all you have done, and I was glad of the excuse to escape for a while.'

'Why is that? Weren't you happy to be reunited with your family?' Anne asked.

'They smother me. I can't move without them wanting to know where I'm going and what I'm doing, and we walk miles to church to hear mass. If I say I don't want to go, then I get called a heathen. Then, there's my great-uncle, Willie – I can't stand him!'

When Anne asked her why, Mildred told her that she would rather not talk about it.

'What about your mother?'

'Oh, she loves it there, enjoys being made a fuss of and dressing up for church with her hat and gloves. She even has her own missal given to her by my grandmother. There's no more news of Daddy yet, so he could be dead.' Tears glistened in her eyes. 'They want me to get in touch with his mother, my other granny, in case she's heard anything, but I don't know where she is, and I doubt that she'd be pleased to see me after all this time. I'm to tell the Liverpool O'Donnell cousins if I do find her. Chance would be a fine thing; they hardly ever helped Mam and me in the past and besides, from what I know of them, I wouldn't trust them as far as I could throw them.'

Anne exchanged glances with Kyle before giving Mildred her attention once more. 'Oh dear. So, what are you going to do?'

'I promised Mam I'd go back before Christmas, so I can't say how long I'll stay here. I'd liked to have stayed until after your wedding.'

Kyle pulled a face. 'I'm glad to be back home. I've responsibilities here, but I presume you can put Mildred up, Anne? She can't go back to the orphanage now.'

'We've a guest staying and are expecting more, but I'll ask Emily whether we can put you up for a couple of nights,' said Anne.

'Of course,' sighed Mildred. 'Then I'll have to find somewhere else.'

'Let's wait and see how things go,' Anne said. 'You can share my bed.'

With that all settled, she suggested Kyle stay for lunch. He and Larry lost no time in discussing the state of the world, especially the state of the economy. It struck Anne that if there was a slump, it might be sensible to have a trip into town to buy clothes for her wedding now. It was possible that come next year, there mightn't be much left in the shops. There had still been no phone call from Alex Murray.

Chapter Twenty Eight

Anne took Mildred with her to C&A Modes in Liverpool and found what she wanted as her wedding gown in no time at all. It was of white viscose, known as taffeta in America and commonly called artificial silk and was first created in the Netherlands. The gown had a V neckline trimmed with artificial white fur and clung to her hips before falling in three layers of frills to just below the knee. Her headdress was in a cloche style with white fabric flowers over her ears and a long trailing veil.

Mildred oohed and aahhed over it, saying she looked like a fairy princess, which surprised Anne no end, wondering where she had seen an image of a fairy princess. She could not believe she had had books of fairy tales at her previous home or the orphanage or in school, so maybe it was how Mildred imagined fairy princesses to look. They then went to catch a train to Ormskirk, rather than returning to Eastham first with the wedding dress as it would cost more money in fares going backwards and forwards. Anne realised it would have made more sense to have gone to Ormskirk first, but she'd had her mind set on buying her wedding dress. Still, the dress was not too heavy, and Lil might like to see it.

Mildred had never visited Ormskirk and enjoyed window-shopping through the streets on their way and

Anne thought how pleasant it was without the clamour of the market stalls and the traders. Anne was surprised to see that the curtains were drawn when they reached the house, and she was filled with foreboding. She rat-tatted the knocker and then there seemed a long wait before the front door was opened to them.

Jane stood there, her face drawn, tear-stained and woebegone. 'Thank God it's you,' she said, seeming not to notice Mildred. 'Mam died in the night, after suddenly taking a turn for the worse. She's gone and I feel so lost. When she worsened in the week I did try and get in touch with Andrew, but he was out on a job. The man on the other end said he'd pass my message on.'

Jane led them into the house, which was more darkened than usual with all the curtains pulled closed and the front room door firmly shut.

'I sent for the vicar and he came and sat and prayed with her.'

Anne placed the bag containing her wedding dress on the table before going over and hugging Jane. 'I'm so sorry about Lil. I wish I'd been in time to speak to her again.'

'She liked you and enjoyed talking to you too and she was so happy that you and Andrew had found us...' Jane's voice broke on a sob. '...so I wouldn't be alone.'

Anne said, 'And you're not alone. We're here and Andrew will be soon as well.' She released Jane and beckoned to Mildred, introducing them formally to each other.

They shook hands, then Mildred said, 'Would you like me to make you a cup of tea, Jane?'

Jane nodded. 'Make a pot, so you and Anne can have one, too.'

'When's the funeral to be?'

'I'm hoping Monday at two o'clock. There'll be a service in church, then she'll be buried in the same plot as her aunt in the churchyard. It's a nice place and some of the graves go back years and years.' Jane sniffed. 'Her grandparents and great-grandparents are buried there.'

'Have you had anything to eat, Jane?' Anne asked.

'I couldn't,' she said.

'Besides, there's no bread,' put in Mildred, who'd been looking around the kitchen. 'I thought of making some toast.'

'Well, I've bought a crusty loaf, butter, marmalade, some cookies and a few other things,' said Anne, holding up the shopping bag. 'You need to eat something, Jane, to keep your strength up.'

Anne wasted no time in slicing the loaf while listening to Jane telling her about Lil's last hours, which seemed to have been peaceful, even though her death had come upon them suddenly. Anne buttered the toast as it came off the toasting fork wielded by Mildred, who had topped up the teapot with boiling water. Soon the three were seated round the table, crunching toast spread with butter and marmalade and drinking tea. Jane asked Anne what was in the bag that Mildred had earlier removed from the table.

'My wedding dress,' Anne replied. 'And before you say it, I know my wedding isn't until next Easter. But with all that's happening in America and even over here on the London stock exchange, there could be a Depression and who knows if there'll be much in the shops next year? Besides, I saw it and really liked it, so couldn't resist buying it.'

'Are we going to get a look at it?' Jane asked.

'If you want to,' Anne said. 'I wasn't sure it was appropriate given the circumstances.'

'You've carried it all the way here, so why not?' Jane said. 'Mam wouldn't have minded and something beautiful will be a good distraction.'

Having been given the go-ahead, Anne wasted no time in stepping away from the table with the bag and changing into her wedding gown and headdress in the hallway.

Having done so, she pushed open the kitchen door and said, 'Ta-da! Here comes the bride!'

'You look lovely,' said Jane on a long indrawn breath.

'You really do,' Mildred said. 'Can I borrow it when I get married? If I get married.'

'And me too,' said Jane.

'Hire it out and you'll make your fortune,' Mildred said.

Anne smiled. 'I hope Andrew's reaction is as good as yours.'

'It's a good job he's not here right now,' Mildred said. 'It's unlucky for the groom to see the bride in her dress before the wedding.'

'I bet during the war there was many a groom who saw the bride in her wedding outfit before they tied the knot,' Jane said. 'There wouldn't be any hanging around with the groom having to go off to fight.'

Anne agreed and, summoning Mildred for assistance, went into the lobby where the girl helped Anne lift the dress over her head. It was packed back into the box along with the veil and placed back in the large holdall.

'I suppose you have plans for the rest of the day, Jane?' said Anne, when they returned to the kitchen. 'You'll need to register Lil's death and get a death certificate. See the insurance man about any life insurance she might have had and also the undertaker.'

'And there's people I need to get in touch with about the funeral,' said Jane with a sigh. 'Such as Cissie and Jessie. I suppose I'd best go to the registry office first and register the death.'

'Do you know where it is?' asked Anne.

'Next to the front gates of the hospital,' Jane replied. 'It won't take me long to walk there.'

'I'll go with you if you like?' Anne said.

'Someone needs to stay home in case people call,' Jane said.

'I could stay for a day or so and keep you company,' Mildred suggested. 'I don't have to go anywhere in a hurry.'

'That would be a great help,' Jane said.

'Are you sure?' Anne asked Mildred.

Mildred nodded. 'I'd like to be of help. Just let Kyle know where I am if you can,' she said.

Anne said, 'I'll do my best.'

'That's settled then,' Mildred said, smiling warmly at Jane.

When Anne left the two girls seemed to be getting on well, considering the circumstances.

Chapter Twenty Nine

On arriving in Liverpool, Anne left the Exchange railway station, careful not to forget her wedding dress, and made her way to James Street station to catch the train to Eastham. She was feeling hungry again and wished she'd remembered to bring one of the cream cookies she had bought. Still, Mildred and Jane could split them between them. She herself must phone Andrew as soon as she arrived back at Emily and Larry's. What would he make of the news about Lil and what would Jane decide to do about the future?

When Emily saw that Anne had bought her wedding dress, she said all the right things about the dress, except to ask Anne if she had she acted wisely in buying it so soon. Larry shushed Emily and told Anne that while she was out, Andrew had phoned and had been relieved to hear that Anne had gone to visit Jane as he had received her message and would come north as soon as he could. Anne realised that Andrew's time was going to be taken up with Jane and that she and Andrew would have little time to see each other. In the meantime, Anne had other matters to deal with when Fiona arrived with Sandy after having visited Alex at his hotel in Chester.

Fiona told Anne how she had tried to act cool, but if the truth was known she had been thrilled that he had driven down from Scotland determined to persuade Fiona to return to Scotland and marry him. He had been offered a new position in Edinburgh and had already been viewing houses, but he wanted her opinion on the two that had taken his fancy.

'That sounds promising,' Anne said. 'And did he tell you why his father came with him here?'

'I presumed he wanted to sort matters out with Uncle Donald, but Sandy said that it was mainly to talk to you.' Fiona gazed interrogatively at Anne.

Anne smiled. 'I wrote to him about Da. He and Alexander Murray were great friends. I wish I'd known he was your boyfriend's father and had got to meet him when I was up in Scotland,' said Anne with a sigh.

'Aye, but there had been no reason to do so then,' said Fiona.

Anne nodded and changed the subject. 'So, how did you leave Albert and Gladys?'

'Disappointed! Albert's also upset that Gordon hasn't sent him an invitation to his wedding.'

'He's no right to be hurt. None of the family was invited to his wedding to Gladys.'

'He said that was different.'

'He would say that,' muttered Anne. 'The truth is that it was less trouble not inviting us all. Anyway, he's going to give me away at my wedding. As for Marjorie and Gordon's, it's going to be low key. They're having the wedding breakfast at Marjorie's place and Emily has volunteered to have Robbie stay here in Eastham while Marjorie and Gordon are on honeymoon in Llandudno.' She paused. 'In the meantime, I'm waiting to hear from

Sandy's father and Andrew's coming north. Jane's foster mother has died.'

Fiona nodded. 'Sorry, I can see you've plenty on your plate but I've something else to tell you.'

'Let's go and have a cup of tea,' said Anne. 'Anyway, how are things with your mother and brother?' She led the way into the kitchen.

'Where's Uncle Donald?' asked Fiona.

'He's always going out for walks, so that's where he'll be.'

She and Fiona were about to sit down and have a cup of tea when Emily came in with Donald, Catrina, Ranald and Larry and Sandy. Immediately Anne stood up and put the kettle on and lifted down cups and sauces, only for Donald to produce a bottle of Scotch whisky and Catrina to hold out a bottle of champagne.

Donald said, 'This gathering is worthy of more than tea, girls.'

'Agreed,' chorused several voices.

Emily disappeared into the living room to fetch glasses. Anne followed her. When they returned it was to find Fiona and Donald were no longer there, and they were told they had gone upstairs to Donald's room.

They did not reappear for half an hour, but Anne thought all seemed well between them. The following morning Anne could not remember how many toasts had been made the evening before. What she could remember was speaking to Andrew on the phone and Fiona saying to Donald, 'So, you're not going to need me back at the farm?'

'I didn't say that – you'll always have a home there,' he said gruffly. 'But I'm presuming it won't be long before you and Sandy tie the knot and you'll be moving to Edinburgh.'

Fiona shrugged. 'And I presume you and Mother will get married and settle down on the farm with Ranald helping out there?'

'If Anne had been honest with us when she visited, I could have provided her with all the information she needed,' he said tersely.

'I doubt you could have done,' responded Anne. 'Alex kept in touch with Hugh long after he left Scotland.'

'And that's what upset me,' said Donald. 'Neither of them bothered keeping in touch with me. I felt that I had not only lost my little sister but my two brothers. Alex had stolen Hugh away from me.'

'That's rubbish,' said Anne and Sandy in unison.

'You could have easily written to Dad,' added Sandy. 'But you held a grudge over a fish.'

'Not really,' said Donald. 'I was just hopeless when it came to emotional stuff and couldn't express my real feelings once Catrina left.'

'Anyway, now is a time for celebration, not raking up sad far-off moments,' said Emily.

After a couple of glasses of champagne, Fiona said to Anne, 'I still haven't told you everything.' She paused. 'Just seeing Sandy got me in a tizzy. It looks like putting some distance between us has done the trick, but it's also made me realise just how much he matters to me. Yet I didn't give him an answer straightaway despite knowing I wanted to accept his proposal. Last week I was determined to fall in with Albert and Gladys's plans for me, but the other day I heard a couple of the maids talking about her.

Apparently, she has been sickly for the last month or so. They think it's morning sickness and she's having a baby.'

Anne felt she could have been knocked down by a feather. 'You're joking!'

'Honest to God! Of course, the maids could be mistaken. But somehow, I think they're right – and that's why they want me in Rhyl.' Fiona gnawed her lower lip.

'Albert and Gladys usually have their own interests at heart, but you underestimate your talents, which they could certainly have made use of,' Anne said. 'As it is, you have the perfect reason to leave the hotel.'

Fiona nodded joyfully. 'Yes, I'm getting married and going to live in Edinburgh.'

'I feel really happy for you,' Anne said, throwing her arms around Fiona and hugging her. 'You've had a lucky escape.'

'Aye, I have,' said Fiona. 'And it's all thanks to you.'

'I don't know how you work that out,' said Anne. 'Anyway, here's Sandy come searching for you.' She smiled at Alex's son and said, 'Some coincidence you being your father's son and Fiona's boyfriend.'

'Fiona did mention after you visited the farm that you were Hugh's daughter.'

'She didn't know at the time that he had adopted me.'

Sandy's craggy features creased into a frown. 'I didn't know that.'

'Fathers don't tell their children everything. I'm hoping, though, that Hugh might have told your father the name of my natural father. My natural mother, Anne Graham, died in childbirth.'

'I've heard the name Anne Graham before,' Sandy said. 'Who from?'

'I remember overhearing part of a conversation Ma and Pa were having and Anne Graham was mentioned; it could have been about Hugh? I didn't hear everything they said because I was told to go and put the kettle on.'

Anne was so excited she could not keep still. 'I hope your father will be open with me about his and Hugh's friendship.'

'He's come all this way, so I'm sure he will,' said Sandy. 'I know he's brought some photographs that I'm sure you'll be interested in seeing.'

'That's wonderful,' Anne said. 'I hope both you and your father consider the journey was worth making.'

'So far, it's worked out for me,' said Sandy. 'Fiona has agreed to marry me.'

'So I hear,' said Anne, 'and I couldn't be more pleased for you both.'

'Dad's here now,' said Sandy.

Anne felt her nerves calm as she gazed up into the searching eyes of Alexander Murray.

'I'm delighted to meet you again, Anne,' he said, while the others left them to talk in private. 'Let me tell you something of my friendship with Hugh.' She listened intently as he began to talk. 'We became scouts together after reading *Scouting for Boys* by Lord Baden-Powell, the hero of Mafeking during the Boer War.' He paused. 'My father was not a lodge person, unlike Hugh's father, so I never became involved, but we still met at scout meetings and went camping occasionally with the scouts. Then Hugh and Anne fell in love, but their parents were against them getting married, even though they were only second cousins, so Hugh left Scotland for Liverpool where he knew he could find work in the sugar works there and be beyond temptation. We wrote to each other occasionally and met up when we attended the World Scout Jamboree in 1920 at London Olympia.'

Anne interrupted at this point to say that she remembered Hugh going to the jamboree.

'It was there he told me about having met Anne again in a pub near Anfield football ground way back in 1912,' said Alex, 'and how their feelings for each other had been rekindled, despite him being married to Sylvia by then. He and Anne had been torn apart by guilt over his adultery and eventually they ended the affair, but even so, he still cared about Anne and one evening he returned to the pub, only to discover that she no longer worked in the bar because she was pregnant. Convinced that the child was his, he tried to find out where she was living but it was like a barrier had been put up. Then dreadful fate stepped in when his small daughter, Flora, died in an accident and his wife was close to a nervous breakdown. A Scots workmate's wife had died in childbirth and asked if Hugh and his wife could take the child.'

'That was Liam Fraser, my fiancé Andrew's father,' Anne said.

'Aye, lassie, Hugh was handed you and in a short space of time, after a conversation with the midwife, he was convinced you were his daughter and that wasn't just because of what she told him but because of your smile. He was heartbroken over Anne's death, regretting she had felt unable to tell him about her pregnancy, but at least he had you,' finished Alex.

'Where was she buried?' asked Anne, shocked that she had never given thought to the last resting place of her mother until now.

'In Anfield Cemetery. Apparently the customers at the pub clubbed together along with the midwife to pay for a decent funeral for her.'

Anne's eyes filled with tears. 'How kind of them.'

'They couldn't afford a memorial stone, so when Hugh discovered that and visited her grave, he paid for one to be erected.'

Anne made up her mind there and then to visit her mother's grave and place flowers on it as soon as possible. 'He never told her parents she had passed away?'

'They were dead by then and her twin sister had left the family home.'

'Her name was Mary and she's dead, too,' Anne said with a sigh. 'She came to Liverpool with a friend in search of Anne, but they couldn't find her.'

'How do you know that?' Alex asked.

'I've met the friend. They ran a sweet shop together until Mary died. Now the friend runs it on her own and calls it Miss Tillymint's Sweet Treats.' Anne fell silent.

Alex stared at her in astonishment. 'As far as Hugh knew, Anne had never told Mary where she was.' He delved into a pocket of his tweed jacket and took out some photographs and handed them to her. Slowly she looked through them, smiling at the shots of Alex and Hugh as cub scouts, then the ones of Hugh with Anne and Mary, as well as the Anderson brothers as young boys.

'But Mary knew Anne was aware that Hugh had gone to Liverpool in search of work,' Anne said earnestly. 'I'd always believed twins were close but Anne and Mary sound very different, despite sharing an upbringing.'

'They were. Mary was the elder by half an hour and bossy with it. Anne was a gentler soul and under her sister's thumb, but she could be very determined if something was important to her. Mary didn't approve of Hugh at all because of his influence over Anne.'

'That's so sad,' said Anne.

'Aye, I still miss Hugh but at least our families will be reunited when Sandy and Fiona are married.'

'I wonder when that will be,' Anne mused.

'June, I should imagine,' Alex said.

'When the bluebells are blooming,' suggested a smiling Anne. 'I hope we'll be invited. I fancy a trip to Scotland then.'

'No doubt you will be,' Alex said, helping Anne to her feet. After a short hesitation, he said, 'I hope you don't mind me asking, but I notice, Anne, that you've made no mention of a letter to yourself from Hugh?'

She stared at him and said, 'That's because I didn't find one.'

Alex frowned. 'That's odd. He told me that he was going to write one for you to read after his death.'

At those words, she made up her mind to go through Hugh's papers once more over the weekend.

Chapter Thirty

Anne decided to keep quiet about what Alex had told her for now as she wanted to tell Andrew first. The following day she and Fiona were up early as Sandy had promised to give them both a lift to Ormskirk for Lil's funeral. Fiona was going along as well, as she had wanted to visit the market town and Sandy was keen to keep her company. As for Alex, he planned to tour Liverpool in Emily's company.

When they arrived at Jane's house, Anne was pleased to find Kyle there, his having come to see Mildred and to attend the funeral. Andrew was there, too, and Anne flung herself into his arms. She realised that despite it being only a short time since they had last seen each other, to Anne it felt ages. She had expected Andrew to be displeased that Kyle had shown up again, and that was true in as much that there was a possibility of the ending to the story of Bridget and Mildred not being the fairy tale that he had hoped.

Andrew told Anne how Mildred had run towards him as soon as he arrived. He had hugged her, asking how she was finding Ireland, but she had pulled a face and said, 'I miss Liverpool. Still, it's doing Mam good, so I'll be going back there for now and it's all thanks to you for saving her life.'

Nonetheless, he was delighted to hear all that Anne had to tell him, as well as meeting Sandy and renewing his acquaintance with Fiona. They all talked weddings and Andrew said that he'd invited his half-brother and his girlfriend and grandmother from Jura, as well as his grandfather from Ireland. 'Of course, they mightn't come, as it is quite a journey.'

'If they can't make it, then we could always visit them when we go up for Fiona and Sandy's wedding in June,' Anne suggested, smiling.

He agreed, adding that he hoped they would come all the same as it would be nice for Jane to meet her Scottish and Irish relatives. 'What does Donald think of Fiona and Sandy getting married?' he asked.

'It no longer matters to her what he thinks. He has her mother and Ranald, so she's free to please herself,' said Anne. 'Let's busy ourselves with our own concerns, which are helping Jane today, and Marjorie and Gordon's wedding, followed of course by our own.'

'You don't have to worry about me. I know you have your job in London and your own commitments,' Jane said, having overheard the conversation. 'But I thought Mildred would be of more concern to the pair of you. She's not happy in Ireland and has no friends there, whereas I do have friends here, and Marjorie has suggested I stay at her house for a while when I've recovered from the funeral and while they're away on honeymoon. I will have a bit of company and that way Robbie can stay at home.'

Yet even as they talked Anne was thinking about the letter Alex had mentioned and what Jane had said about Mildred. Could it be that Andrew was not going to have his happy ending for Mildred and her mother's story? Anne suggested that Jane speak to Kyle who surely knew more about their situation and would be willing to be involved in getting to the bottom of what could be upsetting Mildred. Conscious of Andrew's attitude towards Kyle, she decided not to mention this to Andrew, especially as her fiancé had enough to concern himself with – the funeral and supporting Jane. It was obvious that Jane was going to need all the support she could get to manage without breaking down during the funeral.

She clung to Andrew's arm as they followed the coffin into the church. Anne thought about how Lil had loved Jane exactly like her own daughter and how losing that loving presence was extremely difficult to cope with, however strong and brave a person was. Anne went and stood on the other side of Jane and linked her arm through hers and so together, the three of them led the mourners up the aisle of the parish church. Mildred stayed close to Kyle. Even when Lil's earthly remains were laid to rest in the church cemetery, Jane managed to hold herself together and it was only when she was locking up the house before leaving with Andrew, Anne, Kyle and Mildred did Jane's tears start to fall. Andrew handed her his handkerchief and she wiped her tears away while accepting his arm for support as they set off towards the railway station. Anne and Andrew parted company at Exchange station with Kyle, who was escorting Jane to Marjorie's house as it would be Marjorie's wedding soon and Jane was wanting to get to know her before then. He was also taking Mildred to an elderly neighbour of his who lived alone and was always glad of company. Jane planned on returning to Ormskirk the following morning.

When Anne and Andrew arrived back at Emily and Larry's it was to be informed that a farewell dinner had been arranged at the Adelphi Hotel in Liverpool on Wednesday evening. Donald, Catrina and Ranald had reserved rooms there for a few nights. Sandy and his father would be leaving for Scotland on the Thursday morning.

But before then Ann went upstairs and searched for the letter Alex had mentioned. She emptied everything on the bed and made another search through it all. She even scrutinised Hugh's will again and this time she noticed pinholes in the corner of the first page of the document. She decided her letter from Hugh could have been pinned to the will and removed, no doubt, by Albert. Why should he be bothered about her finding the letter if he had removed it? She felt a spurt of frustrated anger and placed the will under her pillow, desperately wishing she had the letter in her hand.

The following morning, she was up and dressed and having a cup of tea when Andrew woke up from where he was sleeping on the sofa. 'Tea?' she asked, giving him a kiss.

He nodded and took another kiss. 'So, what do you want to do today?' he asked. 'I've decided to travel back to London on the last train this evening.'

Anne understood his reasoning and after all, she thought a carefree day to themselves was just what she needed and not to be sniffed at when there was a party that evening as well. 'Let's go into town, window-shop, have lunch and then go to the Adelphi,' she said.

'That's fine with me,' Andrew said with a grin.

After breakfast with Emily and Larry, who were both working in the shop that day, the young couple left the house arm in arm to catch the train to Liverpool. Andrew told Anne that his grandfather had sent him a generous cheque to help towards wedding expenses. 'Perhaps we could buy my wedding ring and a signet ring for you, as well as presents for the bridesmaids,' Anne suggested.

He agreed, adding, 'Who are you choosing for your bridesmaids?'

'Jane and Mildred – who'd really enjoy being chosen – as well as little Amy for the flower girl if your grandfather's cheque can stretch that far? Sooner or later I'll have to take them shopping for dresses or find a dressmaker and have them made, as well as see about flowers and cars, etcetera.'

Andrew smiled. 'Let's have them all – I'm sure it won't break the bank, as I said it's a generous cheque.'

With that settled, they went ring-hunting which was exciting, and both found ones that they liked and that fitted the bill. With both rings tucked safely inside Andrew's jacket pocket, they had a meal at Berkley Cafe on Church Street and later took in a matinee at the cinema, which was showing *Bulldog Drummond* starring Ronald Colman. The hours passed swiftly. On the way to the Adelphi, they went into Lime Street station and Andrew purchased his ticket for London.

-

The white imposing building that was the Adelphi Hotel was close to Lime Street station and across the road from Lewis's departmental store. The hotel had been built shortly before the war by the Midland Railway Company on the site of a previous hotel opened in 1826.

Andrew and Anne climbed the steps to the front entrance and were met in the foyer by Catrina and Ranald, who led them to a smallish function room where the gathering was being held. Emily, Larry and Donald were already there, and it was Donald who led them to the small bar and asked what they were drinking. Anne decided to forgo anything stronger than lemonade after her last experience of champagne. Andrew chose a pint of bitter. A long table was already set with a white cloth, cutlery, glasses, a Christmassy floral arrangement and candles. Within a short space of time, Fiona, Sandy and Alex arrived and soon they were all invited to sit at table and the first course of cream of chicken soup was served. Anne was seated between Andrew and Alex, and whilst Andrew conversed with Fiona on his other side, Anne asked Alex to tell her more about his and Hugh's time in the scouts. He told her how they had practised woodcraft in the woods close to Cardross and that later, after Hugh had left for Liverpool, Alex had become a scout leader and had taken his troop once a year to Cardross woods to teach them woodcraft, and how on one occasion he had seen Donald and Catrina kissing in the woods.

'Did they see you?' asked Anne.

'I was concealed in the undergrowth, but they must have heard the scouts creeping hither and thither because they didn't hang around. They could have guessed I was in the woods with the lads.'

'So, that's another reason why Donald had a grudge against you,' whispered Anne.

He nodded. 'He might have thought I told Hugh, but I never did.' He paused as Ranald called for silence. All conversation tailed off. A waitress and waiter came and filled the champagne glasses with bubbly.

Ranald raised his glass as the staff stepped out of the way. 'A toast to our kin here in England, and may our ties with them be forever strong.' The words were echoed, and champagne sipped. Then Larry stood and raised a glass for family from over the border and in Canada.

Soup bowls, bread plates and cutlery were cleared away and Donald crossed to the bar and asked for a bottle of whisky for the table for the men and Drambuie liqueur for the women when coffee was served. Then he returned to the table in time for the main course of mutton, tatties and carrots and sprouts to be served.

Conversation was resumed and Alex turned to Emily on his other side, while Anne turned to Andrew. 'Are you enjoying yourself?' she asked.

He raised his eyebrows and said, 'I'm wondering when the band will make an appearance and we'll be expected to dance a Scottish reel or two.'

They did not have long to wait, for soon after a dessert of Cranachan appeared which consisted of oats, cream, whisky and raspberries. During coffee, five musicians made an appearance: two male fiddlers, another with bagpipes, a drummer and a young woman with an accordion who also proved to have a sweet voice. They entertained with Scottish songs until coffee time was over and the table was cleared and moved to the side of the room and the music changed tempo and, as Andrew had guessed, it was time to take to the floor for a reel or two with the band leader guiding them through the steps.

Anne was almost breathless after the first reel, which was the Gay Gordons, but she was determined to have a couple more dances before she went with Andrew to wave him off to London. They managed to slip away without any fuss and after an emotional farewell she stood on the platform until the train vanished into the tunnel. Then she returned to the Adelphi where Emily was looking out for her. They stayed another hour before expressing their thanks for a wonderful evening and then left for Eastham.

—

A fortnight later Anne, Emily and Larry arrived at Marjorie's the morning of Gordon and Marjorie's wedding in plenty of time. Andrew, Jane, Kyle and Mildred were already there. A short time later Teddy and Joan turned up with little Amy. The weather was 'fair to middling' which was a relief to all.

When they arrived at Saint Margaret's Church and had settled in the pew at the front of the church, a short while later the organ began to play 'Here Comes the Bride'. Marjorie smiled happily at Anne, knowing she was looking her very best in a brown suit with a pink cloche hat, matching pink accessories and a bouquet of cream and pink chrysanthemums with maidenhair fern. Gordon wore a charcoal pinstripe suit over a white shirt with a brown and pink patterned tie, topped off with a bowler hat and a nervous smile, standing beside his brother Teddy, his best man. It was not until Marjorie joined him at the altar that he stopped looking anxious, clearly bowled over by his bride's beautiful appearance.

Andrew was calm and performed the role of giving the bride away to perfection. Robbie looked on proudly at his aunt and began to clap as she made her vows, only to immediately stop mid-clap when the vicar scowled at him before carrying on with the service.

At the end of the day, Anne said to Emily and Teddy that she'd had an enjoyable time and she couldn't have been happier for the newlyweds. 'No card or telegram from Albert and Gladys,' Emily said. 'Not that I expected them to.'

'Yeah,' said Joan, who was standing at Teddy's shoulder. 'Yet Marjorie is the right one for Gordon. Level-headed and with no airs and graces.'

They enjoyed a wedding celebration back at Marjorie and Gordon's house, with many flattering and encouraging words spoken by his brother, Teddy, the best man. Soon after, Andrew said his ta-ra's, as did the bride and groom, who went off on their honeymoon to Llandudno.

Anne accompanied Andrew, having every intention of seeing him off at the station, but to her surprise, he said, 'How about us having a walk in Newsham Park before heading for town? I know the weather's turned much colder but I've something to tell you and I'd rather it was in nice surroundings. We've time, so don't look so on edge.'

She wondered what he had to tell her, thinking that maybe it was about their own honeymoon, but to her irritation, he kept her waiting to spill the beans until they arrived at the bridge that crossed over a section of the boating lake. Several ducks were bobbing about and diving under the water; one headed in their direction, no doubt expecting them to throw some crusts. Andrew paused and tugged her to a halt, placing his arm about her shoulders and bringing her snugly against him.

She waited expectantly. 'Is it about where we're going on honeymoon?' she asked.

'In a way - I'm hoping you won't be disappointed. I had thought of taking you to Paris.'

She gasped, and her fingers tightened on his overcoat. 'You said we didn't have the budget. So, where are we going now?'

'Essex.'

'Essex?' she echoed.

'I decided to put the honeymoon money together with my savings and the rest of the money Granddad sent me, as a deposit on a house. I've put an offer in for it and it's been accepted.'

'But what about your job in London?'

'I'll commute like many other workers do - besides which, my job often takes me outside London.' He seized her by the shoulders and held her off from him, holding her gaze intently. 'Do you think you can cope with spending our honeymoon in our own house and turning it into a home?'

A smile warmed her face. 'It's like a dream! What's the house like? How many bedrooms does it have?'

'Three, and a small attic room for storage, as well as having a bathroom and its own garden. It's situated in Westcliff-on-Sea on the outskirts of Southend, the seaside resort.'

Anne was speechless, so she expressed her feelings in a kiss that was long and deep. 'You are a love,' she managed to say once they drew apart. 'My only love.'

'So, you're pleased?' Andrew asked, drawing her arm through his.

'Thrilled,' she said. 'I wish it had been us getting married today, and I could have caught the train with you so that I could see our new home. I presume there's no furniture in the house yet?'

'No. I thought I'd buy a bed and bedding and a sofa and a teapot and a couple of cups once the contract is signed and the present owners move out, and we could shop for the rest of the furniture later. These things take time.'

'Can we have a gramophone?' she asked.

'Let's wait and see,' he said.

'Shame,' she said. 'Metropole records have a competition on right now – if you buy their records there's a chance of winning two thousand pounds.'

He gave a low whistle. 'That would more than pay off the mortgage. I've visited several times and have got to know the next-door neighbours.'

'You are thoughtful,' she said lovingly.

'I want to make you happy.'

'I am happy,' she said.

'Good!'

They left the park and headed for Tuebrook to catch the tram into town.

Anne's head buzzed with thoughts of her wedding, her new home and the missing letter from her father. To her delight, while on the tram, Andrew produced a small snapshot of a three-storey terraced house, but she could not see the downstairs front window because it was blocked by a privet hedge. Andrew told her that that it had a bay window and had been built during Edwardian times.

'I can't wait to go inside,' she said.

'Not long now,' said Andrew, delighted by her enthusiasm.

They snuggled up together as it was cold on the tram. 'Your hair smells lovely,' he said.

'Thanks,' she said absently, having been lost in her own thoughts. She had been wondering whether she should find herself a job once they were settled down south or whether to get herself a dog to keep her company at home if she didn't. She liked animals and thought how a dog would also help her to keep fit by taking it for walks. She would discuss it with Andrew after they were married. They'd have children, of course, but not yet; she was too young.

Christmas came and went and after Andrew returned to London, Anne started counting down the weeks until Easter, but before that it would be her seventeenth birthday in February and Albert had phoned to remind her that he would be there on the day.

Her birthday was a warm day for the season and Anne was strolling around the back garden in the late afternoon, gazing at the snowdrops and the shoots of the daffodils and tulips, waiting for Albert to arrive. She wanted to confront him with what she had discovered about a letter from Hugh, so that she could then relax and be at peace in her mind in the run up to her wedding day.

She heard an automobile draw up outside. Her pulse quickened, and she took a couple of deep breaths before going through the house and opening the front door.

Albert stood at the gate. She stared at him, noticing his new navy pinstripe three-piece suit. 'Hello, Albert,' she said. 'I'd expected you earlier than this.'

'I do have a business to run,' he said. 'As it is, Gladys has stayed behind to see to any problems that may arise.'

'You do surprise me. I thought she'd be here to back you up against me.'

'You've got her wrong. She hates unpleasantness and besides, she believes me quite capable of standing up for myself without any help from her.'

'You'd best come in,' Anne said, holding the door wider and stepping aside.

He entered the house, wiping his feet on the doormat.

'Let's get this over with before Emily and Larry return from their walk,' she said, leading the way into the kitchen.

'I haven't much to say, so it shouldn't take long,' said Albert.

'Well, I have plenty to say, so you'd best make yourself comfortable.' She waved him to the easy chair placed next to the fire and seated herself on the sofa. The brown envelope was balanced on the curved arm and Anne picked it up and placed it on her knees. 'Our father did include me in his will and left me more than you handed to me, as you know, but he also left a letter for me.'

'I suppose Alexander Murray told you about that,' he said, his colour rising.

'Yeah, but I also noticed pinholes on the first page of Da's will.'

'Smart of you,' he said.

Anne smiled tightly, laced her fingers together and placed her hands between her knees. 'I have all the proof I need for my own satisfaction, but I'd still like to know exactly what he said in the letter intended for me that was attached to his will... the letter you probably destroyed.' She laughed mirthlessly.

He leaned forward. 'I nearly did. He was not the good person you believed him to be.'

Her stomach seemed to turn over. 'I know what he was. You said you nearly destroyed it. Does that mean you still have it?'

Albert's cheeks had become even more flushed throughout the conversation, but he nodded. 'He met your mother sometimes on scouts evenings.'

'None of us are perfect and as soon as I was told I was adopted I knew that most likely I was a bastard child.' Anne's voice had risen too. 'At first, I felt terrible about that but then I told myself I wasn't to blame. I needed answers, so I set out on a journey that was interesting and exciting and I was lucky to meet several nice people who were of help to me. Finally I met Da's close friend Alex Murray, who was able to tell me about the relationship between Da and my mother, Anne Graham. He told me that Da knew I was his daughter.' Anne paused. 'What I'd like to know is how you came to know the truth.'

'He wasn't very discreet.' Albert took a deep breath. 'It was after my little sister died and I was visiting her grave with some flowers. There were already some fresh flowers that had been placed there and I caught sight of Dad. I watched him, thinking he must have been the person to put the flowers on the grave, and he obviously hadn't seen me so I kept quiet and to my surprise, watched him lay flowers on another grave as well. After he left, I went and had a look at the headstone and saw the name. I had heard of Anne Graham and knew she was Da's second cousin and I had seen them together on other occasions. I wouldn't have thought much of it but later we heard she had died shortly before you were adopted into our family. Despite us being told you were Liam Fraser's daughter, Dad named you Anne. He also seemed to be dogged by sadness around that time and could only smile when he had you in his arms.'

'So, you put two and two together.' Anne let the words hang in the air.

'I was ashamed to have an adulterer for a father and I told him so. He didn't deny it and asked me not to tell Mother as he and Anne had ended the affair before he knew Anne was having a baby, but had found out her secret when he visited the wet nurse feeding you and Jane Fraser.'

'So, you kept quiet about it all this time,' Anne murmured.

'Of course. I wasn't going to have Mother hurt, but I sometimes think she suspected the truth which is why she could be sharp with you sometimes. Besides which, I made a promise to Da to watch over you because, after all, you have Anderson blood and you are my half-sister. You've proved you have family feeling by the way you helped Emily and Gordon and all the family. I couldn't have done it because Gladys couldn't have coped with the strain. She had spent years looking after her elderly father and she'd had enough.'

'I understand,' said Anne. 'But I'd still like to know what Da's letter to me said.'

'I have it here,' Albert said, taking an envelope from his jacket pocket and handing it to her. 'I had some idea what it might be and didn't want Mother seeing it.'

Anne slit the envelope open and as soon as she read the words *To my darling daughter Anne, you won't get to read this until after I am dead…* her tears began to fall.

…but I want you to know that I have loved you from the moment I set eyes on you and am proud

of the way you have turned out. Your mother's
name was Anne Graham and we loved each other
but our parents were against us being married, but
love will find a way and you are the proof of that.
I wish I could have told you this when I was alive,
but it would have hurt the woman who has been
like a mother to you all these years.

  Your loving Da. xxxxx

She lifted her eyes to Albert's face and tried to thank him for not destroying the letter but was too moved to speak. Instead, she reached up and kissed his cheek. He hugged her.

'I always wanted you to have it,' he said. 'But I was afraid of the truth. I'm sorry. Can I still give you away when you marry Andrew?'

Anne found her voice. 'I think that's only right with Da not being here – and he did trust you enough to wring a promise from you to watch over me. I'd still like to know why you didn't kick up a fuss when I went up to Scotland but maybe you thought I'd never discover the truth even then?'

'Mother was dead, so deep down, I knew whatever you found out wouldn't hurt her. Besides, Uncle Donald and Fiona didn't know the truth about you.'

Anne nodded. 'I presume you spent the money Dad left me on the hotel?'

He shook his head. 'I only borrowed it and always intended on paying it back. Doing the hotel up took a lot of money, but I never spent all of yours. I still have some of it set aside to give you at the right time and I'll make the rest up.'

'I'm glad to hear it. It will come in handy when I'm married.'

There was the sound of a key in the lock of the front door. Knowing Emily and Larry had returned, Anne immediately put the kettle on. The table was already set with cups and saucers and a homemade Victoria sponge cake.

'Well, have you two said all that was necessary to be friends?' Emily asked as she entered the kitchen.

Albert and Anne nodded. 'I shall be giving our sister away on her wedding day, although Gladys won't be there,' Albert said. 'She's having a baby, so needs to take things easy.'

Emily and Anne exchanged surprised looks, then congratulated him sincerely before Emily said, 'Snap, so am I. Larry and I saw the doctor earlier today and it's been confirmed.'

'Goodness, I'm going to be an aunt twice over,' Anne said. 'You're all going to be so busy, you won't have time to miss me when I go down south.'

'We'll bring the children to see you,' said Albert. 'We don't want them missing out on knowing their Aunty Anne.'

Chapter Thirty One

April 1930

Anne rushed to the window as soon as she woke on Easter Saturday and looked out on a blanket of grey fog. 'Damn, damn, damn!' she exclaimed, thinking she and her bridesmaids were all going to be freezing in their dainty dresses. She could only pray that by two o'clock, when she was due to take her vows, the fog would disperse, the sun would come out and the church would be warm enough.

'You should be having a lie-in,' Emily said, having heard Anne moving about. 'By tradition the bride should have breakfast in bed. Larry's gone down to light the fire and put the kettle on.'

By ten o'clock, Anne could see through the window to the bottom of the front garden and the florist's assistant had arrived with her bouquet, the bridesmaids' posies and the guest's buttonholes. Her heart lifted. Next to arrive was Albert in his car, then her Uncle Donald, Catrina and Ranald. Close on their heels came Fiona, Sandy and Alex and bringing up the rear were Teddy, Joan, Amy, Kyle and Mildred.

'It's crowded in here,' Joan said, perching on the arm of the sofa, thanking Albert as he handed her a glass of sherry.

'It's good to be with family,' he said. 'I have to say, Joan, that Amy is looking a picture in her flower girl's frock. She's a real sweetie.'

'I believe you're trying to soft-soap us, Albert,' Joan said, taking a sip of her sherry. 'I hope Gladys is well?'

'She's fine now the morning sickness has passed. You must come to stay and bring Amy with you this time.'

By half past one, the parlour and kitchen had emptied out and the peach-coloured crêpe de Chine clad brides-maids and Amy, the flower girl, were waiting for the horse and trap to transport them to the church nearby. Once they were outside, Anne took a last look at her reflec-tion in the parlour mirror and decided Andrew should be delighted with his bride.

Albert came and stood at her shoulder and said, 'Da and both your mams would be so proud of you.'

'Thank you. Mother would have been delighted to know you're going to be a dad. I never asked you at the time, but how do you feel about it?'

'Honestly? Scared and chuffed at the same time. As the eldest son, I knew Mam wanted me to have a son too, but I'd be just as happy with a girl. Anyhow, enough of such talk. It's your day and a festooned horse and cart has just drawn up outside. Time for us to go.'

Anne took the arm he offered and they left the house together. She was aware of the oohs and ahhs of the neighbours gathered on the pavement to watch her, so she saluted them with her bouquet before climbing into the trap. Within minutes they were at the church where she could see a small crowd gathered in the grounds. She thought she caught sight of Mildred's mother, Bridget, standing next to a youth in a green and brown checked jacket – presumably he was one of the Liverpool O'Donnells – along with the little Chinese boy and the old Chinese woman.

As Anne and Albert joined the bridesmaids, the organ launched into Lohengrin's 'Wedding March', and she felt full of joy that the occasion she had longed for was here at last.

As she proceeded down the aisle on Albert's arm, she caught sight of the midwife, Cissie, and her daughter, Jessie, along with Stanley the pigeon fancier. She smiled at them and wished that Lil could have been there as well. Not only them, but her mother Anne, her father Hugh and her adoptive mother Sylvia, who had all played their part in making her the person she was now. As she approached the chancel and the two men standing there, Andrew turned his head and gazed at her. Their eyes met, and his lips curved into a smile.

She drew alongside him and whispered, 'This isn't a dream, is it?'

'A dream come true,' he said, reaching for her hand.

–

Anne snuggled up to her husband and blinked as the train emerged into the fading light of Easter Saturday. She was glad they had a carriage to themselves. She thought back over the day and remembered the expression on Jane's face when she had caught sight of Kyle again after not seeing him for a while. Jane had left with Granddad Fraser and the members of the family for the Isle of Jura when he had visited Liverpool to visit his son Liam's grave.

Anne wondered if she should have bought an extra bouquet, with one to toss to Jane and one to place on her mother Anne's grave. As it was, Anne and Andrew had visited Anfield Cemetery after the wedding and left her bouquet at the foot of the headstone that Hugh had commissioned in memory of Anne Graham. She had to pray that Jane would see the possibility of a happy future for herself in Liverpool with Kyle. But everything happened for a reason; had her mother not left her home in Scotland in search of Hugh, she wouldn't have given birth to her and her and Andrew would not have a future together.

She closed her eyes and gradually drifted into a doze to the clackety-clack of the train wheels. Andrew roused her just as they were approaching Euston Station. 'We'll be leaving the train in a few minutes, love,' he said,

She blinked up at him, yawned and stretched. 'What must you think of me?' she said.

'I've no complaints,' he said, kissing her. 'I had you where I wanted you, in my arms. But now we need to gather our luggage together.'

She drew away from him and together they prepared to leave the train. She kept glancing about her, trying to take in that she was in London, the capital of England.

'Did I ever tell you,' Andrew said, 'that the first time I came to London, I needed to find my way to Fleet Street and asked a bloke on the street if he could tell me how to get there?'

'And did he help you?' she asked.

'He was an Aussie and was only just starting to find his way about, but he directed me to a bus stop and said that no doubt a conductor would be able to help me.' He paused. 'You do see what I'm getting at, Anne?'

'Yeah, that I'm not the only stranger here,' she said. 'To feel at home, I need to make friends with people just as I would back in Liverpool.'

He nodded and said, 'Now let's go and take the tube to Liverpool Street station.'

'There's a street called Liverpool in London?'

'Haven't I just said there is? It's where we can catch a train to Southend – this way!'

She followed him down to the Tube, not without some difficulty, burdened as they were with their luggage. It was a relief when they were settled in a carriage on the train to Westcliff-on-Sea. Anne was even more relieved when they came out of the station at Southend and stepped into a taxi. Despite snoozing on the train from Liverpool, she was feeling tired out and a little cold; for some reason, she had expected it to be a lot warmer in the south. Gazing out of the taxi window, she could see little of the seaside resort in the dark. When the cab drew up outside her new home it came as a surprise to her to find the lights on and, when they went inside, a coal fire burning in the grate and the larder full of food.

'Who lit the fire and did the shopping?' Anne asked.

'Sally and Cathy probably,' said Andrew.

At that moment, there was a ring at the front doorbell and Andrew hurried to answer it. Anne heard women's voices as well as Andrew's and one of the accents sounded familiar. A few minutes later he reappeared carrying a casserole dish, followed by two women. 'Anne, let me introduce you to Sally and her sister, Cathy. They thought you'd be too tired after your journey to feel like cooking, so they've made us a rabbit stew.'

Anne was almost overcome by the sisters' kindness but managed to say thank you and shake hands.

'At least one of you is from Liverpool,' she said.

'Both of us originally,' said Sally. 'But I left during the war. I was a nurse and married one of the soldiers I looked after in a hospital in the West Country. He was a Cockney from the East End, so we lived in London for a while and then moved out here a couple of years ago.'

'I still live in Liverpool with me son; my fella was killed in the war,' Cathy said. 'But I always come down and visit Sal at this time of year as it's her birthday tomorrow.'

Anne turned on Andrew. 'Why didn't you tell me we had a Scouser for a neighbour?'

'I wanted to give you a surprise,' he said.

'That's men for you,' Sal said. 'Welcome to Essex, Anne. We have football teams and the sea here, so you'll soon feel at home. Southerners aren't that different from us.'

Andrew caught Anne's gaze and winked. 'Neither are the Scots,' he said.

His wink told her differently. Scotland was a different country altogether.